IN THE DAYS before

IN THE DAYS before

RENÉE SHANTEL

Silver Shell
PUBLISHING

ISBN 978-1-964655-07-9 (Paperback)

Cover Design by Kim Wilson
www.theauthorbuddy.com

Edited by Immy Grace
www.fiverr.com/immygrace

Published by Silver Shell Publishing
www.silvershellpublishing.com

For Mum
for sharing my love of books and true crime

1

Jackie rolled her eyes like it was an Olympic sport, and she the gold medallist. "I'm just saying. Maybe if you spent more time looking at people who are actually *here*, you might manage to get yourself a date to the formal instead of showing up like a lonely loser."

Audrey sighed and pinched the bridge of her nose, slumping back further into her hard plastic chair. Twenty seconds. She only had to last twenty more seconds before the upload was complete, and then Jackie could drag her back out into society and instruct her in the ways of being a "normal" girl. *Ugh*. It wasn't like they'd been in the computer lab for hours. She'd asked for fifteen minutes, and she still had three left on the clock. Fifteen minutes to upload her video, do a quick check, and then she'd be done. Was that too much to ask?

Apparently, fifteen minutes was akin to eternity for her best friend. Jackie had scrolled her Instagram feed for the first five, taken a couple of bored selfies to occupy herself for another thirty seconds, then promptly turned the conversation to their upcoming year eleven formal—like they hadn't discussed the same thing that morning, yesterday, and the day before. *And* the day before that. As if life was all about boys and dances and being the best dressed in life.

"What about Marcus?" Jackie went on. She twirled Prada sunglasses around in one hand so carelessly that Audrey was sure the arm was about to snap, and the frames would go flying. "He's kinda cute. Maybe you could flirt your way into him asking."

Audrey fought back another sigh. "I don't want to go to the dance with Marcus."

"Stuart, then. His hair needs some fixing, but–"

"*No.*"

She should have insisted on coming alone. The computer lab usually provided peace and solitude, silent except for mechanical whirring and the occasional electronic beep, and Jackie was disturbing that quiet. Even the two ninth graders who liked to play some sort of war game were less of a nuisance; their noise was an occasional silenced battle cry, the rest contained by headphones. Barely any of the afternoon sun made it through the east-facing windows, making the room an unpopular destination even as spring began to grow warmer and shaded areas became hot property, so Audrey often found herself comfortably alone. Some days, she would have preferred holing up here, researching cases and working on videos for her YouTube channel. It was a much better use of her time than talking about boys.

But that was why Jackie had followed. To make sure Audrey didn't spend her entire lunch hour online like a *lonely loser*. She called it doing her civic duty.

Jackie huffed, sliding her sunglasses back onto her head. They sat like a crown atop hair dark as night. "Well then *who*, Audrey? If you don't find a date soon, you might end up having to go with creepy Newton."

Another eye roll, this time a barely bronze performance from Audrey. "Has it ever occurred to you that maybe I don't need a date for the formal?"

"No. Because you *do* need a date. It's our last big event before we move on to final year, and showing up without a date would just be sa—*are you even listening to me?*"

No, she wasn't. Audrey straightened as the video finished uploading. She held her breath as the browser refreshed to show the new page, and then there it was in all its glory.

She grabbed the mouse and scrolled down, her eyes darting to the title and description, gaze running over them one letter at a time. Scrutinising every character for what must have been the twentieth time at least. She'd been burned once already by a bored troll calling her out on a spelling error, and she'd be damned if she would let it happen again. It was bad enough that her most viewed video was because some anonymous jerk had wanted to make her look like a fool. Even worse, they'd succeeded. She'd tried to believe the *all publicity is good publicity* line, but it definitely hadn't been true in her case. She grimaced. Never again.

IN THE DAYS BEFORE...: Have You Seen Amanda Mulgrave?

"Are you going to sit here and watch the whole thing now?" Jackie groaned, falling back into her chair dramatically. It was truly a tragedy that her parents hadn't allowed her to take drama class for her final years of high school. She was a natural. "Come *on*, Audrey. We've only got half an hour left to get in some sun! Are you seriously going to deprive me of my vitamin D? You know I need the D!"

Audrey slid the cursor to different points in the video, spot-checking for five seconds at a time. She hated the sound of her own voice, but the thought of posting content without double-checking things made her stomach roil. What if there was something wrong with the audio? What would the trolls say if she posted a video and the visual cut out halfway? She'd be crucified, her work considered a joke. A professional would check, and she wanted the quality of her channel to be as professional as possible, even with her lack of decent recording equipment. She wouldn't—*couldn't*—skip over spot-checking. She moved to the last thirty seconds.

Jackie grumbled something in Chinese.

Audrey's own face filled the screen, terribly lit by the last of the afternoon sun that had crawled into her room the previous evening. It threw her background into heavy shadow—her hastily made bed, the stack of notebooks on her dresser, the pile of clothes on the floor by the door. There was nothing she could do about her poor production quality, stuck recording with her four-generations-old mobile phone, but why hadn't she had the foresight to turn on some lights and pick up her clothes? She could practically see the creases forming in her school skirt on-screen and had to force herself not to look down and see how bad it was in person.

On-screen, Audrey was entirely unconcerned about her backdrop as she channelled her inner news anchor. *"Amanda Mulgrave was last seen in Surry Hills on the fifth of October, heading to her evening class at McLennan College. She was wearing a white halter top, light blue denim shorts, and a pair of white sneakers. Her photograph is on-screen now."* It was. *"Please share her face and her story with your friends, and if you or somebody you know have any information you think might help bring her home, please call Crime Stoppers on one eight hundred, triple three, triple zero. As always, thank you for your time, and stay safe out there. See you next time!"*

The screen faded to black, leaving only Amanda Mulgrave's photograph with the least cringy royalty-free music Audrey had been able to dig up. Amanda smiled back at her, eyes shining. Hopeful. Just like every other missing person Audrey had recorded a video for in the past year and a half.

Hopefully, this one would make a difference.

"All right," she conceded. "I'm done."

"Finally." Jackie wasted no time in grabbing her bag and moving to her feet in one quick motion. "I didn't think you were *ever* going to finish with this. I don't know why you even bother."

Audrey tried not to acknowledge the familiar sting in her chest. She clicked to log out of her account and shut down the browser. "It's important work."

"For the police, maybe." Jackie threw her hair over her shoulder. Even in the semi-darkness, it shone like silk.

"Your videos get, like, a hundred views each. *Maybe.* That's not helping anyone."

"But it could," Audrey countered. "You never know."

"Oh, I know."

"You don't." Audrey stood, too, swinging her bag onto her back and following Jackie as she breezed out into the hallway. "All it ta—"

A football went sailing past her ear, so close she heard the whistle and felt the air shift, and she jumped back in surprise. A seventh grader yelled a half-hearted apology as his friend doubled over with laughter, shoes squealing on the linoleum as he made a show of sliding down the wall. Hilarious. Jackie threw them a disgusted look over her shoulder as she strolled away.

Audrey nudged the ball back over to the boys, then hurried to catch up with her best friend. Jackie was on a mission to make it outside as fast as humanly possible, Mary Janes clacking as she made for the double doors that led to the courtyard. Audrey's own tattered sneakers barely made a sound as she ran after her.

"If it were you, wouldn't you want people to bring attention to your case?" she asked breathlessly as she fell into step beside Jackie. "Amanda Mulgrave went missing twenty minutes from here. In the city, Jackie! And her case is recent! You never know when that *one* person might see a video or a report or something and realise they have information that might help. I have a lot of local subscribers—"

"If it were *me*," Jackie interjected, "I would get all the attention I need from the media, thanks. I wouldn't need you and your extra hundred views to help find me. Hell, I'd probably fight off any would-be kidnappers just so you wouldn't have the extra material!"

"That's not funny."

"Neither is you wasting your life making creepy content for morbid freaks." Jackie snapped her fingers. "There's your new tagline. You're welcome."

Audrey bristled, heat rising in her cheeks. "It's not—"

She cut herself off as Principal Evans bustled past them with the young new English teacher hurrying along beside him. They'd both looked over at her rising voice, their faces those of teachers ready to reprimand a student for getting out of hand, and Audrey's face heated more. She grimaced apologetically, shrinking back into herself as Jackie smiled politely, ever the model student her parents believed her to be. If only they knew what their perfect daughter was really doing when they weren't looking.

"Don't go making a scene." Jackie turned the final corner into the brightly lit corridor that led to the exit. Freedom awaited them. "People already think you're weird. You don't want to get labelled as crazy, too."

Audrey ran a hand through her hair—limp and brown and boring next to Jackie's. "Would it hurt you to give me just a little support? The more people hear about these cases—"

Dark eyes flashed as Jackie made a sound of disgust. "Jesus, Audrey, will you *shut up* about your stupid channel? Pretending like you're helping find missing people isn't going to bring your dad back!"

Audrey stopped dead in the middle of the hallway.

Jackie kept walking; porcelain skin glowing as she stepped out into the sunlight. Her sunglasses fell into place like a pair of paid actors. She didn't so much as look back to see if Audrey was following her. She wouldn't. Queen bees didn't care for the workers who'd wronged them.

Message received loud and clear: Audrey had pushed her too far.

But bringing up her father's disappearance was a low blow.

A trio of girls were watching from just past the doorway, their conversation abandoned, obviously having heard everything. Audrey's face burned, but she forced herself to step outside with her head held high, trying not to feel the weight of their stares on her back as she passed. They were eighth graders. What did she care what they thought of her?

Jackie didn't look at her again until they'd both made it down to the basketball court where the rest of their squad had settled, all of them lying in the sun with their heads propped up on bags and folded jumpers. Jackie looked at her long enough to gesture pointedly to their group before dropping down herself and sprawling out with her school bag as a pillow, long legs stretching out to soak up the sun for however long they had left of their lunch break. Audrey sighed and sat opposite her, opting not to take the bait. She didn't want to fight. Not when she was already the odd one out in their gang.

Lenore looked up from her book as Audrey sat beside her. She'd covered up her pale legs to avoid the inevitable burn she would have ended up with, but her curls were fanned out around her in an effort to fit in with the others. "Hey. Where were you guys? We were starting to think you weren't coming."

"The famous Miss Morbid had to put out her latest video for all the world to see," Jackie cut in before Audrey had a chance to say anything. A dark brow rose over the top of her frames. "Haven't you heard she's going to save all the missing people in the world with her five hundred subscribers?"

"Six hundred," Audrey said automatically. Lenore grimaced.

Jackie snorted. "Big deal. I've got forty-five *thousand* followers on Instagram. Now *that's* something."

It was, and it irked her to no end that her best friend had that kind of reach on any social platform, and all she used it for was showing off outfits and make-up looks. How was beauty blogging supposed to make a difference to anyone? She'd asked Jackie several times to promote her channel to her followers, just *once*, only to have her best friend laugh her off. *Ew, why would I show something like that to my fans? Maybe if your channel was about beauty products, you'd get more followers!*

Maybe she would, but that wasn't the kind of content she wanted to make.

"You'd get more if you posted a thirst trap." Danielle winked Jackie's way, her tanned legs stretched out in front of her. She'd folded her skirt up as high as it could go to maximise her sun exposure, and Audrey wondered if it was more for the benefit of the sun or for the guys playing rugby on the nearby field. "You'd be at fifty thousand by the end of the day. Could reach a hundred by Christmas."

"Are you covering that Amanda girl?" Penny pushed her sunglasses up into her blonde hair. She was on her stomach, the latest edition of *Cosmo* lying open in front of her. "The one that went missing in the city?"

A spark of hope sprung to life in Audrey's chest. "Yeah! Have you been following the case?"

Penny snorted. "Of course not. My cousin knew her, is all. It's all he's posting about on Facebook. Kind of annoying, actually."

Danielle's brunette waves popped up at the mention of Facebook. "Oh my God, did you see the photo of the dress I sent you last night?!" She grabbed Penny's leg and shook it eagerly. "I thought it was perfect for you! But maybe in the red?"

"Definitely in the red," Delilah agreed. Her face was to the sky, eyes closed, head tilted back to take in the early afternoon sun. If she wasn't careful, she'd soon be as scarlet as her hair. "The red would look *hot* on you, Pen."

Lenore glanced left at Audrey. *These girls, am I right?*

Audrey leaned back against the metal fence. Unless she decided to take an interest in beauty and fashion, she would get no help here. Lenore understood, but she also didn't do social media, so there was only so far her support could go. Not like the others, who fancied themselves future reality personalities and movie stars. Who probably had a hundred thousand followers between them.

She pulled out her phone and navigated to their group chat, just as the others appeared to be doing. Jackie was already typing swiftly. Audrey looked down, expecting to see the familiar grey text bubble popping up, showing that her best friend was typing into the group chat—probably giving an opinion on the posted dress in text rather than saying anything out loud. As was their way.

But there was no text bubble there, and no new message showed up when Jackie appeared to hit send and wait for a response. Audrey opened her mouth to ask who she was texting but then thought better of it. It was better to let Jackie cool off after their argument. And it wasn't like it mattered anyway. If it wasn't the group chat, she was likely texting her boyfriend.

"It's cute," Penny said, pinching her fingers to zoom out of the photograph on her phone screen. The sunglasses went back on. "We should head into the city this weekend and see if we can find one like it. Are we up for a day of shopping, ladies?"

"It'll have to be Sunday. I've got my grandma's birthday tomorrow." Jackie didn't bother looking away from her phone as she added, "Count Audrey out. She'll be too busy talking about dead people to hang out with the living."

"Missing," Lenore said, loud enough only for Audrey to hear.

Audrey *had* planned on using the weekend to work on her channel, but hearing Jackie say it like that rubbed her the wrong way. So did the smirk on Danielle's face and the pointed look Delilah was giving her. Only Penny hadn't bothered to look up, still engrossed in her phone screen. She had half a mind to tell them to go jump.

But they were her friends, and she could never treat

them like that.

"I'll be there," she said instead.

Jackie snorted. "Sure. If you don't go missing first."

Audrey would never say it, but that might have been preferable.

2

You really need new friends, Audi.

AUDREY SNORTED AT THE stupid nickname and positioned her fingers over her laptop's keyboard.

Are you offering, Mattarati?

Matt sent a crying laughing emoji in response, but Audrey knew it was good-natured. They may not have met in person, but in their year and a half of friendship, she'd often considered Matt to be a better friend to her than any of the girls—including Jackie. He wouldn't care that she was sprawled out on her bed with her hair hastily thrown into a messy bun atop her head, wearing shorts and a tatty old t-shirt that *definitely* didn't go together. He didn't hate all over her content and belittle her work. Hell, that was how they'd met. He was her most loyal subscriber.

Sometimes, it felt like he was her *only* subscriber.

His black and white profile photo was dark and brooding, his admittedly attractive face half hidden in shadow, but she'd always found him to be the opposite of the thousand-word story the picture told. The *Assess the Mess* band poster behind him certainly brightened things, the headstock and neck of a guitar eternally propped up underneath it, giving her creative licence to imagine the kind of music he might make. He always had a smiley face at the ready for her, a kind word when she'd had a rough day. If anything, he was her only source of light when she was looking into her darker cases.

Matt

You know I'd be your friend in a heartbeat. It's a shame we don't live closer to each other. Sure you don't wanna move over the bridge?

Audrey

Not a chance. Everybody knows you North Sydney-siders are snobby little shits.

Another crying laughing emoji, earning another smile from her.

She navigated back to her Word document, looking over the notes she'd made. Two weeks' worth of work stared back at her. She'd intended to have this one completed before the weekend, intended to spend her Saturday fine-tuning and filming and editing as best as she could on her ancient laptop, but Amanda Mulgrave's local disappearance had derailed that completely. She knew the cold cases were important. Knew it better than anyone. But they couldn't take priority over active investigations—especially the ones that were so close to home—so on the back burner, James Anders had gone.

She refused to be discouraged by the fact that she'd woken to find Amanda's video had only garnered twenty-six views overnight, and at least three of them had been from her checking her content over.

Messenger dinged a new response, a tiny sound almost drowned out by the playlist she had on for background noise, and she moved back to it.

Matt

How's the new case coming along?

Audrey

Slow. But it should be ready for next Friday.

There were several beats of silence before the next message came through.

Matt

Have you thought about covering your father's case yet?

Audrey stared at the words.

Matt was the only one of her viewers who knew about her father. She'd opened up to him one night after a particularly terrible week when all the bills had come due at once, and she'd found her mother breaking down in the kitchen. Her friends knew she and her mother struggled with money, that they lived in their tiny apartment only because they couldn't afford the mortgage on their house after her father had vanished, but she never shared with them how dark things could get. How close they sometimes came to living out of their barely-running car. Lenore could sympathise, given she and her mother lived with her aunt and cousin due to their tight finances, but the others would judge her. Would never understand.

Opening up to Matt, Internet-stranger-but-not, had been easy.

And it had felt like the logical next step to tell her fellow crime junkie about her father. He was the entire reason she'd developed an interest in missing persons' cases, and it had always been her intention to cover his story on her channel.

But she'd never managed to plan the video. Had never convinced herself to fall down the rabbit hole that was her father's disappearance. She'd never even googled it, and she couldn't explain why. It wasn't like there was anything the Internet could tell her about the case she didn't already know.

Audrey

Not yet. I think I want to grow my viewership more first. I want to expose his case to as many people as possible. Give it the best chance, you know? Otherwise, it's all been for nothing.

Not for nothing. You're doing great work here. I hope I get to do half as well when I join the force.

Matt had always wanted to become a police officer, to go on to become a detective or an investigator. It was what had drawn him to Audrey's videos in the first place, and it was one of the things she liked most about him. It made him a useful companion to have when she was pulling together her content. Sometimes, he was able to give her another perspective on the cases she was covering. Other times, he found resources she hadn't. They made a great team, and she hoped he'd be as forthcoming when he was officially in law enforcement. Maybe he'd stay on as her researching companion.

If what she could see of his profile photo was anything to go by, he'd make a good cop. He wasn't built like some of the guys Audrey went to school with, but she could tell by those arms that he worked out, and he had the sort of friendly face she imagined people would be comfortable approaching. Even if his eyes were dark, his expression brooding.

Thanks. I really needed to hear that today.

The bedroom door swung open without warning. Her mother stepped in, clearly aggravated, as she held their cordless phone to her ear. There were deep bags under her eyes, and her honey hair was a lopsided mess, likely from being dragged from bed too soon. The result of one too many night shifts at the local hospital. Audrey hadn't expected her to be awake for several hours yet, let alone standing in her doorway on the cordless.

She immediately grimaced and turned her music down. "Sorry, Mum. I did—"

"No, she's definitely not here," her mother said into the phone, fixing her withering gaze on Audrey. "Let me just ask my daughter."

Audrey raised both eyebrows as her mother crossed her arms, tucking the mouthpiece of the phone against her body, muting their conversation to whoever was on the other end.

Before she could ask, her mother said, "Mrs Chen is on the phone, asking about Jackie. I thought we talked about you covering for that girl. Do I need to ground you again, young lady? Will two weeks without your computer do?"

"What?" Audrey stared at her, mouth agape. "I'm not covering for anyone!"

"Oh, really? Because apparently, Jackie told her mother she was staying over here last night." Her mother pursed her lips, looking stern. "Did she stay the night?"

"No," Audrey said immediately. "She didn't. And she never mentioned anything to me about this either."

"Mmhmm. And you wouldn't happen to have any idea where she might have run off to that's so important she needed a cover story?"

Audrey could list a great number of things Jackie would want to keep from her parents, but none that she'd mentioned doing that weekend. "No. Like I said, she didn't tell me anything. She told us she had her grandmother's birthday today."

"She does. That's why Suzy's calling. She hasn't shown up for the party."

"Well, I don't know where she is."

Her mother fixed her with that stare for another few moments before returning the phone to her ear. "I'm sorry, Suzy. Audrey says Jackie hasn't been here, and she's not sure where she might be. Uh-huh… sure. I'll have her give you a call as soon as she figures out where Jackie is."

The phone gave an audible beep as her mother ended the call. She folded her arms again, still looking stern as she fixed those piercing blue eyes on Audrey.

"If I find out you're lying—"

"God, Mum. I covered for her *one* time." That her mother knew of. "I'm not lying. Jackie didn't come over yesterday, she didn't ask to stay the night, and she hasn't been here today." As an afterthought, she added, "I don't even think she's texted."

"Well, I need *you* to text *her* and tell her to get her butt home. She should know better than to test her mother's patience like this." Audrey's own mother sighed heavily. "I swear, that woman's a saint for dealing with that girl."

"Jackie's not *that* bad, Mum. She's just…" Audrey took a moment to search for the right word. "She's free-spirited."

"Yes, well, if you were that free-spirited, you'd be spending all of your free-spirited time in your room."

Audrey looked back at her laptop. A new message

from Matt stared back at her, but she navigated to her group chat with the girls instead. It had gone untouched for several hours. There were a couple of messages from earlier that morning, all between Penny and Danielle as they organised Sunday's shopping trip, but nothing more. Delilah had given a thumbs-up reaction to one of the messages, and that had been it. Not a single word or emoji from Jackie. The activity bubble beside her profile icon wasn't even visible when Audrey looked.

That was weird. Jackie practically lived on her phone. Audrey clicked through to her profile.

Last active 8 hours ago

That was definitely unusual. She opened a new message to Jackie.

She watched the message send, watched its status change to delivered.

And then, nothing.

"I messaged her." She looked back up at her mother, still hovering in the doorway. "I'll let Mrs Chen know if Jackie says she's not coming back for the party or whatever. You should go back to bed. Don't you have a shift tonight?"

Her mother gave a non-committal grunt, shot her

one last suspicious look, and then walked away. Audrey listened for the sound of her bedroom door closing gently before she went back to her messages with Matt.

Matt

You know I'll always be a supporter.
Maybe one day we can help each
other out with cases.

Audrey smiled at the thought—Matt in his police uniform, and her... she still wasn't sure. Join the force and become a detective with him? Become an investigative reporter or a journalist? Or did she want to keep her business online and become a full-time content creator? Matt could be her man on the inside, and she could be his eyes on the ground. And if she dreamed a little bigger, a little more romantically...

She glanced back at her chat with Jackie. Still not active.

Audrey

Sorry for the silence. Jackie's being a
bitch again.

Matt

Hating all over your channel?

Audrey

Worse. She used me as a cover so she
could run off somewhere, and she's
late for her grandma's birthday.

Audrey

> Now my mum's pissed because she thinks I'm covering for her.

Matt

> I'm gonna say it again: You need new friends.

Audrey

> After this, I might consider it.

Matt

> Maybe you'll have to. Kinda sounds like the start of one of your videos, doesn't it?

Matt

> Girl doesn't show up in time for a family event, nobody knows where she is…

He followed up his last message with a gif of a man making spooky fingers at her. Audrey rolled her eyes but glanced at her chat with Jackie again. Unease prickled at the back of her neck. There was still no green circle by her name, no sign she'd come online to check her messages, but that didn't strictly mean there was anything *wrong*. It just meant Jackie wasn't actively looking at her phone.

And hadn't for the previous eight hours.

Stranger things had happened, but… Audrey moved to

the group chat.

Almost immediately, a speech bubble appeared, indicating that somebody was typing. The tension in Audrey's shoulders released.

She'd been stupid to worry for even a second. It wasn't the first time Jackie had pulled a stunt like this, and it probably wouldn't be the last. And, of course, one of the others would know where she was. At least Jackie'd had the courtesy to tell *them*, if not the person who was supposed to be covering for her.

Lenore. Ever the voice of reason. Audrey scrolled

through her messages, looking for Peter's name. She didn't interact much with Jackie's boyfriend, so there could be no doubt in Jackie's mind that she was definitely *not* interested in him, but she was certain they'd exchanged a few messages in the past. Always centred around their mutual connection.

Ah. There.

Peter had been active less than twenty minutes earlier.

Audrey

> Hey, Pete. Is Jackie with you? Her mum's looking for her, and she's not answering my messages. Could you let her know? Thanks.

The message changed to read two seconds after she sent it. He responded almost as quickly.

Peter

> She told me you guys had a girls' weekend planned.

Audrey stared at the message. A girls' weekend? Had she meant their shopping trip on Sunday? It wasn't like Jackie to lie to her boyfriend, so that must have been it. But if she wasn't with the girls now, and she hadn't snuck off to see her boyfriend...

Where was she?

What the hell was she up to?

She went back to the group chat with her friends. She didn't have time to chase after Jackie all day.

> She's not with Peter.

> Whatever. If anybody hears from her, tell her that her mum wants her home ASAP.

She got a thumbs-up from Lenore. The others didn't bother to respond.

She shifted her gaze to the notebook lying beside her laptop. So much for spending Saturday getting her next video done. She rubbed her eyes with the palms of her hands.

There was an alert coming from her messages with Matt. Audrey clicked them open.

> I'm just kidding. You know that, right?

She sighed.

> I know. It's fine. She's probably off drinking or hooking up with some random guy. Probably didn't want to go to her grandmother's party.

> I wouldn't want to go to mine!

Despite the situation, Audrey grinned.

Audrey

> I'm gonna try to focus on getting the script done. I'll let you know when she shows up.

Matt

> No worries. Stay safe out there, Audi.

Audrey

> Always, Mattarati.

The phone rang at exactly ten to nine. Audrey got up with a sigh, pausing the documentary she was watching and slapping on her bedroom light as she went to retrieve it. It was probably her mother calling to check in, as she always did when she was working late in the ER. The woman worried way too much. It wouldn't have been as annoying if she'd at least called Audrey on her mobile as she'd asked so many times, but her mother *insisted* on calling the landline. Probably so she could be sure Audrey really was at home.

But it wasn't her mother on the other end of the line. It was Mrs Chen.

"Hello, Audrey." Jackie's mother's voice was as strong as ever, but Audrey had known the woman long enough to detect the slight tremor, the edge of worry beneath it. "It's Suzy. You haven't heard from Jacqueline yet, have you?"

Audrey's mouth was suddenly dry. It had been hours since Mrs Chen and her mother had spoken. Had Jackie really not shown up yet?

"No, I haven't. She hasn't come home yet?"

"No. And she hasn't called, either."

Audrey hurried back to her room. She moved to her bed, digging for her phone in the covers, and woke up the screen. There were no notifications displayed. She'd been checking it semi-periodically, but there hadn't been any new messages from Jackie. There still weren't. A quick check of Messenger showed Jackie still hadn't checked the previous ones Audrey had sent, and it had been twenty-four hours since her account had been active on the app at all.

Audrey's blood went cold.

"She hasn't been on to check her messages," she told Mrs Chen, her voice small. "It says she hasn't been on since last night."

Mrs Chen let out a shaky breath. Audrey's own breaths were coming quicker, and she had to force herself to breathe properly, to slow down. Nothing bad had happened. Jackie was just... being Jackie. Losing track of time somewhere. Being rebellious on a weekend when she knew it would have the most impact. She'd been saying for years that she wanted to get her parents to back off, to let her be herself instead of the "perfect Asian daughter" they wanted.

But this was a terrible way to do it. Audrey hated the thought of this strong-willed, amazing woman shaking for any reason, let alone for a stunt as stupid as that. If Jackie really was doing this to prove a point, she'd be first in line to give her best friend a much-needed slap in the face.

Mrs Chen inhaled deeply. "All right. I think it's time I called the police."

3

THE CHENS HAD REQUESTED none of the girls come around that evening, but Audrey wished she'd gone anyway. Anything would have been better than lying awake all night, constantly checking her phone for any sign of Jackie, ignoring messages between Penny and Danielle discussing another dress they'd found as if nothing was amiss. Matt had checked in once, asking how things were going, but Audrey hadn't bothered to respond. She wasn't sure how. Things weren't *going* at all.

It had felt like both minutes and hours when the birds started singing, and light crept through her window, signifying the arrival of Sunday. Both increased the sick feeling in her stomach.

Her mother got home sometime around eight, yawning and no doubt exhausted from her shift. Audrey knew what would happen next. Knew her mother looked in on her every morning to make sure she was okay. She braced herself for the moment the door would open, for her mother to realise she was awake, for the dark bags under her eyes to betray that she hadn't slept a wink all night, for her mother to ask what was wr—

The phone rang.

Her mother sighed. It was a weary sigh, a sure sign her night had been extra long. Audrey's stomach backflipped. Maybe she could hold off on telling her mother what had happened. At least until after the woman had managed to get in a solid eight hours of rest. By then, everything would be fine, and her mother wouldn't stress. This would all be a funny story by then.

But then she heard it. One word from the kitchen: "Missing?"

It must have been Mrs Chen on the phone, calling to give an update. Audrey lay still, barely daring to breathe, listening for anything else her mother might say. Maybe Jackie had come home at last, and Mrs Chen was relaying the story to her mother in an exasperated tone. *Girls*, she would say with a sigh, and they'd both laugh.

Audrey grabbed her phone as if she hadn't been dutifully checking it all night. Matt wouldn't be awake yet, but she knew he'd be messaging within the hour. There were dozens from the group chat that she hadn't bothered to read, but when she opened it and scrolled through, she saw none from Jackie. Likewise, Jackie hadn't responded to the one Audrey had sent to their personal chat. And her account still hadn't been active.

She put her phone back on the dresser. It didn't have to mean anything. Maybe Jackie had lost her phone. Maybe she was home after all. Maybe...

"All right," her mother said, her voice soft. She was coming down the hall again, her worn sneakers soft on the floorboards. "Tell them we'll be ready and waiting for them, Suzy. And stay strong, okay?"

Still not home then.

Audrey threw her blankets off as the bedroom door swung open. Despite the early hour, her mother didn't look surprised to see her up.

She still had the phone clutched in her hand. "Why didn't you call me?"

Audrey didn't need to ask what she was talking about. She pushed herself into a sitting position and crossed her legs. "What would have been the point? There was nothing you could do."

"I could have been here with you. Are you all right?"

"I'm fine, Mum." Audrey grabbed a jumper and pulled it over her head. She'd never bothered to change out of her clothes the day before, and she didn't need her mother commenting on it. "I assume we're going to Jackie's house?"

"No." Her mother hesitated. "But the police want to speak with you. They're on their way over now."

Great. Of course they were. Audrey was Jackie's best friend and apparently her cover for whatever it was she was off doing. The police would *have* to question her, even if the Chens had sworn she wasn't involved. Her heart sped up at the thought.

"Is there anything I should know before then?" her mother asked. "Anything at all, Audrey? You won't get in trouble, but I need to know."

Were you covering for her? Do you know where she went? Do you know something that might put you in a compromising position?

Audrey could practically hear the questions ricocheting in her mother's mind. "There's nothing, Mum. I swear it. I don't know anything about this."

She wasn't sure if it was the tone of her voice, the fact she obviously hadn't slept that night, or whether her mother had simply decided to believe her, but the woman simply nodded and didn't question her any further.

"Fix yourself up," she said gently. "I'll be in the kitchen when you're ready to come out, but don't rush yourself."

Audrey listened to the sound of her mother's retreating footsteps, wishing she could crawl back under the covers and get some proper sleep. This had to be a joke. Jackie had probably decided she hadn't had enough attention for the week, and this was the perfect way to fill her quota. That was all.

She'd probably gotten the idea from their discussion on Friday. Because for them to talk about Jackie going missing as a hypothetical and then have it happen less than twenty-four hours later was *extremely* unlikely. Jackie probably thought it was hilarious. Audrey scowled. She was going to be giving Jackie an earful for it—for making her mother worry, for concerning her friends, for wasting precious police time and resources. This was beyond selfish. It was cruel.

Maybe she was doing it to prove her point: that Audrey couldn't do anything to help find her.

It was exactly the sort of stunt her best friend would pull.

Gravel crunched as a car turned into the parking lot of her apartment complex. She unfolded her legs and moved to the window, looking down to see if... yes. It was the police arriving, lights off, and sirens silent. Despite this, she knew half the neighbourhood would know they were here before the clocks hit nine. There were more than enough gossipy old hags in her building alone. She could practically feel Mrs Adderson peering through her curtains a level below.

There was no fanfare as the two officers, a man and a woman dressed in identical blues, climbed out of their cruiser and made their way inside. Just the sound of heavy footfall echoing up the cement stairs in their building's hallway and then the ancient, failing doorbell of the apartment.

Audrey couldn't stay in her room forever. The police would grow impatient, and her mother would drag her out, and that wouldn't look good for either of them. She turned away from the window and chanced a glimpse of her reflection in the mirror. Bedhead. Pale complexion. Her outfit something dug out of a charity bin. But she couldn't be bothered fixing herself up. She just wanted to get this over with.

Her mother had already invited the two officers into the kitchen and was in the middle of pouring coffee by the time Audrey stepped into the tiny space. Their kitchen was cramped at the best of times, and now, with the broad-shouldered male officer sitting at their table and his equally built female partner leaning in the opposite doorframe, the room was more than over capacity. The man, dark-haired and on the younger side, accepted a steaming cup from her mother with quiet thanks, but the middle-aged woman silently waved off the offer. Audrey shuffled from one foot to the other, debating whether or not she really could avoid having to join them.

As if sensing her thoughts, the female officer looked her way, and her eyes softened immediately.

"This must be Audrey," she said.

Audrey's mother set two more mugs on the table and looked over. She was still in her dark blue scrubs, but she'd at least had the energy to fix her hair.

"Yes, that's Audrey." Her mother waved her over. "Come on, hon. This is Detective Sergeant Flanagan and Detective... Senior Constable O'Rourke?"

The female officer, O'Rourke, nodded. "Detective works in a pinch."

"Hello, Audrey," Detective Flanagan said, his deep voice gentle. "I assume you know why we're here?"

Audrey nodded, her mouth dry. *Oh, God*. This was really happening. She could feel the blood draining from her face. Her head spun.

Detective Flanagan offered her a reassuring smile. "Do you mind if we ask you a couple of questions about your friend?"

Audrey opened her mouth to tell them sure, she didn't mind. But she couldn't get the words out. She nodded again instead and moved to the seat at their tiny table that her mother had pulled out for her, dropping into it wordlessly. The scent of coffee washed over her, turning her stomach. She swallowed the bile that threatened to rise.

Her mother sat beside her, hand within reach. Just in

case Audrey needed it.

Detective Flanagan wrapped his hands around his coffee mug. It was navy blue, almost the same shade as his vest, and didn't match any of the other mugs in their chronically mismatched kitchen. "Mr and Mrs Chen tell us their daughter was meant to be staying with you on Friday night. Is that what happened?"

"No." Audrey's hands were shaking. She folded them on the table to steady them. Jackie was going to be in *so* much trouble for all of this. "I haven't seen Jackie since school got out on Friday. This isn't the first time she's told her parents she was going to be staying with me when she wasn't, but she usually tells me when she's going to be using me as a cover. She didn't say anything about it this time."

"Did she message you at all that night?"

Audrey thought back. She wished she'd brought her phone to the kitchen with her so she could open Messenger and check. "No. I don't think so. She might have said something in our group chat, but I don't remember."

"Group chat?"

"With us and the rest of our friends. There are six of us."

"We're going to need to speak to your friends, too," Detective O'Rourke said. Audrey glanced at her, then looked back at Detective Flanagan as he took out a pen and notepad. He slid them across the table to her.

"Please," he added, giving his partner a look. "It might be helpful. In fact, we were hoping you could make a list of anyone you think Jacqueline might have spoken to and of places she might have gone. Does she have somewhere she usually goes when she asks you to cover for her?"

"Her boyfriend's place usually." Audrey pulled the notepad and pen to herself but made no move to write anything down. "But I already spoke to him yesterday. He thought Jackie was with me."

O'Rourke crossed her arms, a frown marring her already wrinkling face. "Her parents didn't mention a boyfriend."

Audrey made a point of not looking at her mother, who was definitely going to disapprove of what she was about to say. "They don't know. They don't like the idea of her dating when she should be focusing on her studies, and she's pretty sure they wouldn't approve of Peter if they met him, so... She keeps their relationship a secret from her family."

Movement caught Audrey's eye. Detective O'Rourke was jotting something down in her own notepad.

"What can you tell us about Peter?" Detective Flanagan asked, drawing Audrey's attention back to him. The sunlight was catching in his hazel eyes, making them golden. "Does he go to school with you? How long have he and Jacqueline been dating?"

"Yeah. He goes to school with us." Audrey thought about it. "They've been dating since... eighth grade, I think? Maybe ninth. It's been a while."

Jackie was going to murder her when she found out about this. If the police didn't tell the Chens about Peter, she knew her own mother would, and three years of a perfectly good relationship would go down the drain. Between disappearing for two days and having a secret boyfriend, Jackie was going to be grounded for life. Her parents wouldn't be letting her out of their sight until she was forty.

"And what's your opinion of Peter?"

Audrey started. She knew exactly what Detective Flanagan was implying. It was textbook. The partner of a missing person was *always* the first suspect.

But they weren't always the culprit.

"He's a good guy," she said adamantly. "I've never seen him be anything but good to her. He definitely doesn't have anything to do with this."

Detective O'Rourke's pen moved furiously across her notepad, not pausing for a moment as she asked, "Is there anything between you and the boyfriend? Something that might have caused trouble between the three of you?"

"Is that really relevant?" Audrey's mother demanded as Audrey said, "No, there's nothing between me and Peter. We don't even talk unless Jackie's there making us talk to each other."

Detective O'Rourke nodded but made no further comment.

"Do you think Jacqueline might have run off to spend the weekend with him?" Detective Flanagan asked instead.

Asking her something she'd technically already answered. Was he trying to catch her in a lie? She wished she had Matt beside her to navigate this. "I mean, maybe. But she usually says something, and like I said, Peter told me he hadn't heard from her."

Detective Flanagan was nodding, but Audrey was sure the only part he'd heard was when she'd said Jackie might have spent the weekend with her boyfriend. She'd bet her entire measly savings that the police would be questioning him as a suspect before the end of the day.

"All right," he said. "Go ahead and make us that list of names and places. What can you tell us about them?"

Audrey made the list, taking the time to explain each name and place as she went: Penny, Danielle, Delilah, and Lenore—the group chat, their friends from school; Peter Fitzsimons, Jackie's boyfriend. Again, she itched to have her phone back in her hand. It would be easier to think about who Jackie might spend the weekend with if she'd had the names right in front of her, helping her move through the fog in her mind. Places were just as difficult. Where did Jackie go when she wasn't with their group? The mall? Her grandparents' house?

Her mother sat in silence, watching Audrey write as she sipped her coffee. She was probably going to interrogate Audrey herself the moment the police left.

The list was a great deal shorter than Audrey would have liked when she handed it back to Detective Flanagan, but he seemed satisfied as he looked it over and tucked it into his vest pocket. The pen slipped in beside it.

"We're going to look into everything you've given us," he said, "but we'll probably have more questions for you later. So don't skip the country, all right?"

The grin and easy-going attitude told Audrey he'd meant it as a joke, but she was too wired to care. He seemed to realise it, too, because he took a card from his pocket and one from his partner and slid them across the table to her instead. Detective O'Rourke didn't look half as friendly. She was already inching towards the door.

"If anything comes to mind," Detective Flanagan said gently, tapping the cards, "you can call us anytime."

Audrey looked at them wordlessly, stark white cardstock with printed black text and the NSW Police logo. She could feel the weight of them already, the expectation that would come with carrying them. Jackie would probably consider what she'd already said a betrayal. Taking the cards would be the final knife in her best friend's back.

"I'll make sure she calls," her mother said softly, moving the two cards to rest between them on the table. "Thank you for coming, detectives. And please, keep us updated."

"We'll do our best, ma'am."

Audrey went on staring at those cards as her mother escorted the detectives out. *If anything comes to mind.* But what could come to mind? That she thought Jackie could be doing this for attention? What would their response have been if she'd said that? Would Detective Flanagan have lost the easy smile? Would O'Rourke have gone full bad cop and started demanding answers from her?

She rubbed her hands over her face, her head spinning with a single, unwelcome thought: *what if this is really happening?*

What if Jackie was really missing?

4

SHE'D BEEN SURE JACKIE wouldn't stay gone long. That her best friend would run off for the weekend, give everybody a good scare, and show up again on Sunday night, laughing and asking what everybody's problem was. She was so sure of it that she'd spent all of Sunday afternoon rehearsing what she was going to say to show Jackie exactly how pissed off she was. Matt would be proud of the speech she'd prepared.

Audrey barely took the time to look in the mirror as she dressed on Monday morning. She needed to get to school, to see Jackie's ridiculous prank come to its end, to put all the unease of the weekend behind her. The Chens hadn't called again, and Jackie's social media was still inactive, but Audrey was taking both as a good sign—of course her socials wouldn't be active. The second she got back from wherever she'd been, her parents would have confiscated her electronics and confined her to her room. She'd be saying goodbye to her social life and influencer dreams in one fell swoop.

And Audrey didn't feel sorry for her in the slightest.

She power-walked on auto-pilot towards their usual

morning meet-up spot, under the old eucalyptus tree out in front of the school's main building. It was still early, twenty minutes before the first bell was due to ring, but Lenore was already there. She had a book propped open on one knee, but her eyes were unseeing as she stared down at the page. She looked up through soft brown waves as Audrey sat beside her, the same worry Audrey had felt all weekend reflected back in her blue eyes. At least they weren't alone in that.

"Have you heard anything?"

Audrey shook her head. She'd been hoping Lenore would be the one with an update for her.

Instead, Lenore looked crestfallen. "The police came to talk to me yesterday. I told them everything I could think of, but... I don't think I was helpful."

"You never know." Audrey gave her what she hoped was a reassuring smile. "We might tell them something we don't think is important, but it might help them find her."

"Is that how it usually works in the cases you cover?"

It took Audrey a moment to process what Lenore was asking. In all the chaos of Jackie's disappearance, she hadn't thought much about her YouTube channel. It was strange. The channel was her life's work, but it had gone straight to the back of her mind when she'd learned Jackie hadn't made it home. Nothing was more important than that. Not even the half-finished case she'd left somewhere on her bedroom floor.

"A lot of the time, yeah," she said. "Like... a woman might not think her neighbour is a bad guy, but she calls the police to let them know he has a car that matches the description of the one they're looking for in relation to an abduction. She calls to tell them so they can rule her neighbour out in case they get more calls about him, but then he turns out to be the guy they're looking for."

Lenore remained silent, her eyes unfocused as she gazed out at the students filing off the two buses that had pulled up. Audrey looked at them, too. There were already a lot of students milling about the front of the building, laughing and chatting and catching up with friends after their weekend apart. It was surreal. Audrey's entire world had changed in the space of those two days, but everything in front of her had stayed the same. People were smiling, flirting, straightening uniforms and fixing their hair, but all she felt were the butterflies doing backflips in her stomach.

"Do you think anybody knows yet?" Lenore was watching the other students, too. The surreal normalcy that surrounded them. "They put out an Amber Alert yesterday. I saw it all over social media. And the police would have to tell the school, right?"

Audrey nodded. They would, if Jackie's parents hadn't done it already. She'd been so focused on the idea that Jackie would show up at school that she hadn't taken the time to consider what was going to happen if she didn't. Of course the school was going to be informed. There would probably be some kind of announcement about it. The police might show up to talk to students, and counsellors would be offered to anybody who needed them. Audrey and her friends would probably all be made to speak with one. She grimaced.

She'd seen the Amber Alert too, in the brief moments she'd gone in to check Jackie's various profiles for signs of activity. Jackie would hate the photo her parents had chosen of her, looking like a perfect, studious daughter, her hair worn straight down and her face void of make-up. Audrey had half a mind to contact the police with a more appropriate shot of her friend. But that wasn't her place. Maybe she would speak to the Chens about it instead if things went far enough for it to become a real problem.

The rest of their group showed up as one.

Penny and Danielle were as animated as ever, chatting up a storm as they breezed through the front gates like schoolyard royalty in their Mary Janes and perfectly pressed uniforms. They'd clearly taken the time to arrange their hair and make-up to their usual standards—God forbid they leave the house without looking perfect for their adoring fans. Danielle had even taken the time to dye her hair over the weekend, the obviously fake blonde catching the eye of more than a few people as they passed. Like clockwork, she winked at Tyson Branwell as he passed them, batting her fake eyelashes for good measure. Like he gave a damn about anything but her bra size. Penny waved in the direction of her on-again, off-again boyfriend, even though they were having an off period. He didn't deign to wave back.

Life really was getting on like normal. Lenore sighed and closed her book at the sight, giving Audrey a look. *Are they serious?*

Delilah trailed behind them, her hair limp and her eyes not holding their usual spark. She looked how Audrey felt—like she didn't know what day it was; like this couldn't be real life. She'd slapped on some eyeliner and a layer of lip gloss, but the rest of her face was void of its usual colour. Even the freckles she hated so much were on full display.

At least one of them looked like she cared that Jackie was missing.

"We're going to Jackie's after school," Penny declared as she reached them. She said it with her usual air of authority, a clear indication the decision had already been made whether they were onboard or not. Typical Penny. "We'll meet back here after fourth period and head over. If you're late, we're going without you."

Lenore frowned. Considering she'd been friends with Penny the longest of any of them, she should have been used to the domineering attitude by now. "Do you think that's a good idea? Her parents are probably going to be busy dealing with the police and—"

She stopped short when Penny shot her a withering glare, lowering her gaze back down to the cover of her book. Her nails were digging into the cover.

"Where do you think she is?" Danielle asked. Audrey's attention shifted to her, and she was surprised to find the new blonde looking at her. Danielle's voice was sharp, her tone demanding. Her bright eyes sparked with challenge. "You're obsessed with this kind of crap, right? You probably know more about it than we do."

Audrey bristled. "Just because I have an interest in true crime, doesn't me—"

The first bell rang, cutting her off abruptly. Audrey

didn't move. Neither did her friends.

Their tiny vice principal hurried through the sea of students making their way inside, struggling through the bottleneck in the doorway to make her way towards where Audrey and her friends were. Audrey sighed. Maybe they should have met somewhere private this morning instead of the same spot they'd been meeting since they'd started high school. Five years of sitting under the same tree every morning of course meant the faculty knew exactly where to find them. Their vice principal's presence proved it.

She had a feeling they weren't going to make it to first period.

"Ladies." Ms Masters's eyes moved from one face to the next, quickly taking in their grim—or, in the case of Penny and Danielle, *annoyed*—expressions. "I'd like you to follow me to the office, please."

Delilah went first, not a word spoken to any of them. Danielle rolled her eyes in the most obvious way possible, looking like she might spit out a "Do we *have* to?" before she hooked her arm around Penny's and followed suit. Audrey waited for Lenore to join her before she moved, slinging her school bag over her shoulder and trailing Ms Masters as she hurried back into the building. Lenore looked about as enthused to be getting out of class as Audrey felt. Any other day, it might have been a blessing, but this morning... she didn't want to think about what was happening. Could she go back to burying her head in the sand and pretending everything was fine?

The faint scent of Mrs Chen's perfume lingered in the air in Mr Evans's office, taking Audrey back to afternoons spent in Jackie's kitchen while her mother treated their group to traditional Chinese cuisine. When was the last time they'd done that? When would they get to do it again? She must have just missed the woman, and guilt settled in her stomach. How was she holding up? How was Mr Chen handling things? She should have called before school to check in. Maybe going to see them later wouldn't be the worst idea after all.

She wondered whether Mrs Chen had been escorted by the police officers standing around the room.

Audrey looked them over as Ms Masters ushered her and her friends into the office and gestured for them to take seats. Was it her imagination, or had extra chairs been brought in for them? There definitely weren't usually this many. She settled into one beside Lenore, setting her bag down as her eyes ran over the uniformed officers. She recognised Detective Flanagan, his back straight and his hands folded in front of him, but Detective O'Rourke was nowhere in sight. Was that a good thing? Maybe she was following up on a lead.

Mr Evans was in quiet conversation with one of the officers, but he broke off and returned to his desk as the girls were seated.

"Good morning, girls, good morning," he said. Not even nine on a Monday morning, and the man already looked like he'd been working a full week and then some. His hands were steady, but his expression was laced with exhaustion. "I've been informed that you all know what's happening with Jacqueline Chen."

"Have they found her yet?" Delilah interjected before

anybody else could speak. Her gaze drifted over to the police on the other side of the office. "Is she dead? Is that why the police are here? Did you bring us in here to tell us she's dead?"

Audrey's heart stopped. *Dead*. She refused to consider the thought.

"She hasn't been found," Mr Evans said gently, his weary face softening, "and I assure you that when she is, we will do our best to ensure the five of you are the first to know. After her parents, of course." He cleared his throat. "Now. You're here this morning so we can have a little chat, and I can explain a few things to you. Firstly, the officers you see here are going to be taking a look around the school this morning and talking with any students who wish to speak with them. Your parents will be made aware of their presence here. They may pull you aside throughout the day to ask you questions, but I want it to be clear you're under no obligation to speak to them. If you don't want to answer their questions, you don't have to, but I do hope you will so they can find our Jacqueline."

"We'll answer them." Lenore glanced briefly at the officers, shifting uncomfortably in her seat. "We don't have anything to hide."

Mr Evans nodded. "It's also very possible that reporters might show up at some point. We're going to do our best to keep them away, but the police are asking that you keep your interactions with them to a minimum. For now, it would be best if Jacqueline's parents handled anything relating to the media, and the five of you kept your distance."

Audrey looked at her friends. Lenore would keep her nose clean easy enough, but Penny, Danielle, and Delilah, to a smaller degree, had all sat up straighter at the mention of reporters. Any one of them would be glad to get in front of a camera and give an interview, even if the subject wasn't one they were particularly happy about. Audrey had to fight back a snort. How the tables had turned. Anything for their fifteen minutes of fame.

"I'm going to be holding an assembly this morning," Mr Evans went on, oblivious to their eager reactions. Audrey hoped the police didn't read more into it. Or maybe she hoped they did. "Most of the student body probably already know, but it would be wrong of me not to say something. I'm giving you fair warning because I know this means your group is going to be getting a lot of attention, and if any of it gets to be too much for you, I want you to come to me immediately. Do I make myself clear?" The five of them nodded automatically. "Good. I'd also like to remind you that Mrs Pillott will be on standby should any of you find the need to speak with a counsellor. I recommend you all make time today."

Audrey grimaced. Mrs Pillott was annoying at the best of times. No way was she going to waste her time talking to the woman when there would be more important things she could be doing—like assisting the police or extending her list of people Jackie might have spoken to or places she could have gone.

"We'd also like to ask if any of you have seen anybody around that may have made you uncomfortable," Mr Evans said. "Perhaps a man approached your group?

Somebody who may have been watching from the streets?"

Lenore paled. "You think somebody abducted her?"

A chill ran down the length of Audrey's spine. She hadn't wanted to entertain *that* idea either. But the longer Jackie went not showing up...

"People watch us all the time," Danielle said with an unconcerned shrug. "It's kinda the way we like it."

Speak for yourself.

"Yeah, and Jackie is Instagram famous," Penny added. She was casually examining the ends of her hair, looking for split ends. Audrey wanted to reach over and slap her hands down. "She has all sorts of creeps hitting up her inbox all the time. I told the police that yesterday." She gave a short laugh. "This is gonna be great for boosting her numbers."

Holy cow, she was stupid. At least Penny had thought to tell the police about Jackie's obsession with becoming a social media influencer because it had completely slipped her mind when she'd been speaking with Detectives O'Rourke and Flanagan. Of course that might be important. Probably more important than knowing Jackie had a boyfriend. She wouldn't have described Jackie as being *famous*, but she definitely had quite the following. Enough that it might have landed her in trouble. Especially since she didn't take Internet safety anywhere near as seriously as Audrey constantly insisted she should. She had all the knowledge to be safe but little of the drive. She could have said the same of Penny and Danielle—all three of them had major Main Character Syndrome, their heads filled with the notion of *that'll never happen to me.*

Audrey hated herself for wanting to tell Jackie, "I told you so."

"We're looking into that," Detective Flanagan said from the corner. Audrey's eyes drifted to him. He met her gaze. "We asked Penelope this yesterday, but would any of you happen to know the passwords to Jacqueline's social media accounts?"

The girls all shook their heads, with Danielle piping up, "Can't you just open her phone? We know her passcode. She should already be logged in to everything."

"Her phone isn't in her house, so we're working under the assumption that it's either with her or she's lost it somewhere. And her parents haven't managed to locate her laptop. It's possible she might have taken that with her, too."

Audrey tried not to hear the things Detective Flanagan wasn't saying: that Jackie's phone might not have been lost, but dumped. That her laptop might have been taken in an attempt to conceal evidence. She wondered if they'd tracked her electronics already. That was a real thing, right? Would it still work if the phone was turned off or someone had broken it? She made a mental note to ask Matt later. If anyone would know, it would be him.

"Can't you just hire a hacker to get into her accounts or whatever?" Danielle asked, at the same time that Delilah said, "Why do you need to get into them?"

"So they can check her message history," Audrey said.

Four heads swung her way. Mr Evans and Ms Masters looked at her, too. None of the officers looked surprised.

"That's right." Detective Flanagan nodded once. "There may be nothing there, but the only way for us to know for sure is to look. It's possible she may have been speaking to and making plans with somebody none of you knew about."

Penny snorted. "Jackie tells us everything."

Audrey bit her tongue. She used to think that, too.

"I'm sure she did, but we still need to rule the theory out. So if you think of something that might work for her password, please let us know."

Audrey could do that. Or at least, she hoped she could.

"All right." Mr Evans cleared his throat. "Do you ladies have any questions before I let you get back to class?"

Audrey had dozens of questions. She knew her friends did, too, but not one of them spoke up. Danielle shook her head; Lenore averted her eyes.

"Very well. I meant what I said. If there's anything you need today—and I mean anything at all—please let me or these officers know."

"Can we skip class and hang out in the courtyard all day?" Penny asked, pouting for good measure. Audrey wanted to hit her again.

Mr Evans didn't even flinch. "Nice try, Penelope. Back to class, all of you. The assembly will be held during second period."

5

PENNY GRUMBLED AS THEY left Mr Evans's office, as if she'd been personally wronged by his denial of her request. Audrey did her best to ignore it. Her mother had offered to let her stay home before she'd left for work that morning, but Audrey hadn't been able to stand the thought of sitting around in her empty apartment all day, waiting for news that may or may not come. She wanted to be on the ground, in the midst of things, where she could be helpful. Penny's parents wouldn't have given her that same option. They were both hard-working, absent parents who expected their children to work as hard as they did, and that meant missing as little school as possible.

She wondered if Penny had even bothered to tell them Jackie was missing.

Audrey couldn't imagine her own mother not knowing. The woman would have known there was something wrong, even if Mrs Chen hadn't called the previous morning. But Penny's parents weren't the most observant or the most available. It wasn't that they didn't care. They were just too busy to be there for their daughter or for her younger brother. They worked hard to provide their children with a big, beautiful house and all the opportunities they could ever want, but it came at a cost. If Penny cared about the lack of closeness, she'd never let on. Audrey hated the idea of it.

Danielle was probably in a similar situation, with her parents being as busy as they were, but she would still take the time out to make sure they knew what was going on. Delilah's parents would know, even if she didn't want them to. The same went for Lenore's mother, who was as attentive as Audrey's, and Lenore had the added bonus of living with her cousin, too. Roxanne avoided their group like the plague because she couldn't stand most of them, but she was always civil to Audrey in the hallways. Roxanne would have seen the Amber Alerts, and would have made sure her mother and aunt were aware. Audrey was glad Lenore had her to turn to.

Penny and Delilah parted from the rest of their group as they reached the stairs, heading up towards their biology class while Audrey, Lenore, and Danielle made a right turn to get to theirs. Jackie should have been with them, and now, heading to class without her, Audrey felt her absence more than ever. Her laughter should have been echoing down the cement hall as their group split. Teachers should have been sticking their heads out of classrooms and shushing her. Instead, they were accompanied by excruciating silence. Even Penny had stopped talking. The missing presence was so great it stole the breath from Audrey's lungs.

If their classmates didn't already know about Jackie's disappearance, the three of them walking into class late without her was going to broadcast it loud and clear.

Audrey gripped the strap of her bag and took a deep breath.

Danielle swung the door wide and strolled into the room with her head held high, no knocking or offering any sort of apology for interrupting the lesson as if there was nothing wrong at all. Like Jackie would have done, Audrey noted. Jackie was a queen, and this was her court. And in the queen's absence, the princess of the realm had stepped up to take the throne. Audrey missed a step in her surprise. Danielle may have been confident, but she was usually more self-aware than this. Maybe the situation with Jackie was affecting her more than she'd let on.

Lenore looked uneasy but followed Danielle into the classroom. No point in being later than they already were. Audrey hesitated another moment before trailing behind the two, slipping the door shut quietly behind her. She could do this. They all could. How bad could it be?

Bad.

Everybody turned to stare—from the boys in the back to the nerds in the front row to stern old Ms Dennings, ungraded quizzes spread across her desk at the head of the room. Even the kids who usually wouldn't stare were staring. Audrey swallowed dryly and waited for the bombardment of questions that were sure to follow, the demands to know what they knew and what was going on and where the hell was Jackie?

There was dead silence.

It was a heavy silence, the kind that filled a space when several people suddenly stopped talking about somebody the second they entered a room. Audrey would have bet every cent she had that her classmates had been discussing Jackie before Danielle had opened the door. Had probably been talking about the rest of their group, too. She doubted they would have stopped if it had been anyone but the three of them now standing in the doorway. She hoped they didn't look as lost as she felt.

"Ladies," Ms Dennings said. She peered at them over half-moon frames, her expression softer than Audrey had ever seen it. It was strange, coming from a teacher who pursed her lips so much they had practically disappeared. "Please take your seats."

Lenore went without a word, head lowered, her hair falling across her face like a curtain. It was a smart move on her part, letting her avoid people's eyes with ease. Audrey followed, but with much less success. Her hair was tied back today, so try as she might, she couldn't help but catch people's eyes as she passed them. Her classmates' gazes burned back at her, full of curiosity and questions and a little doubt for some. She tried to keep her eyes on the ground, but the weight of their stares fell heavy on her shoulders.

She tried extra hard not to look at Jackie's empty seat.

It was bad enough that she had to slink into her own beside it. At least when she'd been at home or in Mr Evans's office, Jackie's absence was easy to explain away—she was simply not there because she hadn't needed to be. But now, sitting on the familiarly uncomfortable stools they'd always complained about together, it suddenly felt more real. Jackie was *supposed* to be here. She was meant to be sitting on that stool, groaning about how the hard wood was going to flatten her butt, sighing in irritation as she looked at the clock over the chalkboard.

Audrey's throat grew tight. Tears stung the backs of her eyes.

Keep it together, girl.

Danielle made for her seat in the middle of the room, meeting eyes left and right as she went. Challenging them. Daring them to speak. Audrey watched her warily. Was Danielle wearing more make-up than usual? She hadn't been paying much attention before, but the windows in the science lab were perfectly angled for the morning sun to catch the glimmer in her friend's eyeshadow as she walked down the centre aisle. Her palette had never held much sparkle before.

One of the guys had noticed, too. He whistled at Danielle from the back of the room. "Lookin' good, baby! You wanna *disappear* with me?"

Danielle let her bag fall to the floor with a bang.

"All right, arseholes." She immediately had the attention of everyone in the room, Ms Dennings included. She even had the nerve to smile around at them all. "We know you want to know what happened with Jackie over the weekend, so go ahead. Ask all of your questions, or forever hold your peace. This is a one-time offer before I decide th—"

"Are you freaking serious, Dani?"

Audrey started at the interruption, her attention darting to Lenore. She was in her usual spot beside Danielle but looked as though she'd rather be anywhere else. Her expression was one of disgust as she glared at the desk in front of her. Her hands were balled into fists; there were angry tears forming in her eyes.

"This isn't the time to make yourself the centre of attention." Lenore's face was flushed; she still wasn't looking at Danielle. "Jackie is *missing*, for Christ's sake, and you're going to use it as an opportunity to make yourself the face of the investigation? What do you think you're going to get out of it? You think this is going to make you Miss Popularity? Stop acting like the whole goddamn world revolves around you. Just sit down and shut the hell up!"

Danielle's jaw dropped. There was an intake of breath all around the room.

Audrey stared. Lenore was *not* the type to make a scene in front of a class. Hell, she would barely do it in front of their own group. She was a doormat by her own admission. Audrey could count on one hand the number of times she'd seen Lenore stand up for herself against somebody, and she'd never seen her do it publicly. She'd seen Penny tear her down one insult at a time, from the way she dressed to the way she did her hair to the way she'd rather bury her nose in a book than a guy's crotch, and still, Lenore hadn't cracked. To see it happen now...

Voices erupted all around the room. Ms Dennings cleared her throat loudly in an effort to stop them. It had zero effect.

Danielle's gaze hardened. "Ex*cuuuse* me? What the hell did you just say to me?!"

Lenore almost tripped in her haste to get away from

Danielle, dragging her bag as she moved across the room. All eyes were on her. She would have hated it if she'd noticed, but it looked like she was too caught up in her escape to give much thought to the people around her. Audrey had a feeling that was the only reason Danielle didn't make a move—she was the kind to start grabbing hair and screeching when she felt she'd been wronged, but even she knew better than to get physical in front of so many people.

Lenore practically fell into Jackie's seat beside Audrey, her shoulders hunched, and her head bowed so much that practically all of her hair was in her face now. It wasn't enough to hide how red her face had gone.

Danielle's eyes were wild. She opened her mouth to say something.

"That's enough!" Several of Audrey's classmates jumped at Ms Dennings's outburst, Audrey included. What a morning this was shaping up to be. "I understand you girls have had a difficult weekend, but I'll not have you disrupting this class any further! You can save your arguments for recess, or you can spend this period in the principal's office. Is that clear?"

Danielle scoffed and sunk into her own seat, looking put out. She shot one last glare Lenore's way, then refused to look at either of them again.

Voices filled the room again, but they were quiet, whispering. People kept turning in their seats to look their way. To look between Danielle and Lenore—Lenore, who was the least likely person in their group to raise her voice or lose her temper.

Audrey nudged her gently. "You okay?"

Lenore turned her head just enough to peer out at Audrey through a curtain of hair. There were definitely tears in her eyes now, fat and angry and threatening to fall.

"I'm fine." Lenore swiped a palm across her eyes. She was definitely not fine. "I knew at least one of them was going to pull a stunt like this, but I didn't think it would be so soon. And I just... I don't want them making this all about themselves. They should be focused on finding Jackie, not on the attention it can get them."

Audrey thought back to the looks she'd seen on the other girls' faces at the mention of the media that morning and grimaced. Anything for their fifteen minutes of fame. Longer than fifteen minutes, if they could manage it. They were probably going to milk the situation for all it was worth. And there wasn't a damn thing she could do about it.

When Jackie made it back, she would no doubt do the same.

"We'll keep them under control." She glanced across the aisle. Danielle was on her phone, posting something to her ten thousand or so Instagram followers by the look of things. "Somehow."

Lenore nodded. "I hope you're right."

Audrey didn't have the heart to tell her she was pretty sure she was wrong.

6

Mr Evans fought for quiet as the entire student body filed into the gym. He stood on the stage looking exasperated, repeatedly yelling, "Please lower your voices and take your seats!" as his students did anything but. Penny swore she could see more of his already thinning hair dropping right off his head from the stress of it all. His efforts were drowning in a sea of sound, and he threw up at his hands as if he knew it. Most of the noise was entirely unavoidable, that of leather shoes on polished wood and plastic chairs scraping as people seated themselves, but the rest was pure teen chaos.

Audrey sat second from the end of a row with her friends, all of them silent. Danielle had made a point of sitting as far away from Lenore as possible, and if Penny or Delilah had noticed, they weren't asking about it. Lenore sat in the aisle seat beside Audrey, also pointedly not looking in Danielle's direction, her hands folded neatly in her lap. She'd calmed down since her outburst in class that morning, but her eyes were still teary and rimmed in red. She hadn't spoken much since their few exchanged words.

Audrey sat back and looked around. She spotted some

of her classmates from first period chatting to their friends who hadn't been in the same class, all of them turning as one to stare at Lenore, who paid them no mind. By lunch, Audrey had no doubt the entire school would know about her friend's outburst. Already, there were kids from other grades staring, too. But the more she looked, the more she reasoned the staring had to be because of Jackie—because *everybody* was looking towards her and her friends, and there was no way word of Danielle and Lenore's little fight had spread that quickly. The only people not openly staring at them were the eight or so police officers stationed around the room.

She focused on them instead. Some were standing still, backs to the wall, arms crossed, their eyes scanning the sea of students. A couple were walking the perimeter slowly. Looking for somebody in particular or observing the group as a whole?

Audrey's breath caught. They might have thought somebody from the school was involved in Jackie's disappearance! Her heart raced at the thought. Did they suspect one of her classmates? Or a teacher, maybe? Mr Michaels had always been overly friendly with some of the girls. Was that something she should be reporting to Detective Flanagan? At the very least, it couldn't hurt, right?

"Thank you, everybody." Up front, Mr Evans had finally been handed a microphone. The volume always felt far too loud for their little gym, but it did the job of finally getting all those voices to quiet. "I know a lot of you are already aware of what happened over the weekend, but some of you aren't. We'll be sending letters home with everybody today for you and your parents to go over, and I welcome any questions you may have in regard to the contents. For the sake of clarity, we're going to tell you everything that we know today so we don't have any more of these disgusting rumours floating around."

Disgusting rumours? Audrey hadn't heard anything. But Penny scoffed and mumbled something under her breath that sounded a lot like, "Yeah, as if she'd ever run off with that ugly douchebag."

A number of people heard her and turned to stare. A few teachers shot disapproving or sympathetic looks her way.

"Let's start with the basics," Mr Evans went on, none the wiser. His eyes moved to a set of cards he was holding. "One of our year eleven students, Jacqueline Chen, disappeared over the weekend. Her mother saw her last on Friday evening. Jacqueline told her mother she would be staying at a friend's house that night but that she would be back the following afternoon for a family celebration. She did not show up at her friend's house for their sleepover, and nobody has heard from her since."

He sounded like he was reading from a script. He probably *was*. Clearly, he was hesitant to deviate from his cards, likely due to the limited information the police had provided him. It did nothing coming from a man who was a hopeless public speaker at the best of times. It was the main reason their assemblies were so tedious and dull, the main reason most of the student body didn't pay attention. But people were paying attention today. Apparently, the subject of Jackie's disappearance was interesting enough that people could overlook Mr Evans's lacklustre delivery.

Audrey wanted to add that the slumber party hadn't been planned and that Jackie had been using her as a cover so she could run off who knew where. It was an important distinction to make. But the police knew already, and she supposed that was what mattered.

"It is entirely possible that Jacqueline decided to run away from home without telling anybody, but it is equally possible that she has had an accident or become a victim of foul play. You'll have noticed today that we have a police presence on campus. Those officers are here to ensure your safety and also for you to speak to should you have any concerns or any information about Jacqueline. In a moment, I'll be inviting Senior Inspector Pearson up to speak with you. I want to assure you that you should not be afraid to speak to him or any of the officers you see in the hall. If there's something on your mind you think might be beneficial to their investigation, please do not hesitate to speak with them."

Audrey thought she could hear whispers starting up in various parts of the gym, but she didn't have time to try to make them out as Mr Evans gestured for a uniformed officer with salt and pepper hair to take his place centre stage. Even without being able to see his badge and rank, the man gave off an air of importance that made Audrey sit up a little straighter.

"Thank you, Principal Evans," the man began. "Good morning, West Drummond High. I'm Senior Inspector

Grant Pearson, and I'm the senior contact for the operation at your school today. As your principal has informed you, one of your classmates is missing, and it's imperative to our operation that we have your full co-operation in our efforts to find her.

"I would first like to make it clear that while we do hope you'll speak with us and bring any concerns our way, you are under no obligation to do so. You have the right to remain silent." Many students laughed at this. Audrey did not. Inspector Pearson didn't smile. "If you want to speak with us but wish to have a parent or guardian present while you do so, that is your right, and we are more than happy to accommodate you. Nobody will be formally questioned without a parent or guardian present.

"I know a lot of you are going to have questions, and I will be more than happy to take them at the end. But first, I'm going to talk a little about the theories we're working with to see if they might jog something in your memories. Any piece of information you have might end up being the key to solving our mystery and bringing Jacqueline home safe."

Bringing Jacqueline home safe. Audrey latched onto those words. If the police were saying that, then there was definitely hope. Those words relaxed her friends, too. Some of the tension went out of Lenore's shoulders; Delilah's face softened.

"We are, of course, looking into the theory that Jacqueline might have disappeared of her own accord," Inspector Pearson said. "It's always a possibility, and we find it to be more common among teenagers. However, we don't believe it's what happened here. Although Miss Chen appears to have taken her phone and computer with her when she left, she did not pack anything else of importance."

Audrey wondered how the police could be certain of that. As much as she adored Mrs Chen, the woman didn't know half the things her daughter was up to. Jackie's prized possessions to her mother were probably the photograph of her with her grandparents or the violin she only played when she had to. She'd have to ask the Chens if she could take a look in Jackie's room to see whether any of the *truly* important objects were missing—her favourite bottle of perfume, the autograph she'd managed to score off some K-Pop star, the necklace Peter had given her for their first Valentine's.

Peter. She glanced around the hall, searching for him.

He was tall enough that locating him wasn't a struggle. She spotted him in the last row on the opposite side of the gym, his jaw tight as he listened to Inspector Pearson drone on. His back was straight, his shoulders tense, and his attention was on the front of the room so he wouldn't have to look at any of the multiple people who had turned to stare at him. The same people who were shooting looks across the room to where Audrey sat with her friends. Nosy creeps. She did her best to ignore them, too—to only focus on Peter.

He looked agitated. Annoyed. Like he'd rather be anywhere else than in the tiny, stifling gym, sitting through this assembly. *Same, Pete.*

"It is also possible that Jacqueline had an accident after

she left her home on Friday night." Inspector Pearson looked around the room, and she got the impression that he was trying to look at every student individually as he spoke. It felt like he was looking right at her when she returned her gaze to the front. "We're looking into this and investigating areas around her home where she might have encountered trouble.

"But the main theory we are working with is that Jacqueline may have been abducted."

This time, the murmuring that sprung to life wasn't subtle. Inspector Pearson was silent for a minute, letting students express their surprise. It was the teachers who started calling for quiet, shushing people left and right, waving angry hands at groups of students until they settled.

Inspector Pearson waited until the room was silent before he began speaking again. "Oftentimes, abductions are committed by family members or someone the victim knows. Fewer still are committed by complete strangers. But in modern times, these crimes are being committed by a new kind of person. Can anybody tell me who that might be?"

Audrey had a feeling she knew where this was going. So did a seventh grader, clearly, because the girl called out, "Strangers on the Internet!"

"That's right." Inspector Pearson nodded. His voice turned grave. "Since the advent of the Internet, strangers have been finding more and more creative ways to lure their victims away from the people and places that they deem as safe. I want to see a raise of hands. How many of you speak to people online that you didn't meet in the real world? That includes video games and live streams. Keep those hands up."

A lot of hands went up. A *lot*. Audrey reluctantly raised her own hand, knowing it would be a lie if she didn't. She interacted with her YouTube comments on occasion when she actually managed to get them, but she probably wouldn't have counted that. But Matt? She had to count Matt. After all, he'd quickly become a great friend to her, even though they had never actually met. They talked almost daily.

"Put a finger down," Inspector Pearson said, "if you've ever told these people that you live in or around West Drummond."

Audrey grimaced. This would look bad on her part, but... she put down a finger.

"Put a finger down if any of your social media accounts are set to public."

On and on it went: put a finger down if you have public photos of yourself in your school uniform; put a finger down if you geo-tag your photos or check-in to places publicly; put a finger down if your online friends know your real name.

By the time Inspector Pearson had finished with his little game, Audrey had put all five fingers down and then some. Her friends had, too, though Penny and Danielle gave each other pleased looks about it, as though they had won the game. Audrey knew better. Of their group, Lenore was the only one with fingers still up.

"Put your hand down if you still have at least four fingers

up," Inspector Pearson said. "The rest of you might be surprised to learn that you're being unsafe online."

Audrey could feel the argument on her own lips. *Not me*, she wanted to say. Matt was the only person she was so open with, and even though she had come to trust him over the years, she would still never give him her home address or phone number. They knew where the line was in their friendship—she would never allow him to cross it, and she knew he would never ask.

Not like Jackie and Penny, who were constantly posting images that revealed too much. Not like Danielle, who flirted up a storm with every guy who sent her a message—if she deemed them attractive enough, anyway.

"Everybody wants to believe they can trust the person on the other end of their messages," Inspector Pearson said, "but the truth of the matter is if you haven't met that person in real life, they could be anybody. It's easy to lie from behind a screen. We're constantly pushing for Internet safety to be taught in schools, and we highly encourage you to speak to your parents about this and look into it for yourselves. If you think you're already being smart about it, I'm challenging you to step up your game."

"Are you saying that Jackie Chen was talking to some forty-year-old fat guy online?" somebody called out. A few people laughed.

"I'm not saying that at all." Inspector Pearson wasn't smiling. Did he ever? "This is simply a theory that we're looking into. And even if she was abducted by somebody she was speaking to online, that doesn't mean it has to be an overweight man living out of his mother's basement."

More laughter. "Young people can be just as dangerous. Don't think you're safe just because that kid you're talking to really does turn out to be your own age."

"What if somebody approaches us pretending to be a police officer," a girl closer to the front of the room asked, "but they're not really a police officer? Is there a way we can tell if they're real or fake?"

"Certainly. You can always ask an officer to show you their badge before you speak with them. If they refuse to show you their badge, it's likely they're not really a police officer, and you should seek safety immediately. Alternatively, if you're concerned a badge may be fake, you can always place a call to their Local Area Command and give the badge's number for confirmation purposes."

Audrey's head was spinning by the time the assembly came to an end. Inspector Pearson had answered questions until people had stopped asking before Mr Evans had finally dismissed them, letting them head out to a quick recess. She told Lenore she'd catch up with the group in their next class. She wanted to catch Peter before he disappeared into the crowd, and with people already rising and heading for the exits, it was going to be a struggle.

She pushed through the masses, making their way towards the doors, heading for the place where she'd seen him last. She knew he was probably already gone, somewhere in the middle of the bottleneck, if not at the head of it, but she had to try. She squeezed between two groups of people and came out at the end of the aisle where he'd been sitting. Where he was thankfully still standing, waiting back with his friends.

Up close, Peter looked as exhausted as she felt. He seemed more relaxed now they weren't being forced to listen to an Internet safety lecture, but there were heavy bags under his dark eyes that definitely hadn't been there when she'd glimpsed him on Friday morning. She wondered if he'd slept much over the weekend and hated herself for not checking in with him, too. They may not have been friends, but she was better than that.

One of his friends saw her coming and gestured her way.

Peter turned. Audrey gave him the friendliest smile she could, doing her best to ignore the eyes that followed her. "Hey, Pete."

"So she really is missing, huh?"

He sounded resigned. His buddy gave his shoulder a squeeze before filing out of the aisle behind him with their other friends, leaving Audrey and Peter to speak alone.

"Yeah. Crazy, right?" Audrey hesitated a moment before asking, "So you don't know where she might be? Or, I dunno, you wouldn't happen to know her social media passwords, would you?"

He shook his head. "Cops already asked me yesterday. I've got no clue. Me and Jackie... we were sorta cooling things off. Or at least, I was trying to."

Audrey blinked. That was news to her. Jackie had never been able to shut up when the topic of her and Peter came up, and she'd never given any indication that things between them were anything less than perfect. She'd seen them together on Friday morning, Jackie slipping her hand into Peter's and kissing his cheek like she did every morning. But had Peter reciprocated? Now that she was thinking about it, she couldn't recall.

Have you been hiding things, Jackie?

Peter rubbed the back of his neck. "Will you keep me updated on shit?"

There. There was the worry he was trying to hide flashing in his eyes briefly. It softened something in Audrey. Cooling off or not, he still cared about Jackie.

"Yeah. Of course I will." Audrey considered him. "When you say you were cooling things off—"

"Miss Herringbone?"

Audrey turned to Detective Flanagan, who had made his way over to her and Peter easily now the crowd had mostly dissipated. He kept his hands loosely in the pockets of his blue slacks, but he couldn't quite reach the casualness he was going for. A flutter of nerves rose in Audrey's stomach. Something about his stance was off-putting. He was too poised.

"Detective Flanagan," she said. "Did you need something?"

"Yes. I was hoping we could chat. Would that be all right?"

She looked back at Peter. He gave her a half smile, half grimace before ducking out to follow his friends, heading for the double doors that led back to the main building. He barely waved at her over his shoulder as he went, leaving her to face the cop on her own. Rude.

"I'm all yours, Detective," Audrey said as she turned back. "Did you have anything in particular you wanted to chat about?"

"Yes, actually." Detective Flanagan fixed her with a long

stare. "I was hoping we could talk about your YouTube channel."

7

Detective Flanagan led her to the vice principal's office. Audrey tried not to look as uneasy as she felt as he held the door and gestured for her to take the seat opposite the desk. She'd never been called into this office before, but it didn't stop her from feeling like she was in trouble, especially given the circumstances. This wasn't going to be an ordinary conversation. How had he found out about her YouTube channel? What did he want to know about it? Was he going to ask her to put out a video for Jackie?

Her heart gave a little start. Would she even be up for doing that?

She should have been. If it had been another of their classmates, somebody Audrey wasn't as close to, she would have done it already. She was always telling anyone who would listen that the first twenty-four hours were the most important in any missing persons case, that the sooner she could get her videos up after a person was declared missing, the better. She'd worked late into the night to get Amanda Mulgrave's video done, had gone to school with only three hours of sleep and a USB stick so she could finish editing the video over recess and lunch and get it up before the end of the day, but she hadn't spared a minute to think about putting together one for her best friend.

She should have used her Sunday more wisely. She could have gotten a video up for Jackie by late afternoon if she'd set her mind to it. Why hadn't she started as soon as it had been confirmed Jackie was missing? How many people would have missed seeing the video and providing helpful information because of her delay?

What was the point of her channel if she didn't use it for its intended purpose?

To his credit, Detective Flanagan looked more relaxed now. He sank into Ms Masters's seat heavily, his gear looking extra bulky today, even if it didn't show in his expression. He'd grabbed a polystyrene cup of coffee as they'd passed the main office and was casually stirring it as he considered her carefully. It was a different look from the one he'd been giving her on the weekend. That look had been sympathetic, friendly. This look was much more aware.

She considered him for the first time—really looked at him. He was younger than most of the other officers she'd spotted in the gym but still old enough that she knew he'd been on the force a while. Late twenties, maybe? Definitely younger than her mother.

He took a sip of his coffee, grimaced, then set the cup down and returned his gaze to her.

"Your school's coffee is worse than the shit we get at the station. I didn't think that was possible."

Was he trying to lighten the mood? Audrey cracked a

smile. "I don't drink coffee, but I've heard it's bad here."

"Consider yourself lucky." Detective Flanagan pulled out his notepad and pen, setting them on the desk beside what was probably now an abandoned cup. "Before we begin, I have to ask. Would you like your mother to be present for this? I'm not officially questioning you, but I can have her picked up and brought in immediately if you'd like."

Her mother? Her mother was probably busy at work, and even if she wasn't, why would Audrey need her? She'd done nothing wrong. And only the guilty called for back-up. "No, that's fine. I'm happy to answer anything you have to ask."

"All right. So you have a YouTube show."

So he was old enough to get the terms wrong, apparently. "It's a channel, not a show."

"Channel, then. Tell me about it. What do you post on there?"

Audrey frowned. Why was he bringing up her channel if he didn't know what kind of content she posted?

"I'm sorry, Detective Flanagan, but how is this relevant to us finding Jackie?"

"It's relevant, Miss Herringbone," he said, "because the police had to find out from external sources that you run a YouTube channel dedicated to covering the cases of missing persons."

Okay, so he did know. "Is that a bad thing?"

"Not at all," he said. "In fact, I think it's great. The police don't always have enough time or resources to keep up with these cases, so any help we can get from the public is welcome."

"Then I don't understand why we're talking about this now."

Detective Flanagan folded his arms and looked at her squarely. For a moment, she could almost see her father in his posture. "Why didn't you tell me about your channel when we spoke on the weekend?"

Audrey frowned. "It didn't occur to me to bring it up. I was so focused on Jackie being missing, and you were asking me all these questions about who she might be speaking to and where she might be that I practically forgot I had a channel at all. I honestly haven't thought about it much all weekend. I haven't even looked at the notebook where I write down all of my ideas and stuff for the cases I'm going to cover. It just... doesn't feel all that important right now."

"What is important right now?"

"Finding Jackie, obviously."

Detective Flanagan nodded. "And have you started making a video for her?"

Oh no. He was going to ask her to do it, wasn't he?

"No," she said quietly. "I hadn't really thought about it until now, honestly. I know I probably should, but..."

I don't know if I could handle it.

Detective Flanagan nodded again, jotting a few things down in his notepad. "And are you holding back on releasing a video about her because of the argument the two of you had the day she disappeared?"

Audrey froze. "What argument?"

He looked back up at her. "We've had multiple witnesses

report that you and Miss Chen had an altercation on Friday afternoon during your lunch period. That she said she would never want you to report on her missing persons case on your channel, and that you were not pleased about it. Is this true?"

Witnesses. Altercation. Audrey's blood ran cold. "What?"

"It's a simple question, Miss Herringbone. Did you or did you not have an argument with Miss Chen on Friday afternoon regarding reporting about her on your YouTube channel?"

"It wasn't about that, exactly." Audrey twisted her hands together in her lap. Was this really happening? Was she being *questioned?* "It was about my channel as a whole. Jackie doesn't agree with the content. None of my friends do. They think it's stupid and that my channel should be about fashion or make-up or something like that. Jackie's always saying I'd get more viewers that way, but she doesn't care that I don't give a crap about any of that. My channel's subject matter is important to me. I just wish she could understand that."

Maybe now she will.

"So it annoys you that Jacqueline doesn't approve of the stories you cover?"

There was no point in lying. "Yeah. It does."

"Enough for you to want to get rid of her?"

If Audrey had thought her blood had gone cold before, it would have been nothing compared to how cold it had gone now. Her heart pounded in her ears. Had she heard him right? Was he really accusing her of... "Of course not!

I would never hurt Jackie! Are you *crazy?!*"

"Miss Herringbone, if you cover these kinds of cases as thoroughly as I hope you do, then you know we need to explore every option made available to us," Detective Flanagan said. He hadn't even flinched at her raised voice. "The fact of the matter is you and Miss Chen had an argument on Friday afternoon in which you directly mentioned her going missing, and that same night, she did, in fact, go missing." He gave her a hard look. "If you were researching a case and you heard this fact, what would you think?"

Audrey didn't want to admit it, but the answer was obvious. From an outside perspective, this looked incredibly incriminating. She couldn't blame whoever had reported their disagreement to the police, whether it be those eighth-grade girls she had encountered or somebody else in the hallway, but that didn't mean she had to like it. The comment had obviously been taken completely out of context. Of course she hadn't meant it literally. Detective Flanagan had to know that. There shouldn't have been a single person in the world who would think she could have done anything to Jackie.

"If it's okay with you," he said, jotting down another few things in his notepad, "I'd like to take a look at your channel."

"That's fine," Audrey said automatically. "My handle is *Auds Talks Crime*. You can look at whatever you like. I have nothing to hide."

She winced as the words left her mouth. That was what guilty people always said.

"Is there anything you'd like to tell me about your channel before I look at it myself?" he asked, glancing up from his notes. "Do you have a particular video that's the most popular? Or maybe you have a favourite case you've covered?"

"My most popular video is about the Beaumont children." And it was only popular because she'd misspelled it as 'Baumont' and caught the eye of a troll. A mistake that would follow her to her grave. "No favourite cases."

"And have you ever received any... *strange* comments I might find?"

Strange comments? Audrey frowned again. "No? My channel doesn't really get that much attention. I'm still building an audience." To give it a more positive note, she added, "That doesn't stop me, though."

"I'm glad to hear it." Detective Flanagan pocketed his notepad and pen once again. "All right, Miss Herringbone. I think that'll be all."

She should leave. She should get up and walk away before Detective Flanagan thought of any more questions to ask her—questions that she hadn't prepared herself to answer, questions that might make her look bad if she answered them wrong or not at all. But there was something she needed to ask him before she went anywhere.

"Detective?"

He took another cautious sip of his coffee and looked at her over the foam rim of the cup. He didn't speak, but the acknowledgment was clear.

Audrey hesitated, but she had to know for sure. "Do I need to think about getting a lawyer?"

Detective Flanagan set the cup down once more. His expression was soft, but it did nothing for her pounding heart. Any other time, she might have liked him. He had a friendly, approachable face and didn't give off the same aura of high and mighty as his partner had on the weekend. He was someone she'd have felt comfortable calling with questions for her videos if things had gone well. Now, it looked like there would never be a chance for that.

"You're welcome to be represented by a lawyer if that makes you feel more comfortable." He traced the rim of the cup with a finger. "You should definitely speak with your mother about this, though. This wasn't an official questioning, but I can't promise things will stay that way. If our questions for you become more serious, she might feel better if you had a lawyer on standby, and any advice I might give could be seen as a conflict of interest should things develop in an unsavoury manner."

It wasn't a yes, but it wasn't a no, either. Her body went cold.

She nodded, standing quickly and scooping up her bag as she went. She would definitely ask her mother what she thought was best. But the idea of lawyering up felt wrong, incriminating. She'd done nothing wrong, and hiding behind a suit would make people think she had. But not getting a lawyer, not answering a question right...

And the fact that he'd bothered to ask these questions at all meant something. Either she was a suspect, or they thought she was involved somehow. Why else would he want to know about the fight? About her channel?

For the first time since she'd met him, she could not wait to get away from Detective Flanagan.

8

"It's completely crazy! I can't believe he would think that!"

Mrs Balford hissed a *shh!* at Audrey from across the library, the annoyance on her face clear. Usually, Audrey would have recoiled at this, at having disappointed a teacher—even if that teacher was the librarian nobody liked—but today, she couldn't find it in herself to care. She was too riled up from her conversation with Detective Flanagan, too anxious about the things he'd implied.

She, a suspect in her best friend's disappearance. It was wild!

Penny, Danielle, and Delilah had gathered in the library at lunch when she'd asked, which was a first. Their usual stance on the school's poorly lit, aesthetically displeasing library was they wouldn't be caught dead in it, and why would they spend their lunch hour indoors when there was sun to be had and boys to be seen—or boys to be *seeing* them. But they were quiet today, their complaints non-existent, even if Penny was flicking invisible mothballs off her skirt. Maybe the staring had started to get to them, too.

Lenore hadn't come. She'd texted back that she was taking the chance to visit the school counsellor over lunch instead.

"It makes me sick to think about it," Audrey went on, albeit in a lower tone of voice. "How could they ever think that I could be a suspect in all of this? She was my best friend!"

Penny looked up from her mothball extermination and raised an eyebrow. "*Was?*"

All three of her friends went from bored to alert at lightning speed. They gave her wide-eyed, startled looks. Danielle's jaw practically hit the floor.

"Oh my *God*," she hissed. "You *did* do it, didn't you?!"

"Of course not!"

"Everybody's saying it," Penny said, crossing her arms and giving Audrey a disgusted look. "Everybody knows you got pulled aside by the police while we were in the gym, and everybody knows about the fight you and Jackie had on Friday. Did you really say that shit? About her going missing and you covering it on your stupid channel?"

"I was trying to make a point," Audrey said. By the looks on their faces, that wasn't going to help her. "She was saying that I was stupid for wanting to get my video on Amanda Mulgrave up so quickly and that it wasn't going to make a difference anyway, so I asked her if she went missing, wouldn't she want every possible person drawing attention to her case to help find her?"

"And then she went missing that same night." Penny was outright glaring at her now. There was fire in the brown of her eyes. "Conveniently, while she was supposed to be at *your* house."

"She was never coming to my house!" Audrey hissed, ignoring another withering glare from the librarian. Didn't she know they were in the middle of a crisis? "She never told me she was coming, so I assume she was using me as a cover and didn't bother to tell me about that either!"

"Right." Penny laughed bitterly. "So she never showed up at your house that night. I guess that rules you out as a suspect then since your mum can back you up on that and give you an alibi." She gave a sarcastic little gasp, clutching a hand over her heart. "Oh, wait. She *can't* do that, because your mum works all the time. So you were home alone when Jackie was supposed to be showing up at your house, and you *have no alibi*."

Audrey gaped at her. Was this conversation really happening?

She looked to the others. Danielle mirrored Penny's furious expression. Delilah looked torn; her hands held tight against her chest as she fidgeted. Audrey's stomach dropped. Yes, this was really happening. Their faces told her everything she needed to know.

"You actually think I did it," she whispered.

Danielle snorted. "Well, if the shoe fits..."

She wanted to shout that it *didn't* fit. That her goal in life was to *help* people, not hurt them! That she'd never do anything to Jackie, especially for something as stupid as gaining a few followers or making a point. She wasn't like that. She wasn't like *them*.

"Let's get out of here," Penny said. She stood gracefully, looking down her nose at Audrey. "Wouldn't want to let the *murderer* over here make us disappear, too. Think of all the views her channel could get if all her gorgeous friends vanished!"

"I haven't posted about this on my channel." Audrey's words fell on deaf ears. The girls were already climbing to their feet, grabbing their things and preparing to leave her there. Alone. "And nobody's saying she's been murdered. She's *missing!* She's still alive!"

"Apparently, that's not what you think," Danielle spat, "seeing as she *was* your best friend."

They wouldn't let her get another word in. Penny and Danielle led the way, marching towards the doors of the library, Penny's ponytail swaying with each step. Delilah didn't look back as she followed, her shoulders hunched and her head down. Audrey watched them go with a sinking feeling in her gut.

Was this what it felt like to be abandoned?

A group of ninth graders were staring at her from across the library, their expressions a mixture of pity and disgust. When she looked away from them, she found another group staring at her, looking the same. A group of girls were peering down at her from the mezzanine.

She suddenly felt extremely exposed. Did *all* of these people think she'd had something to do with Jackie's disappearance? Did they think she'd *murdered* her best friend?

The hairs on the back of her neck stood up.

"That couldn't have been easy."

Audrey looked to her left, to the end of a stretch of shelves, and spotted the light-haired boy looking her way as he leaned against the aisle, arms crossed over his chest. She didn't know Jackson Miranda all that well—knew he was generally well-liked, was casual friends with Peter, and played for the school's soccer team—but she'd never had much cause to interact with him. She half expected him to sneer at her, to follow up his comment with something like, "Was killing your best friend easier?" But he wasn't looking at her like she was a monster. He wasn't looking at her like he suspected her of wrongdoing at all.

"I meant your friends turning on you like that," he clarified, nodding towards the door of the library. "You'd think they'd be more sympathetic with everything that's happened and not turn on their own. But I guess you're not the wolf pack everybody thinks you are."

Audrey frowned. "You heard all that?"

"Everybody did." Jackson looked around pointedly. "You weren't exactly being quiet."

He was right. *Everybody* was looking her way when Audrey glanced around, none of them bothering to hide it. She may as well have been an exhibit at the zoo. Even Mrs Balford was still staring, her look the most disapproving of all, but hopefully, that was from the disturbance Audrey had caused and not because the woman thought she was suspicious. She sighed deeply and rubbed her temples. Would that make her look better or worse to people? Did it even matter?

"I'm in the conference room back here," Jackson said, jerking his head towards the wall behind him. Audrey had never ventured that way, but she knew there was a small, private room behind it where some of the more dedicated students would often meet to work on group projects. "You're welcome to join me if you want to get away from all the eyes on you."

Who was she to turn down the only offer of companionship she was probably going to get?

The conference room wasn't the nerdy hideaway her friends had often claimed it would be. The chairs were plush and clean, purchased in the school's standard shade of navy blue; the walls were covered in an assortment of book-related posters, some of them looking like they dated back to the eighties. There was no window, but the lights were bright and warm. The space was small, but it was inviting.

Jackson returned to his seat at the head of the lone, long table that occupied the space, and Audrey took in the small pile of papers he'd piled neatly in front of him. The word *application* stood out, bold and capitalised across the top of a page. An emblem on the letterhead caught her eye—one for a local university.

"You're applying?" she asked.

Jackson shrugged. "Thinking about it. My parents insisted it was time to start looking at where to go since we've only got a year left. I figured I'd apply to this one as a back-up to keep them happy. Couldn't hurt, right?"

"Sure, I guess that's true." She set her bag on the floor and dropped into the seat adjacent to him. She hadn't thought much about university yet. She didn't really see the point when it would be more convenient to get a job to help her mother pay the bills. Besides, she didn't need to start her life with that kind of debt. Especially when she had no idea what she wanted to do in the first place. "What are you planning on studying?"

"Criminology and forensic psychology."

If she'd still been holding her bag, she would have dropped it. "Say what?"

Jackson smirked. "Didn't expect that, did you?"

"No, I didn't. I didn't know you were into that kind of thing."

I thought you were just another dumb soccer player, was what she didn't say.

"A lot of people are. They're just not as open about it as you." Audrey frowned, but Jackson went on with, "And I don't mean that as an insult. It's great that you're open about your interests. But you have to admit, it gets you some judgy stares and people crossing the corridor to get away from you."

That *had* happened once after she'd started going public and telling people about her channel. One of the younger girls—highly religious and very timid—had made a point of lowering her head, moving as far to the right of the hallway as she could, and scuttling past Audrey as if she thought she might catch the plague. Jackie had found the entire thing hilarious and had showered Audrey with a mixture of *I told you so*'s and hissing at her while she made the sign of the cross. Audrey had spent the rest of the day feeling like a leper.

"It's important work," she said for what felt like the millionth time. Her mantra for every time somebody made her feel wrong about what she was doing. She refused to let self-doubt creep in.

"It is," Jackson agreed. "I saw your video on the Amanda Mulgrave case. Did you hear they found her yesterday?"

Audrey blinked in surprise. No, she hadn't heard. "I haven't really been watching the news or reading social media since..."

"Right. I guess your feeds would be full of Jacqueline now, anyway, wouldn't they?"

Audrey nodded. "So where'd they find her?"

"Amanda? Locked up in her boyfriend's house." Jackson shrugged. "I'd like to give the whole *not all guys are bad* speech, but it's hard when this kind of shit happens literally every day. It's always the ones you think are the nice guys, right?"

"Nice guys are dicks."

"And apparently, best friends are prime suspects."

Audrey winced. "Does everybody really think that?"

Jackson toyed with his pen. "Opinions are split. I think it mostly depends on how people saw you before—as the nice girl who never gets into trouble or the weird girl who talks about dead people online."

She didn't bother to correct him. "Which side of the debate are you on?"

Jackson grinned. "I definitely think you're weird."

Audrey rolled her eyes, but his joking tone was the first thing to put her at ease since she'd spoken with Detective Flanagan. A little of the tension went out of her shoulders, and the sick feeling in her stomach lessened a fraction.

"I don't believe it at all, in case that wasn't clear," he said.

"We've been classmates since, what? The second grade? And in all that time, I don't think I've ever seen you be mean to anybody. You felt bad for stepping on a dead mouse, for Christ's sake."

"Ugh. You remember that?"

"Of course. There isn't a mean bone in your entire body," Jackson said. "No way in hell did you do anything to Jacqueline."

Audrey smiled just a little. After watching three of her friends literally turn their backs on her, it was nice to know that she had at least one person on her side.

Jackson clasped his hands in front of himself and gave her his full attention. "So. How are you planning on convincing the police that they're barking up the wrong tree?"

"What do you mean?" Audrey asked, surprised. "I wasn't planning on doing anything. I figure they'll see it for themselves soon enough, and everything will be fine. They have to know that I'm innocent. What is there to worry about?"

"You don't cover much beyond missing people, do you?" Jackson raised an eyebrow. "Do you always only focus on the people themselves, or do you look at the investigations that surround their cases, too?"

"I find all the relevant details about their cases, and I present that to the public. There's no need to know the ins and outs of everything."

"I beg to differ." Jackson leaned back, one arm slung over the back of his chair. "For example, I know that when cops are investigating a crime and they come across somebody they think is an ideal suspect, they can get tunnel vision. Their minds narrow, and they start looking for evidence that can tie that suspect to the case instead of looking for any kind of evidence that might introduce a *new* suspect. So many people are falsely accused of crimes that they didn't commit, but because the police are so set on believing it was them, they end up going to prison for it anyway. That, or the cops and the media make sure their lives are a literal living hell."

She knew that already. "That's not going to happen to me. Detective Flanagan only questioned me today because he had to. They'll look into me and my channel, they'll see I'm not hiding anything, and they'll get back to looking for whoever is really behind this."

"Speaking of—what do you think happened to her?"

Audrey blinked. "I... don't really know. I've spent most of my time trying *not* to think about what could be happening."

If she was being honest, she didn't want to let those thoughts consume her. There were a lot of deep, dark paths her mind could go down if she started wondering, and the longer Jackie stayed missing, the darker those roads were going to get. Better to not let her mind wander too far. At least not yet.

"Do you think it could have something to do with the guys she's always chatting with?"

Audrey shook her head. "She wasn't talking to anyone online. That I know of, anyway."

Jackie had never mentioned anything like that. Even though the police were considering it a possibility, Audrey wasn't so sure. An online hottie was exactly the sort of thing Jackie would have bragged about to the group, but she only ever talked about Peter. She spoke to different people all the time—randoms on Instagram and Facebook, people who wanted to collaborate with her, fans of her pages—but never anything serious. She might have had some questionable morals, but she wasn't a cheater.

"Don't try to defend her," Jackson said, his voice calm. "You don't have to keep lying for her. She makes it pretty obvious she thinks she's queen shit, and she's chatting up guys online. Even Pete knows about it."

"She was probably just chatting to friends or something. What makes you think she was chatting up a guy?"

"Guys," he said, emphasising the plural. "She sits in front of me in English. I saw her do it. And before you say it, no, she definitely wasn't texting Pete. He was in the class."

Audrey didn't know what to say to that.

Was this the reason Peter was trying to cool things off? Maybe Jackie was the only one who thought their relationship was perfect. Or maybe they'd both checked out of it, and Jackie was clinging to the image because they'd always been Mr and Mrs Perfect. She was all about her image, after all. Even in front of their little group.

Maybe Peter could tell her more. She'd never taken him as the kind of guy to let Jackie walk all over him, so he'd definitely confront her if he suspected she was chatting up other guys. Right? The logical part of her brain said yes, definitely. He'd know whether it was true or not. He might even know who she'd been talking to.

The darker, more crime-orientated side of her brain said something else.

Maybe it was enough for him to want to hurt her.

9

IT HAD BEEN THE longest Monday ever. Audrey practically dragged her feet as she left her final class of the day, mental exhaustion weighing her down as she made for the nearest exit. It was hard to say what the worst part had been. The constant, pitiful staring? Her friends turning on her? Jackson telling her Jackie had been interacting with faceless guys online? The fact that the police might suspect she had something to do with Jackie's disappearance?

That. That was definitely the winner. Her stomach backflipped just thinking about it.

But maybe Jackson's information would help. Jackie chatting up guys on social media was exactly the sort of thing the police would be looking for—evidence that she might have gotten herself into trouble by trusting the wrong person. Audrey tried to picture it: Jackie agreeing to meet up with one of her Instagram followers, likely one posing as an attractive uni student-aged local who knew just what to say to flatter her. That, at least, wouldn't be hard. A well-placed comment about her eyes, about how they'd love to tangle their fingers up in her hair...

But it was a hard sell. Jackie wasn't stupid. She loved

watching those catfishing shows, and she had Audrey constantly reminding her that her followers couldn't be trusted. That it could be *anyone* behind the keyboard. She didn't give out her address or her phone number. She didn't even use her real name online. She was Internet-safe. They all were.

Then again, after hearing what Inspector Pearson had said at the assembly today, maybe she needed to reassess that thought.

Lenore fell into step beside her, a folder full of class work clutched tight to her chest. She looked better than she had that morning, though her blue eyes were tired. "Are you coming to Jackie's?"

Jackie's house. Right.

Audrey looked ahead. The other girls weren't waiting at the staircase, which meant one of two things—either they were late to their own meeting, or they'd chosen to go on ahead without Audrey and Lenore. Audrey knew they would do it to her, especially after what had happened at lunch. But would they abandon Lenore like that?

Yes. Absolutely.

"I don't know if I'm still welcome." Audrey glanced sideways at Lenore. Possibly the only friend she had left. "Didn't the others tell you about what happened at lunch?"

"Oh, they told me." Lenore shrugged. She looked truly unbothered, and Audrey relaxed, some of the tension in her body releasing. "For what it's worth, I think they were out of line. I know you. We all do. You *definitely* didn't have anything to do with this. You made it your life's mission to try to stop things like this happening in the first place!"

A couple of heads turned in their direction, and Lenore shrunk back into herself, blushing.

"And besides that," she went on more quietly, "you've known the Chens the longest of any of us. If you're not going, then I'm not going to intrude on them. Jackie's mum will probably slam the door in our faces if you're not there."

Audrey very much doubted that sweet old Mrs Chen would slam a door in anybody's face, whether their visit was a welcome one or not, but she didn't say that.

The others were late, of course. Audrey wanted to ask at what point *fashionably late* became just plain rude, but she didn't need to be stirring up any trouble that might carry through to the Chen house. Penny and Danielle both made a point of giving her disgusted looks as they brushed past, arm in arm, the latter hissing something that sounded an awful lot like *psycho bitch* as she went. Audrey gritted her teeth and breathed deeply through her nose.

One of us is definitely a bitch, she wished she could say, *but it's not me.*

Delilah gave them a sheepish look as she brought up the rear. "You guys coming?"

Lenore nodded.

Audrey texted her mother as they walked, letting her know she was headed to Jackie's and would be home later than usual. Not unheard of. She probably should have called, especially given the circumstances, but she knew what her mother would think if she spotted Audrey calling while she was at work. She'd panic. She'd think something was wrong. Audrey didn't want her mother worrying. Not when she should have been focusing on her patients in the ER. Definitely not when they already struggled to pay their bills.

Maybe it was better she was heading to Jackie's. Her mother could rest easier knowing she was with her friends.

The people she *thought* were her friends.

Jackie lived in the opposite direction to home, closer towards East Drummond and the snobbier parts of their suburb. Penny was two streets further, Delilah another one back, and Audrey always wondered if they knew how envious she was of them and their beautiful homes. She'd lived in this area once, too. Back before her father had disappeared, the lion's share of their household income with him, and her and her mother's lives had gone to hell. She didn't begrudge her mother for having to give up the house or the finer things they'd had in life, but she'd be lying if she said she didn't miss it. Almost as much as she missed her father. But that was life.

The Chen household was eerily quiet on the outside. Audrey had expected to see police cars, neighbours, maybe a news crew or two, but there was nothing. The street was empty. A complete ghost town. It looked like every other Monday afternoon she'd walked these footpaths, minus the woman across the street who was usually headed home with her primary school-aged kids at this time. But maybe they'd headed to a park instead. Their absence didn't have to mean anything sinister.

It was easy to imagine nothing was out of the ordinary

as they approached the house. It could be just another normal afternoon spent giggling over cute guys in boy bands and debating which Hemsworth brother was the hottest.

Maybe Jackie had made it home during the day, and they really *would* be walking into that.

"Not even *one* reporter?" Danielle scoffed. "Jackie'd be pissed if she saw this."

Audrey bit back the comment she wanted to make and swung open the Chen's painted white gate. The pebbles that lined the tiled path were today all over the place, knocked loose by who knew how many sets of boots over the weekend. She nudged a few back into place as she led the way to the door, but it looked no less messy for it. Black stones mixed with brown and dozens of the white rocks had been kicked into the grass. They stood out the way she imagined snow would, bright and out of place in the Sydney sun. Mrs Chen must have hated seeing her little garden such a mess. If she'd had the energy to step outside at all.

Audrey rang the doorbell. It echoed loudly behind the closed door, bouncing down the wood-panelled hallway beyond, straight through to the kitchen where Mrs Chen spent most of her afternoons. Would she be in there now, keeping to her regular routine? Or would she be—

A breathless Mrs Chen flung the door wide, her dark eyes wild and... hopeful, Audrey realised. Jackie's mother had been hopeful when she heard the doorbell. But the look lasted for only a second before it fell, Mrs Chen quickly taking in their faces. The lack of one face in particular. Her expression said it all.

Jackie wasn't home. Her mother had been waiting, hoping her daughter would make her way back from wherever she was, maybe that she'd skip home from school with her friends like she did every other day. Of course she'd be hoping that. Just as Audrey had been hoping, as unlikely as it may be, that they would find Jackie at home with her parents, safe and sound. They should have called ahead. They should have warned Mrs Chen that they were on their way and asked permission to visit. Showing up like this, without Jackie among them, had been cruel.

Mrs Chen looked like she'd aged ten years in a matter of days. The lines around her eyes were deeper, more prominent. Her hair, the same pitch black as Jackie's, looked like it was going grey. She's always looked so youthful to Audrey, more like Jackie's sister than someone old enough to be her mother. Now, she looked older than her years.

"Oh. Hello, Audrey. Girls." Mrs Chen forced a smile. Her eyes glimmered with a fresh wave of tears. "Won't you come on in?"

Not even Danielle had a snide remark as they walked single file down the hall into a kitchen that had seen better days. By Mrs Chen's standards, the place was in shambles—dirty dishes piled in the sink, a wok crusted with burned remnants on the stovetop, and several half-drunk cups of tea scattered around the room. Mr Chen's newspapers were on the kitchen table, two days' worth still wrapped in their delivery plastic. Seeing even one, unwrapped and unread, was unusual. He wasn't present, but judging by the fact his lunch bag was thrown in a corner on the counter, he hadn't gone to work.

The Chens were not doing well.

Jackie's mother waved her hands at the cluttered table. "Please, sit. I'll make us all some tea."

Lenore stepped past Audrey, who had come to a standstill in the kitchen doorway and moved to take Mrs Chen's arm gently. "Why don't you sit, Mrs Chen? I can make the tea."

Audrey expected Mrs Chen to protest. *Guests will never need to raise a finger in my house.* But she must have been so exhausted from catering to people all weekend, so exhausted from waiting and waiting for Jackie to stumble on home, that she only gave Lenore a thankful smile before sinking into a creaking wooden chair and sighing.

Penny shoved past Audrey to take the seat beside Mrs Chen.

And that was fine. Audrey couldn't stand the thought of sitting at that little wooden table where she and Jackie had spent so many afternoons as children enjoying pineapple buns and almond cookies while they did their homework, and their mothers drank tea. Couldn't stand the thought of sitting there and pretending everything was fine when everything was *not* fine, and Jackie *wasn't* here.

Her head spun. She gripped the counter to keep from falling.

Her hand nudged a ceramic mug, knocking it into another. Tea sloshed in both. There were dishes all over, she reminded herself. Either from being forgotten or from Mrs Chen's lack of motivation to keep her kitchen clean, it didn't matter. It was something she could do to help. Something she could focus on while she steadied herself. She gathered both with one hand, swung by the table to gather a handful of finely patterned plates in the other, and carried the whole lot to the sink.

Lenore's eyes drifted her way as they worked—one making tea and one washing dishes, while Penny and Danielle played their roles as concerned, comforting friends. Their voices were surprisingly gentle as they spoke with Mrs Chen. Audrey glanced over her shoulder at them. She hadn't known what to expect after the day's events, but she was glad it was this. Mrs Chen looked like she needed a kind hand after the weekend she'd endured. Delilah slipped into the last chair like it was made of glass, looking as unsure as Audrey felt about their being there. She said nothing, clasping her trembling hands in front of her and letting the others do the talking. It was strange to see her so quiet. Jackie's disappearance had clearly shaken her.

Not as much as it had shaken Jackie's mother, of course.

"None of you have heard from her at all?" Mrs Chen asked, seeking out each of their gazes individually. Audrey met the woman's eyes, and Mrs Chen held hers with a pleading expression. "It's so unlike her to go this long without at least calling."

Penny's dark expression loomed from behind Mrs Chen. "It is, isn't it? Are you *sure* she didn't show up at your place on Friday night, Audrey?"

Oh, hell no. She wasn't going to play this game.

"Very sure," she said, her eyes never leaving Mrs Chen.

"Actually, I was wondering if it would be okay if I took a look in Jackie's room. It's just..." How could she say this without making herself sound superior? "I thought I might be able to catch something the police might have missed?"

Mrs Chen was waving a hand before Audrey had even finished asking. "Of course, of course. You're her friends. You know her best. If anybody will know if something's amiss..."

"It will be Audrey," Lenore agreed as she carried two mugs to the table, setting one first down in front of Mrs Chen before offering the other to Delilah. "Maybe we can give her some time to take a look."

"She shouldn't go alone." Danielle was smirking as she said it. "If something turns up missing, the police might get the wrong idea and think she's got something to do with it. One of us should definitely go with her." She made a show of cracking her neck. "I suppose I—"

"I'll go." Delilah stood quickly, sliding her tea to Danielle instead. "I'm sure we won't be long."

She made for Jackie's room before anyone could get another word in. Audrey wiped her sudsy hands on her skirt before following Delilah down the hall, ignoring Danielle's glare burning into her back, making a right into Jackie's room as naturally as she would have into her own. It was stupid that she held onto one last fragment of hope—that traitorous thought that just *maaaybe* Jackie might be hiding out in her bedroom, waiting to yell, "Gotcha!" when they entered—but that hope was dashed when she and Delilah stepped into a lifeless space.

No Jackie.

Delilah wrapped her arms around herself and sat on the neatly made bed. "Sorry. I don't think I could have spent another minute out there."

"It's fine." Audrey paused, looking her friend over. "Are you okay?"

"Not really." Delilah trailed a sneaker along the cream-coloured carpet, somehow still fresh and clean after two years. "It's just a lot, you know? Being here and everything that's happening." She shook her head. "Can we just get this over with so we can go home?"

Audrey nodded.

It was clear Jackie's room had been picked through. There were books out of place, folders askew on her usually neat desk, and a storage box left at the foot of the bed when it was usually kept under. She had no doubt the police had done a thorough job, and she wasn't anticipating uncovering a secret stash of love notes or anything, but there were other treasures to check for.

She went through her mental checklist of Jackie's prized possessions and marked them off as she found them: her Chanel was still sitting proudly on her vanity; the necklace from Peter was tucked safely into the hidden drawer in her jewellery box; the K-popper's autograph was still safely preserved in its frame. Even the smaller things were still in place. None of the photos Jackie kept taped to her wall in the shape of a heart had been removed. Her favourite boots were nestled comfortably in her closet. Everything looked to be accounted for.

Except for Jackie's laptop.

Sure enough, the computer wasn't in any of its usual places. It wasn't out in the open on the desk. Wasn't tucked out of sight under Jackie's pillows. Her school bag was sitting in her desk chair, but the laptop wasn't in there either. Its carry case was also noticeably absent from its usual place hanging on the back of the door.

She looked under the desk and frowned. "The charger's gone."

That was unusual. Jackie only took her laptop's charger with her to study sessions or on weekend trips, times when she knew her computer would be getting a lot of use without her being able to get it home to recharge. Clearly, she hadn't intended to be home Friday night, but had she anticipated being gone longer than that?

Audrey stood, drumming her fingers once along the desk. It felt traitorous to voice the thought, but… "Do you think she might actually have run away?"

She would have loved living Jackie's life, but she knew her best friend didn't always feel the same. Jackie was always complaining her parents were too strict. That they expected too much of her. That they were too busy shaping her into their idea of perfection to stop and listen to what she wanted for her own life. To Jackie, her life was often a prison. Or so she claimed.

So maybe she *had* run away. Maybe she'd taken her phone and her laptop to keep pursuing her dreams of becoming an influencer but left every other aspect of her life behind—right down to her signature scent.

Delilah was silent for so long that Audrey looked over to make sure she was still there. She was, looking uneasy as she gripped the comforter on either side of herself, frowning so deep the lines on her forehead were bound to stick permanently. Her gaze was laser-focused on Jackie's pristine carpet.

Audrey grimaced. Here she was focusing on the friend that was missing when another of her friends was suffering right in front of her.

She sank down beside Delilah slowly. "Listen. I know you're probably mad at me and all that, but... you know you can talk to me, right? We're in this together. All of us."

Delilah remained silent for a long while. Her hands clenched and unclenched the bed covers, almost like she was nervous, hesitant to say whatever was on her mind. Audrey stayed quiet. She knew what it was like to need a minute to sort out your thoughts.

Delilah opened her mouth.

"Are you guys done in here?" Penny asked, practically swinging herself through the open doorway. Her brown eyes moved from Audrey to Delilah. "We should go before our parents start sending out the search parties."

Delilah stood quickly—as quickly as she had in the kitchen—and hurried from the room before Audrey could ask her what she'd been about to say. The action was so sudden she wondered whether she'd imagined that Delilah was about to speak.

Penny gave her one last dirty look from the doorway. "Sorry not sorry for stealing your next victim, freak."

Before she could even think of a comeback, Penny had slammed the bedroom door in her face.

10

AUDREY STARED AT THE message, her phone balanced precariously on a knee as she absently picked pineapple slices off her reheated pizza and dropped them into her mouth. Matt had sent it first thing that morning before her alarm had even sounded, like he'd known she was going to need it. She hadn't responded, hadn't even looked at it throughout the day, but looking at it now was a weight off her shoulders. It was proof that no matter what Penny or Danielle thought of her, Matt had her back. Just like he always had. Her heart stuttered at the thought.

Even with the Messenger app set to dark mode, her phone's screen gave her more than enough ambience for stewing in her thoughts. She didn't want the light. Didn't want to look around her room and see the pictures of her friends placed everywhere, from the peeling closet door to the frame around her mirror. Her mother would have tutted and said something about her ruining her eyes, but

Audrey didn't have the energy to care. Today had been too long. Too mentally and emotionally draining. Too full of unwelcome surprises. Maybe if she ruined her eyes, the rest of the world would take pity on her and cut her some slack. At least for a few days. Was that too much to ask?

For a teenage girl? Probably.

She closed her eyes and took a deep breath. Now would have been a great time to be into yoga or meditation or *something* that could help take the load off her shoulders. She let the breath out through her nose, counting backwards from ten like she'd heard some influencer recommend, and tried to let go of everything that had happened. Her friends turning their backs on her? Gone. Detective Flanagan accusing her of having something to do with Jackie's disappearance? Like water off a duck's back.

She pushed the last of the air out of her lungs. She didn't feel any better.

Her phone vibrated on her knee, and she opened her eyes to peer down at it.

Matt

How are you holding up? How did
school go today?

I wish someone would burn the place down, she wanted to say. And she could. Matt would understand. He'd always understood whenever she'd vented to him about something—her friends, her mother, her *life*. But if she really was a suspect in Jackie's disappearance, the last thing she needed was the police to see messages like that on her phone. With her luck, the school *would* catch fire, and she'd be arrested for sure.

As if Matt knew the headspace she was in, he prompted her again.

Matt

> Feel free to vent. This is a safe space, Audi.

He really did know her. Maybe better than she knew herself. Definitely better than Jackie knew her. She didn't give him nearly enough credit, this boy whose face she'd never even seen properly. His half-shadowed profile picture looked back at her, unsmiling but a comfort all the same. She wondered if he looked like that right now—his dark hair half in his eyes, his expression bored. Was he sitting in darkness, too?

She wiped her greasy hands on her shorts and plucked the phone from her knee.

Audrey

> School sucked. Me and my friends got called into the principal's office as soon as the first bell rang. There were cops all over the school today talking to people, and they had an assembly so our principal could tell everybody what was going on. Some inspector spoke to us about why Internet safety is so important.

Audrey

Then, right after the assembly, one of the cops who came to my apartment on the weekend pulled me aside again and wanted to ask me some questions about a stupid little argument that me and Jackie had on Friday. You know, when I told you we argued about my YouTube channel? He was asking about that and asking why I never told the police about my channel in the first place, and it sounds like they actually think I'm a suspect in Jackie's disappearance.

Audrey

And then it gets EVEN WORSE, because when I went to talk to my friends about it, they turned on me, too! They actually think that I did this to get more views on my channel or something! Well, maybe not Lenore, and I think maybe Delilah is struggling with everything, but Penny and Danielle definitely hate my guts right now. It's all just UGH.

She forced herself to stop. She'd go on ranting for hours

otherwise, and whether he'd invited her to vent or not, Audrey didn't want to do that. It was getting late, and she didn't need to go riling herself up. Her mother would never leave it alone if she got home at midnight and found Audrey still wide awake, mashing her keyboard in a frenzy.

Matt took a minute to read everything she'd already written. No speech bubble popped up to show that he was writing, but his status bubble remained green. He was definitely still there, probably taking his time digesting everything. She took a moment to finish the remainder of her pizza, stale crusts and all, and set the plate on her bedside table.

Matt

Holy shit. That's one hell of a day.

Audrey laughed dryly. Yeah, it really had been.

Matt

I'm sorry to hear about your friends. That's a really shitty thing for them to have done to you, Audrey. Especially when you're going through the same trauma they are.

Matt

But as for those accusations about you having something to do with Jackie's disappearance, did you show them our messages from that night?

Audrey frowned.

What do our messages have to do with Jackie's disappearance?

Nothing. That's the point. They're timestamped until something like two in the morning, so that might help you prove you were too busy chatting with me to be able to do anything to your friend. And if you're lucky, there might even be geo-tagging on them. It's not solid proof, but it's a start.

Audrey hadn't thought about that. Why hadn't she told Detective Flanagan that she had a kind-of alibi for Friday night? She couldn't possibly have been doing anything to Jackie when she and Matt were messaging back and forth every sixty seconds. They'd been watching a true crime documentary together, the latest they'd found on the Zodiac Killer, and the commentary had been constant. It was better than if they'd been on a call together.

Something they'd never done. But maybe soon.

You didn't even consider that, did you?

She could practically hear Matt chuckling from behind

the screen. In her head, it was a rich, musical sound that made her stomach flutter.

Matt

> It's fine. You've had more important things on your mind. Like finding your friend.

This was why she needed Matt. Why she valued their friendship so much, even if they'd never met in person. He was the fresh perspective that she needed on everything—her life, her cases, her fears. She could no longer count on one hand the number of times he'd helped her take a step back and reassess a situation, giving her more material to work with or helping her solve a problem that had felt impossible. She could only hope that one day she would be able to return the favour, when he was a detective, and she was... whatever she was going to be.

Audrey

> Thanks, Matt. What would I do without you?

Matt

> You're a smart girl. You'd figure it out.

She wasn't so sure about that, but she appreciated the support all the same.

Matt

> But I'll say it again. You really, REALLY need new friends.

Audrey sighed and rubbed her hands over her face. How many times had he said it now? How many times had she agreed, only to do nothing about it? He probably thought she'd walked right into this situation, that she was the cause of her own misery. Of course her friends thought she was behind Jackie's disappearance. They already thought she was weird. They knew she had an interest in true crime. How big of a jump was it to think she might have kidnapped someone? Especially if they thought she was as obsessed with getting likes and views as they were.

Did they think she was going to come after them next?

Audrey

Is this the part where you say I told you so?

Matt

Of course not. This is the part where I say I'm sorry your friends are such shits. Except Lenore. She always seems cool when you talk about her.

Audrey smiled.

Audrey

She is.

Matt

Tell me more about what you're thinking.

Matt

You said Danielle was struggling? Maybe you could talk her around. Then you don't have to feel like EVERYBODY is against you.

Audrey

Delilah. And… maybe?

Audrey

I don't know. It felt like she wanted to tell me something, but she stopped when Penny came into the room. So whatever it is, I guess she doesn't want Penny to know. Which could either mean she wanted to tell me she was on my side, and she knew Penny would hate that, or…

Matt

Or maybe she's struggling with a guilty conscience.

Audrey snorted.

Audrey

Absolutely not. Delilah's not capable of doing something like this. And struggling with things doesn't make somebody guilty.

Matt

Having a guilty conscience doesn't make her guilty either. She might be feeling guilty because she thinks she could have stopped things. It could mean she knows something. Maybe she knows where Jackie really was that night.

Audrey

Do you think she could?

Matt

Anything's possible. I can't say anything for sure because the only perspective I'm getting on things is yours. But she's your friend. Trust your gut, Audi. If you think she wanted to tell you something, you should probably follow up on it. Even if it turns out to be nothing, at least you'll know.

Audrey

And if she wants to tell me she hates me?

Matt

Then you don't need her in your life.

Audrey fell back against her pillows, letting her phone settle in the blankets beside her. Matt was right. Of course he was. But that didn't make things any easier to stomach. These were her friends they were talking about, the girls she thought she'd be having brunch with into their forties after they were all married and successful in their careers. In her mind, Jackie had always been at the forefront of these daydreams—a successful lawyer like her parents wanted, with a lucrative beauty business on the side, an adoring husband, and two perfect kids. She was driven enough to have it all.

And she still would, Audrey promised herself. Because she was going to figure out where her friend was, and she was going to bring her home.

She trailed her fingers along her comforter, seeking her phone where she'd let it fall. Her greasy fingers found the screen. She tapped it once. Twice. Debating.

She lifted the screen back to her face.

It took a little scrolling to find her personal messages with Delilah. They were much further down the list, slotted back in May when she'd wished her a happy birthday.

Delilah's status said she'd been active only two minutes prior when Audrey tapped the messages open. Good. Maybe her response would be quick.

Delilah's status became active almost immediately. The message Audrey had sent changed to *read*.

And then nothing.

She waited a minute. Then another. Delilah's status moved from being active to the app counting the minutes she'd been gone, and Audrey let out a breath. So she didn't want to talk. That was okay. She was probably as exhausted as Audrey herself. Maybe she just wanted some time alone.

Peter was active.

Her lunchtime conversation with Jackson came to mind. There was no time like the present to see how much Peter knew.

She opened her messages with him instead, thumbs poised over the keyboard as she contemplated the best way to ask him what she wanted to know. She didn't want him to feel like she was only talking to him because she wanted information, so...

Audrey

> Hey, Pete. How are you holding up?

A glance at the time told her it was getting late—approaching ten-thirty, which was past her appointed bedtime for a school night. She doubted Peter was the type to listen to his parents about something as trivial as a curfew if he had one at all, but maybe it was a little late to be texting. She didn't want to come across as rude. He'd probably blow her off until morning, anyway.

The message status changed.

Peter

Doing fine. How 'bout you?

Before she'd had a chance to respond, he'd added to his message.

Peter

> We don't have to do the small talk. Jack told me you talked. I know why you're texting me.

She frowned at the screen. She probably owed Jackson thanks for giving Peter a heads up that she'd want to ask him about Jackie's online activities. Of course he would—the two of them were friends. And if he already knew why she was messaging...

Audrey

> So you did know, then? About her talking to guys online?

Peter

> Of course I knew. She wasn't exactly smart about it. She'd do it sitting right next to me. I find it hard to believe that you DIDN'T know.

Peter

> You don't have to keep lying for her. It's basically working against the police at this point. Isn't there a law against that? Obstruction of justice or some shit?

She didn't have time to be impressed that he knew that.

He read her messages immediately, and she waited with bated breath for a response.

Sixty seconds passed. Ninety. Five minutes.

It took her fifteen to realise Peter wasn't going to bother responding.

11

THE WEEK DRAGGED ON, every day another without news on Jackie. The police hadn't returned to the school on Tuesday morning, but the atmospheric shift they'd brought with them remained, permeating the air and putting a damper on even some of the most obnoxious teens. That had sucked, but not as much as the lack of presence meaning people had free rein to torment her.

If Audrey had thought she was getting looks before, it was nothing compared to now. Penny had been right when she'd said everybody knew—about the argument, about Audrey being questioned, about *everything*—and some of the student body had taken it upon themselves to decide that meant she was guilty.

And guilty people got no sympathy.

She pushed through the days with her head down and her shoulders braced for both physical and verbal abuse. There'd already been one instance of the physical. A senior guy had flung a container of scrambled eggs at her and said something about murdering more innocents as she'd headed to her final class—an action that had him bowing as he was sent to the principal's office, his friends laughing and cheering—and Audrey found herself wary of the fact that it could happen again at any moment. And maybe next time, it would be something heavier than eggs.

Everything was made worse by her friends. When she'd tried to join them for lunch on Tuesday, Danielle had started screaming—literally *screaming* bloody murder, attracting the attention of every person on the school grounds and the couple walking with their dog and toddler across the street. Penny had cackled with delight, her usual manicure suddenly looking more like a witch's talons. Delilah had kept her head down, avoiding Audrey's gaze.

Only Lenore had given Danielle a disgusted look, muttering at the girls to *grow up* before grabbing her things and following Audrey off the court. Her reward had been to cop half the sandwich thrown at them, the mayonnaise coating the back of her blouse as they traipsed inside in search of a bathroom.

She hadn't told her mother any of this. Hadn't asked her about hiring a lawyer either, figuring she both didn't need the woman worrying about needing to bring in *more* money or thinking Audrey couldn't handle a little heat. Because she could. She could hold out for a few days until the police found Jackie, and all of this blew over. The end had to be near.

By Thursday, Jackson had started joining them, having witnessed the harassment first-hand, and he was enough of a deterrent that people started to leave them alone.

The weekend wasn't the respite she'd been hoping for. She'd remained curled up in bed until well past ten on Saturday morning, but it hadn't been a relaxing lie-in. Every second of wakefulness had been spent wondering when the police were going to come for her. When would she hear the sirens wailing? When would Detective Flanagan and his partner come banging on the door, ready to handcuff her and take her away? Not even binge-watching true crime with Matt could calm her thoughts. Sunday was no better. She'd set out to work on the script for her latest video and ended up jumping between chatting with Matt, Lenore, and Jackson. Anything to keep her mind off the rest of the world.

Still, Jackie didn't appear.

Monday afternoon, Jackson met Audrey at the main entrance and escorted her out of school, almost working as a shield to get people off her back. The abuse might have lessened as the new week had begun, but Audrey still flinched whenever she caught a sudden movement and looked around corners carefully before she stepped around them. She was still getting disgusted looks. People were still shouting horrible things at her. Threatening her.

She wanted to scream at Jackie—scream at her to *come back* and prove to all these people that she'd had nothing to do with her best friend's disappearance. More than a week of no news had done nothing for anybody.

"You want a lift?" Jackson asked casually. He jingled a set of keys at her. "My car's parked around the corner, and considering there's potentially a psycho on the loose..."

Audrey followed him to his car wordlessly. Anything to get away from the toxic environment school had become.

She let him drive her away from it, not caring where they were headed as long as it wasn't back. What had happened to school being a safe place? When had everybody decided that, yes, she was definitely behind Jackie's disappearance? What had she done to these people to make them think that she was not only capable but also *willing* to do such a thing? What did they even think she'd done with her?

Even some of the teachers had started looking at her like she was a criminal.

She'd considered going to Mr Evans with her complaints, but what was the point? She wouldn't be a victim in his eyes. If the police told him she was a suspect, everything would change. He wouldn't ask people to stop hassling her. He'd probably encourage it in the hopes that one of his students could be the one to get her to confess to this crime she hadn't committed. She could only imagine how good that would make the school look to the media. *School Uncovers Girl Behind Mystery of Vanished Classmate!*

"Hey," Jackson said. "Get out of your head, huh?"

Audrey grimaced. Was it that obvious?

Yes, she realised. It was. One of her hands was tugging at the ends of her hair, and the other was almost white-knuckled on her bouncing knees. She pulled them both into her lap at his words, fighting the urge to keep fidgeting. This wasn't her. She could keep her cool.

"Sorry," she said. "Where are we going?"

"Wherever you like. My place is empty if you want to get away from the world for a while. My parents both work long hours."

Audrey just nodded. Jackson drove on.

Going home sounded like a nightmare right now. If her mother wasn't home, Audrey would end up sitting in a bedroom filled with photographs and memories of a friend she couldn't find. A friend people thought she'd...

Her home might be considered a crime scene soon. If it wasn't already. Audrey frowned. If Detective Flanagan had already begun to question her, then it was likely they were already thinking that, wasn't it? It was the last known place Jackie was supposed to be. Were there police waiting for her to arrive home? Had they already filed for a search warrant?

Would they get it?

"You're doing it again."

Audrey dragged herself back out of her head. "Sorry."

"Don't be sorry." Jackson glanced her way. "You've obviously got a lot going on up there. Why don't you come inside and tell me what's up?"

He'd pulled up outside a modern-looking home on a quiet street, and she hadn't even noticed. She looked it over in silence—freshly painted window frames, clean red bricks, a power-washed driveway. This was the sort of home she dreamed of living in someday. Preferably one that she owned, instead of having to live pay cheque to pay cheque like she and her mother did now. She'd occasionally had dreams of her YouTube channel getting big enough to earn her some money so she might someday buy her mother a home of her own. But at the rate she was going, that was never going to happen. She'd be spending the rest of her days in a prison cell if she wasn't careful.

Crap. She was in her head again. She tried cracking a joke to break the awkward silence she'd created. "Oh, I don't know. The cops have been telling us we shouldn't be running off with total strangers, no matter what they tell us or how nice they are."

Jackson gave a snort of laughter. "Right, of course. Because it's not like we've known each other for years, right?"

"Exactly."

Jackson winked and climbed out of his car. Audrey didn't hesitate to follow suit, dragging her bag along with her. Jackson *was* practically a stranger to her. In all of those years, they'd never really said much to each other; she had never once seen his house, and she hadn't known he had any interest in studying criminology or forensic psychology. But she knew he was a nice guy. Top of his class, despite being a "dumb jock". Well-liked by everybody at school. And right now, besides Lenore and Matt, he was her only friend. And she definitely needed all she could get when it came to those.

She followed him up the white stone walk, listening to gravel crunch under their feet as they moved towards the entrance. It reminded her a little of the Chens' front path, and she made a mental note to make it back to Jackie's house to fix up the mess the stones had been in when she'd last been there. It was the least she could do.

Jackson slid a key into the lock and swung the door open, stepping aside and gesturing for Audrey to enter first.

The house was as nice on the inside as she'd expected.

Dark wood floors, walls a shade of off-white, everything fresh and clean and new. It was all Audrey expected a modern family home to be, complete with ornately framed family portraits hung tastefully along the walls. It was the sort of home she imagined she'd live in now if her father's disappearance hadn't up-ended her life.

The door snapped shut behind her, and Audrey turned to find Jackson watching her.

"It's not much," he said with a shrug, "and my mum considers herself a bit of an interior designer, so don't mind if some of the rooms look a little different."

Audrey nodded, stepping aside so that Jackson could glide past her. He threw his keys into a little glass dish on a cabinet beside the door and beckoned for her to follow him.

They journeyed down the hall and into a tidy, fancy living room with leather chairs that looked like they had come right out of an Ikea display. Jackson dropped onto one and put his feet up as though he was not at all aware of how expensive the chairs probably were. Audrey lowered herself opposite him much more carefully, keeping her feet away from the leather so there was no chance she might damage it with her shoes. She was almost too afraid to put her bag on the pristine rug.

"So, talk to me," Jackson said, watching her from his casual position on the couch. He looked much more relaxed here, his shirt loose and his hair a slight mess from the heat and humidity outside. Summer was well and truly on its way. It was much cooler inside of his house. Air conditioning, of course. It would be more surprising if the house didn't have it. "What's worrying you? Talk it out."

Talk it out. It sounded like something Matt would say.

"Well, there's the obvious," Audrey said. "I'm worried about Jackie. And I'm worried about people thinking that this is all my fault because they all think she was supposed to be at my house that night. But she never was. I swear it. She never asked to come to my place, and she never told me she was going to be telling her mum that's where she was. If she'd mentioned it, I would have asked where she was really going and what she was planning on doing." She pinched the bridge of her nose. "I was so annoyed with her that Friday I didn't even bother to ask what her plans were. Maybe that was why she didn't tell me anything. Maybe if I'd asked, she would have told me, and then we wouldn't be where we are right now. She'd be home safe, and this entire investigation wouldn't be happening."

Jackson raised an eyebrow. "You shouldn't feel guilty for not asking what her plans were that night."

"Please. That's only the beginning of it."

"All right, then let's try a new tactic," Jackson suggested. "Instead of focusing on everything that's worrying you, tell me how you're planning on fixing all of those things."

"How I'm planning on fixing them?"

"Exactly." He stared her down. "Like, how are you planning on helping to bring Jacqueline back home? Have you started planning your video for her yet?"

Audrey stared back. "My video for her?"

"Yes. Your entire YouTube channel is dedicated to helping find missing people. Your best friend is now missing. I would have thought the next step here would be obvious."

"I wasn't planning on making a video for her. And now it would probably make me look like even more of a suspect." As an afterthought, she added, "And it would be stupid safety-wise. She's too close to me, and I don't want people to use information from her case to be able to figure out more of my personal information."

"You know," Jackson said slowly, "ignoring her case might actually have the effect you're trying to avoid. All of your viewers already know you live in Sydney and that you cover all the local cases here as soon as you can to help get the word out." He shrugged. "You ignoring Jacqueline's case would look suspicious. It's probably already starting to. Girl your own age goes missing, and you don't even mention the case to your viewers? They're going to know something's up."

She hadn't considered that. Could he be right? "The police questioned me about my channel. About an argument that Jackie and I had about it."

"And did they tell you that you couldn't make a video about her?"

Audrey opened her mouth to say that was exactly what Detective Flanagan had said, but... that would have been a lie. Detective Flanagan hadn't said that at all. In fact, he had agreed Audrey's work was important. He hadn't told her to go ahead and make the video, that he thought it would be a good idea for her to do so, but... he also hadn't told her *not* to.

"You're thinking about it," Jackson said. It wasn't a question.

She was. Now that she was away from school, in a fresh environment with somebody who didn't think she was guilty, she entertained the thought. She could see the entire thing coming together in her mind already. She wouldn't even need to do any research on the case—she knew what Jackie's cover story had been for the evening, she knew the moment her mother had started to worry about her, she knew the event that Jackie had failed to show up for. She knew exactly what kind of person Jackie was and the kinds of things that she would or would not have done when it came to running off with some stranger, if that was what this had come down to.

But there was one thing holding her back.

She bit her lower lip. "If I make a video about Jackie, people are definitely going to think I'm guilty of something. People are saying I made her disappear so I could use her to gain more views on my channel. If I do this now, it makes it seem like that's true."

"And what's more important?" Jackson asked. "Making sure people don't think of you as some air-headed girl who's only after views online or making sure your friend comes home safe?"

Audrey looked at him. He looked back at her.

And in that moment, she knew exactly what she needed to do.

12

Jackson already had everything she needed. He owned a DSLR camera that was much fancier than the old second-hand ones she'd been eyeing online, as well as both a microphone and a borrowed ring light his mother used for her occasional Zoom meetings. His laptop was top-of-the-line, the kind of machine she could only ever dream of owning, and it was already loaded up with video editing software that far exceeded the free program she'd been struggling with for the past year. She marvelled as he brought it all out—like *he* was the professional content creator who regularly set up a studio space, not her. She hoped the envy wasn't painted too obviously across her face.

They had everything set up within ten minutes, her stage a black leather couch against a simple background of white with a few lively plants, and it was only when she sat down to write a quick script that the gravity of the situation hit her.

She was really about to do this. She was about to make a video about Jackie.

At least working with Jackson around was easier than

trying to do it with her best friend watching. Jackie was constantly interrupting, trying to draw her attention to something more "appropriate", like a new beauty guru she'd discovered or a make-up look she wanted to try on Audrey right that moment. Jackie would put her down for what she was working on, calling it disgusting or telling her she was too young and pretty to be reading about things that were so morbid.

In stark contrast to this, Jackson remained completely silent while she worked.

She wrote for a solid fifteen minutes, jotting down memories and everything else she could remember in the lead-up to the police coming to talk to her, then did her best to group them into a list that didn't look like it was written by somebody who had no concept of organisation. She needed her notes to have some kind of order to minimise the risk of her forgetting anything and to reduce the amount of time they needed to spend in post-production. Workflow was as important as the finished product.

"All right," she said at long last. "I think we're ready to go."

"You sure?"

Audrey gave her notes one last look over. She'd done her best to structure the script as much like her usual videos as possible, starting out with trying to humanise Jackie for her viewers before launching into the days before her disappearance and then finally leading up to the disappearance itself and any theories that law enforcement might have. On that front, at least, she was going to keep things as vague as possible. If the media weren't aware, then neither should she be. Especially since she wanted to play out this video as if she'd never met Jackie.

Maybe then people wouldn't think she was using it to gain more viewers. Because sure, if she posted this video and told the world that she was Jackie's best friend, the views would most likely start pouring in as the word spread. But that wasn't the kind of attention she wanted for her channel—she didn't want people who would show up for the spectacle, stay in the hopes of there being drama, only to then depart when Jackie was found, and the media frenzy died down. She needed viewers who wanted to be there for the people she was reporting on.

She nodded. "I'm ready."

Jackson turned on his mother's ring light and adjusted its positioning, then set the DSLR to record. He gave her a thumbs-up.

Audrey looked down the lens... and froze.

Was she really about to do this? With all the things people were saying about her?

What did it matter? This was her job, and she had a duty to her viewers—and to Jackie, whether her best friend liked it or not. Jackie needed her help, and this was the best way she knew how to give it, even if Jackie had always thought her channel and its purpose were stupid.

Wouldn't it be ironic if she posted this video now, and it was exactly the thing that helped find Jackie? She almost smiled at the thought. But what were people going to say about her doing this in the first place? Especially when she and Jackie had argued about it the week before.

Jackson was watching her internal battle in silence, his arms crossed over his chest. His look wasn't one of impatience or judgement but one of understanding. Audrey met his gaze. Even without him needing to say it, she could hear him telling her to get out of her head, to focus on the task at hand.

"...will you film this one with me?"

Jackson's eyebrows went up in surprise. Audrey was surprised at herself. She'd never asked anybody to be in one of her videos. Not even Jackie, ignoring the fact that her best friend would mostly definitely have given her a resounding *no, gross!* She'd daydreamed about doing a video with Matt once or twice, both of them filming in their own homes and joining the videos together to create one, but she'd never shared the thought with him. And she had never considered asking anybody else.

But here she was now asking Jackson, who a week ago had barely been on her radar. The thought of him sitting beside her, being her companion through this video, lifted a little of the weight off her shoulders. She could get through this if she had somebody helping her. It felt a lot less daunting when she considered that she would not be doing it alone.

Jackson gave it a moment of thought before nodding. "All right. If that's what you want. Just tell me what you want me to do or say."

He came around to sit with her. Audrey spent a moment composing herself, working out some way to sit that didn't make them look awkward or too overly comfortable. Should she angle her body towards him?

Cross one leg over the other? Jackson settled himself, facing the camera at a slight angle—almost as if they were talking to a friend. A complete natural. Audrey mimicked his position and took a deep breath.

She could do this. She *had* to do this.

"Hey, everyone," she started, the usual greeting for her videos. "I'm back today with another recent case, unfortunately. A local girl has gone missing, and we need *your* help finding her. For those of you who don't know me, my name is Audrey, and I'm joined today by my friend Jackson. It's something a little different for the both of us, so I hope you don't mind."

Jackson gave the camera a little salute but didn't say anything. Cute.

Audrey opened her mouth to speak again, to start talking about the case, but nothing came out. Her heart pounded in her throat. Her own breathing was too loud. She could practically hear the sound of her rapid-fire blinking as her nerves began to rise. *Jackie.* She had to do this for Jackie. But her mouth wouldn't move, wouldn't let her get the words out. She gripped the couch, the leather squeaking beneath her sweating palms.

"We're here today to talk about Jacqueline Chen," Jackson said suddenly, breaking Audrey out of her minor panic. She closed her mouth and let him take over. Focused on getting her breathing back under control. "Jacqueline is a sixteen-year-old girl from Sydney who left her parents' house on Friday night and hasn't been seen since."

She listened to him talk about Jackie in the way she'd intended to: describing her as a person, not a victim—as a girl who was interested in fashion and beauty, a girl who was always working to further her reach on Instagram, where she dreamed of becoming an influencer; a girl with many friends, who describe her as a true leader, as the life of the party. Every now and then, he glanced down at Audrey's own notes and parroted what she had written back to the camera. He even managed to throw in a few things she hadn't written—things he'd learned from Peter, no doubt.

She was going to thank him profusely for this. There was no way she could have made it through that. Her heart was still thundering, though she'd managed to get herself back under control. She wiped her palms on her skirt.

Once Jackson was done talking about Jackie as a person, he looked at Audrey. Questioning her resolve.

"In the days before her disappearance," she jumped in immediately, "Jackie's life was entirely normal. She'd gone to look at formal dresses with her friends on Wednesday night—prom dresses, for those of you more familiar with the American version of this event—but friends report she hadn't found the right one yet and was going to be looking again that Sunday. Before that, she was due to celebrate her grandmother's birthday on Saturday. By all accounts, this was something she didn't want to miss."

On and on she went—about how both of these things were signs that Jackie hadn't run away on her own, as these were plans that she was making for her future. She spoke about that Friday, the last day that Jackie had been seen, and how nothing at all had seemed amiss. How Jackie had walked away from the school that afternoon, and it was the last time any of her friends had seen her.

"That night," she said, "Jacqueline told her mother she was going to a friend's house to stay but that she'd be back by Saturday afternoon for her grandmother's birthday celebrations. Unfortunately, Jacqueline's story about heading to a sleepover was a lie, as her friend stated no such arrangement had ever been made.

"Nobody knows where Jacqueline was headed when she left her parents' house that night. It cannot be determined whether she left on foot or got into a car with somebody or whether she might have caught public transport or a rideshare to get to her destination. This makes Jacqueline's case extremely important to get out to as many people as possible, as the search radius is unknown and could stretch across the entire city or further. So please, if you're watching this, ask everybody you know whether they've seen Jacqueline Chen. You never know when somebody you know might have seen something.

"Jackie is of Chinese descent and has medium-length black hair and dark eyes. She was last seen leaving her parents' house in West Drummond, in Sydney's inner west. Her intended destination was unknown. Her image is on your screen now. Please memorise her face, keep an eye out for her, and ask all of your friends and family to do the same."

Audrey steeled herself. Almost there. "And that brings us to the end of today's video. As always, please stay safe out there, and if you have any information at all, contact Crime Stoppers on one eight hundred, triple three, triple zero. We'll see you next time!"

She forced herself to smile at the camera for a long moment before sinking back onto the couch cushions. Jackson stood effortlessly and walked back around to the camera, shutting off their recording. Audrey breathed a deep sigh. It was done. They had done it. The video was recorded, and the hard part was over.

"Do you feel any better?" Jackson asked her.

Audrey nodded. She *did* feel better. Lighter. Jackie was still missing, and everybody still hated her and thought she was a freak, but having this weight off her shoulders was huge.

The next weight wouldn't lift until the video was edited and posted.

Jackson wasted no time in getting started on that. He took the memory card from the camera and plugged it into his laptop, sitting back on the couch beside Audrey and angling the laptop so that she could see the screen, too.

"So, I've gotta ask," he said as they waited for the video to download. "What made you get started in this? Why the interest in missing people? I think most other people I watch online cover murders. I'm surprised your channel doesn't stand out more with the brighter subject."

"Probably because it *is* a brighter subject," Audrey said bitterly. She hesitated. How much was she willing to reveal? "I got started in all of this because my father went missing when I was a kid."

Jackson raised an eyebrow. "Your father is a missing person?"

Audrey nodded. "Technically. He had to fly to Perth for work when I was eight or something. Mum knew he was going to be busy, so she didn't think anything of it when he didn't call the whole week. But then he never came home when he was supposed to."

"But he made it to Perth for the job?"

"We don't know," Audrey admitted. "Dad worked for himself, so there was no boss we could call and ask. And he wasn't the most organised guy in the world, so he didn't leave a contact number for us to be able to reach anybody in Perth." She shook her head. "We had so little information back then that the police couldn't really do much. They opened a case, and they contacted the police in Perth, but... We never heard back from anybody."

"Christ. That can't have been easy."

"It wasn't. Mum was only working part-time back then, and there were no full-time positions open at her hospital. She wanted to stay at our old place so Dad would always have somewhere to come back to, but we couldn't afford the mortgage. We ended up losing the house."

"I'm sorry."

Audrey shrugged. "It was a long time ago. And besides, it was just a house. I'd rather have my dad back."

Jackson nodded. "Have you covered his case on your channel?"

Audrey was shaking her head before he'd finished asking. "I started the channel with the intention of covering it eventually, but I always wanted to wait until I had more of a following to give his story the best opportunity to reach people, y'know?" She nibbled on her lower lip. "And if I'm being totally honest, I'm a little scared about what I might find when I start to do the research."

Jackson gave her a hard look. "You're afraid you'll cover his case and turn up a body."

Audrey grimaced.

"It's my worst-case scenario," she admitted.

"Understandable," Jackson said. "Do you want me to help you start?"

Audrey's heart gave a jolt. "*No*. No. Definitely not. I'm not ready for that yet, and... that's definitely a case I need to cover on my own."

She'd always been sure of that, at least. She wouldn't even ask Matt for help doing the research.

"All right." Jackson moved the cursor on his laptop down to the app bar and opened their program. "Let me know if you change your mind."

Audrey knew she wouldn't, but she appreciated the offer regardless.

Jackson cracked his knuckles and shook his fingers out. "Let's get this bad boy edited and out into the world, shall we?"

13

AUDREY WASN'T SURE WHAT she'd been expecting. For the video to blow up? For the comments to start pouring in? For the view count to shoot through the roof as soon as they hit publish? None of that happened, of course, but she was still disappointed when the video simply showed up on YouTube and existed. It was no different to when she posted any of the others. But this was Jackie, and, if she was being honest, she'd been hoping for some magical solution to her friend's disappearance. For a miracle. Seeing nothing was disheartening.

Jackson drove her home when she asked. There was a message from her mother waiting on the fridge, telling her to call if anything changed or if Audrey felt like she needed to talk to someone. She sighed and left the note there, heated up some leftovers in the microwave, and headed to her room to eat. She booted up her old laptop, cringing at how obvious its snail pace was now that she'd spent an afternoon on a new MacBook, and immediately navigated to YouTube to see if the video had fantastically begun to gain views yet. The number six stared back at her.

Not six thousand. Not even six hundred. Just six.

She sighed.

She logged into Facebook instead as she ate half-cold spaghetti, clicking her messages quickly so she didn't have to look at the photographs of Jackie that were all over her feed. It was the first thing to pop up—that Jackie-but-not-Jackie portrait the Chens had chosen for the media release, front and centre, with *MISSING* printed beneath it in scarlet. Her hair was still worn straight, her face still bare of make-up. Nothing like how she would look in the real world. Nothing that would help people recognise her. Jackie hated that photo. It was everything she wasn't.

She should talk to the Chens about that.

On a usual weeknight, she'd have at least a couple of messages from her best friend waiting for her, and their absence still hit hard even a week later. Tonight, there were only a handful of messages from Matt. Audrey frowned. That was odd. Even though her friends had stopped talking to her after the incident on Monday, she usually still saw a thing or two pop up from the group chat, the girls too eager to share pictures of dresses and memes to care much if Audrey saw them. Were they not using it anymore? Had they abandoned it and started another chat just to keep away from her? She scrolled through to look.

No, it was worse than that. They had booted her out of the group chat entirely.

Her heart sank.

It had surprised her when they hadn't done it immediately, but to wait a week and *then* start treating her like she was diseased? That was petty.

She did a quick check of their profiles. Lenore's she could access just fine, but Penny, Danielle, and even Delilah had all either unfriended or blocked her. She was willing to bet it was the latter. Not that it made a huge amount of difference when most of their posts were set to public, a necessity for them to gain all those likes they needed to live. She tried not to let it sting, but it did. A lot. They'd been friends for so long, it was hard to comprehend they were really going to up and abandon her like this over a theory. And a hurtful theory at that.

She couldn't even take solace in her *when Jackie gets back* thoughts. It didn't matter if they came grovelling and begging for forgiveness once they found out she was innocent. How was she supposed to look at them the same after they'd ditched her? In a time when they should have been banding together for their friend?

Her video, with their social media reach, could have been the answer to their prayers. Together, they could have brought Jackie home. Instead, she was sitting alone with her six views, and Penny was probably about to drop her weekly *Penny for Your Thoughts* ramble that would somehow land in the thousands.

Messenger chimed, and she navigated back to it with a little flare of hope. But no. It wasn't any of the girls messaging her. It was another from Matt. At least she never had to worry about him blocking her.

Matt

I saw the video.

I thought you kept it together really
well, and it was probably smart that
you didn't let on you knew the girl.
Interesting seeing you work with
someone else. Friend from school?
How are you feeling?

Trust Matt to know that she wouldn't be fine after
doing the video. She took another bite of her dinner and
typed back quickly.

I'm okay. Doing the video was hard,
but it needed to be done, and
Jackson made it a little easier.
He's friends with Jackie's boyfriend.
Honestly, I feel better now knowing
that it's over with, and I won't have
to think about it anymore. Bit of a
burden off the shoulders, you know?

I'm glad to hear it. I can't begin to
imagine how stressful this has been,
especially since it's not your first
time going through it.

Is it okay if I ask if this is bringing up
bad memories for you?

Audrey drummed her fingers along her knee. She didn't need to ask what he meant. It had been almost ten years, but something like that... it never went away.

Audrey

> Sometimes. I really felt it when I visited Jackie's house. It was like it was in the air or something, and it took me back to when my dad disappeared. The house was quiet, and Mrs Chen had let all the dishes build up, and her garden was a mess. I know that sounds weird, but she LOVES that garden. It's like her second child. She never lets it get out of hand, and now it's all over the place.

Audrey

> My mum did the same. I remember for almost a week straight, we were eating takeout straight out of the boxes because we didn't have any clean dishes until my grandmother took pity and cleaned them, and Mum didn't have the energy to do things like laundry. I'm pretty sure we didn't even shower for the first few days.

You just get so busy thinking about what's happening, everything else ends up on the back burner.

It had been a dark time. She couldn't remember how long it had taken for things to start improving, but normalcy had come gradually and painfully. After the neighbours had stopped visiting. After the police had stopped giving them updates. After they'd given up on trying to keep up with the mortgage and moved.

I'm sorry I asked.

Audrey shook her head before remembering Matt couldn't see her. Not for the first time, she wished he could. Wished he was here with her, a physical presence rather than a virtual one. He probably gave the best hugs.

Don't be. I'm okay. Really.

As okay as she could be given the circumstances.

Anyway, things weren't the same with Jackie. Audrey had been a child when her father vanished, and times had been different—she hadn't fully understood what was happening, and she hadn't known how she could help. They certainly hadn't had the power of social media on their side. Her mother had never been an Internet-orientated person before then, and she hadn't had the time to learn when she was a newly single mother.

Things might have been very different if they'd been able to access the resources they had today.

Hope flared in her chest at the thought. They were living in an age where disappearing was next to impossible, with CCTV on every corner and everybody having access to a camera on their phone. It was only a matter of time before Jackie's face would pop up somewhere or somebody would recognise her from the photos online. They just had to wait it out. It would happen any day now.

Matt

> Have there been any new leads? There's nothing in the news, but I figured if anybody would know, it would be you. Have you spoken to that detective lately?

Audrey

> Not lately. The police were only at my school for that one day, and I haven't heard from any of them since. And nothing yet. I think they're looking at a stranger abduction, but they're being vague.

She drummed her fingers on the keyboard.

Audrey

> They asked us if we knew her account passwords.

> They want to get a look at her messages, see if she was talking to someone online.

> Jackson and Peter both say she was talking to guys.

She wondered if they'd told the police that. Peter probably had. It would explain why the police were eager to get into Jackie's accounts.

> And did you know her passwords?

> I did for her laptop. But not for her accounts. But I'm going to try to guess my way in.

She looked to the top of her screen, to the logout button she'd never bothered to use. It stared back at her.

She could have been preparing her next video. She *should* have been doing homework. But she knew the email Jackie used for her accounts, and trying to gain access to her messages seemed more important than anything else right now. There could be evidence waiting to be uncovered. The faster the police got it, the better. She should have attempted this *days* ago. The answer to where Jackie was could be *right there*.

I'll message again later. I'm not sure how long this is going to take me, but I'll need to focus.

Be careful. You might find something you don't like. Either way, let me know if you find anything. I'll be here. Good luck, Audi.

She gave him a thumbs-up and backed out of their messages.

She'd known Jackie longer than any of the other girls. They'd been through all of life's ups and downs together. She'd been there to sympathise when Jackie's parents had started getting stricter about her studies, and she'd been there when Jackie had discovered beauty bloggers and make-up. She knew all the important dates in Jackie's life—birthdays, anniversaries, even the day her childhood parakeet had passed away. If anybody was going to have any luck guessing her password, it was definitely Audrey.

She moved to grab her notebook and a pen and started jotting down everything she could think of. The date Jackie and Peter had first started dating. The dates of all the girls' birthdays. The names of Jackie's family members, her old bird, her online alias. She was going to need to keep track of everything she tried if she ever had a hope of—

Jackie's status was active.

Audrey stopped breathing.

Her eyes had to be playing tricks on her. It was getting late; she was sitting in the dark, and she was still amped up from doing the video. She shut her eyes, digging her palms into them, giving them a rest. That was all they needed. Her mind was alive. It was just her eyes seeing what wasn't there. She prepared herself for the disappointment she knew was coming when she opened them again, and Jackie wasn't online at all. She'd probably seen that little green bubble because she wanted it so bad.

She opened her eyes.

Jackie was *still* active.

Her heart soared. It was real. It was *real!* She clicked open the window quickly, typing so fast that on the first try, she fumbled all her letters, and the sentence didn't make sense. She had to backtrack, force herself to take a breath and start her message over. Slower this time.

Had anybody else noticed? How many messages was Jackie being flooded with right now? The giggle that bubbled out of Audrey was almost hysterical with relief. All those thoughts of giving Jackie hell for all she'd put them through vanished in an instant. She was just glad her best friend was *back!* The Chens must have been thrilled. Even more than she was!

The message status changed to *read*.

Audrey grinned. She couldn't help it. This was the best feeling ever. She was going to be riding this high and the high of everyone realising she was innocent into next year!

She could only imagine the story Jackie was going to be telling. Had she disappeared of her own free will? Had she been kidnapped? Had she fallen and hit her head while out for a walk? Audrey could see her now, sitting in the Chens' kitchen, telling her parents all about how she'd spent the week in a hospital with no memory of who she was, getting called Jane Doe by doting nurses and friendly doctors. It was exactly the sort of tale she'd tell. Audrey might even let her get away with it. This time.

But then Jackie's status went dark, like someone had put it on invisible mode, as quickly as it had become active.

And in the hours that Audrey watched, it didn't turn green again.

14

ONE PHONE CALL TO the station the next morning told Audrey that Detective Flanagan was at her school. She didn't question her luck—it was about time the universe gave her something good to balance out the bad it had been throwing her way—just pulled on her uniform, grabbed her things, and hurried out of the apartment.

Detective Flanagan was stepping out of Mr Evans's office as Audrey approached. He fit right in with his police blues, the same colours as her skirt and blouse, almost like he was just another student in for a day of learning. If it hadn't been the standard police uniform, she would have assumed it was on purpose to get her and her classmates to feel more comfortable around him. She raised her hand in a half-wave to get his attention, but he'd already spotted her and was heading her way.

"Miss Herringbone," he greeted her. "I was hoping we could have another little chat this morning. Your principal was going to call you out of your first class, but I suppose this works better."

"Good," Audrey said, "because I wanted to talk to you, too."

"Excellent. Shall we step back into your principal's office, then?"

Detective Flanagan pushed the door back open and gestured for Audrey to enter first. She hurried over.

Mr Evans glanced up from his desk, looking surprised to see her.

"Miss Herringbone," he greeted her as Detective Flanagan gently closed the door behind her. "We weren't expecting you so soon. Please, take a seat."

Audrey sat, slipping her phone out of her back pocket eagerly as she did. She'd checked on Jackie's messages again that morning, but there'd been nothing more since last night. Just the shining new status that declared her to have been active ten hours earlier. Detective Flanagan came to stand beside the desk, between herself and Mr Evans, and crossed his arms over his chest. He nodded once at Mr Evans, giving him the go-ahead for something.

Mr Evans looked back at Audrey. "Would you like to explain to us what you were thinking last night?"

Audrey blinked. Of course they already knew. This was an active missing persons investigation—she was stupid not to have considered they'd be monitoring Jackie's accounts for activity, waiting for her to come online so they could contact her themselves. Had she interrupted their operation? Was that why Detective Flanagan was looking at her like a disappointed uncle?

"I'm sorry," she said. "But did you really expect me not to message her? She's been missing for over a week, and I wanted to know what happened to her!"

Mr Evans's brow furrowed in confusion; Detective

Flanagan raised an eyebrow.

"Excuse me?" the latter asked.

"Jackie," Audrey clarified. When neither of them looked like she was making things any clearer, she added, "When she came online last night?"

"She was online?" Detective Flanagan was suddenly all business, pulling out his own phone as he straightened. "Did she say anything to you?"

"No, nothing. I figured she was home and asked where she'd been, but she never responded. She was active for... I don't know, a minute, maybe?"

She watched his thumbs fly across the keypad of his phone at a speed that would have impressed even her friends. Her heart sped up. So they *hadn't* known then?

"I don't know what you're talking about, Miss Herringbone," Detective Flanagan said calmly, confirming her suspicions as he pocketed his phone once more, "but this has nothing to do with Jacqueline coming online. I've let my colleagues at the station know, and they'll look into it. But in the meantime, we need to talk about the video you posted last night. The one detailing Miss Chen's case."

"What were you *thinking?*" Mr Evans demanded, his tone every bit as agitated as Detective Flanagan's was calm. "And dragging another student into it, too!"

Audrey blinked in surprise. Then blinked again.

The video. Of course they were talking about the video. She'd been so focused on Jackie having come online that she hadn't taken the time to think about the video that morning. Had it gained many views? Were there any comments? Had it struck a chord with anybody who thought they might have seen Jackie? Had it gone *viral?*

"You will take it down immediately," Mr Evans said, his tone stone cold.

Audrey's heart skipped a beat. She stumbled over her defence. "Mr Evans, Detective Flanagan—I haven't done anything wrong. I didn't mention any details that the public didn't already have access to, and I made sure not to mention that I knew Jackie in any way. And besides, it would have looked strange if I didn't cover her case. I cover *every* local case because I know how important it is to do that and how important it is to do it quickly. My viewers would have thought it was suspicious if I didn't post about her. I didn't do this for views or anything!"

Even though she was hoping for them.

"Be that as it may," Mr Evans scowled, "I find this extremely inappropriate, and I will not have such rubbish bringing more unwanted attention to this school. You will take the video down and be done with it, or I will contact your mother."

Audrey grimaced. That was the last thing she needed. She hadn't even told her mother about her channel.

"Audrey." Detective Flanagan's tone was softer. She flicked her gaze to his much kinder expression. "The boy in the video. Did he ask you to do this?"

"Jackson? No." She frowned. "Well, I guess, in a way. But he knew it was something I needed to do. He helped me prepare everything and then did the video with me when I asked him to, so I didn't have to do it alone. Which was nice, by the way, since you turned my friends against me and now none of them will speak to me. So yeah, I did it. And I feel a whole lot better because of it. It's like this giant weight has lifted off my shoulders. And I like knowing that the video is out there and that it might help bring Jackie home, so no. I will not be taking it down, thank you very much, Mr Evans."

Even *she* was surprised by her defiance.

Mr Evans's face went red. "*Miss Herringbone—*"

"Audrey," Detective Flanagan said again. It was strange hearing him call her by her first name. "We're not saying your work isn't important or that the video you did for Jacqueline isn't a good thing, but there are other things at play here. This is an active investigation into a missing teenage girl. We still don't know what might have happened to her, and as such, we don't know whether or not there is further risk to the remaining students at this school."

A chill ran down her spine. Further risk?

"You didn't say I couldn't do it." But there was doubt settling in her stomach now. Her voice came out barely louder than a whisper.

"I didn't. But by putting that video out, you could be making yourself a target for an unknown perpetrator, and that is the absolute last thing that we need right now."

Audrey stared at him. Jackie had once made a joke about how she was probably making herself a target for kidnappers and serial killers by drawing attention to their crimes, but to hear this kind of talk coming from a police officer, in regard to an investigation that was so close to home...

"You want me to take it down."

"At least for now," Detective Flanagan said. He, at least, looked apologetic. "I should have been clearer the last time we talked, I'm sorry. I want to assure you this request has nothing to do with the subject of the video and everything to do with your safety. We just can't afford to have another missing student on our hands. All of our resources need to be put into finding Jacqueline. Do you understand?"

Audrey nodded. "I understand, Detective."

"Good." He gave her a long look. "The sooner you can take the video down, the better, but we'll give you until the end of the day. How does that sound?"

"That sounds reasonable enough."

"Excellent. You're free to go, Miss Herringbone."

Audrey stood quickly, suddenly not as eager to be near Detective Flanagan or Mr Evans. Especially the latter, who was still red in the face and looking as annoyed as she had ever seen him. She all but fled the man's office, letting the door slam shut behind her as the principal snapped something at the detective. It got her a few startled looks in the corridor, but she hurried past those students without looking back.

She should have known this would happen. Of course Mr Evans would be worried about the reputation of the school, especially when Jackie's disappearance was already making them look bad. It was his job to protect the school and its image, to make sure they continued to get enrolments for the new year, and her video wouldn't be doing it any favours. It was bad enough that they still had the media out there today, even if it was only a lone reporter hoping for a break in the case. He didn't need to be worrying about what she was posting online, too.

Stupid, stupid, *stupid*.

At least Detective Flanagan had been nice about it. His words were concerning, though. Did they really think whoever had abducted Jackie was hanging around the school, watching them? Did they think the guy would strike again with a police and media presence?

They probably couldn't take the chance either way.

She found Jackson as he was coming into the main building, the blinding morning sunlight behind him framing his hair like a halo. He looked surprised to see her as she weaved through clusters of other students to get to him.

"You're in early."

Audrey nodded. "I needed to talk to Detective Flanagan. Jackie came online last night."

Jackson raised an eyebrow. "Jackie did?"

"Yes. Only for a minute, but it definitely happened. I messaged her, but..."

"She didn't respond," Jackson finished for her. It wasn't a question. He crossed his arms and casually leaned against the wall they'd moved towards, letting other students bustle past. "What makes you so sure it was her?"

Audrey frowned. "Who else would it have been? Nobody knows her passwords."

Jackson gave her a look of disbelief. "Come on, Audrey. I thought you were smarter than that. You don't need her passwords to get into her accounts. Just one of her devices that's already logged in."

Like her missing phone or laptop.

Christ, she *was* stupid. In all the excitement, she hadn't even considered it might not be Jackie on the other end of those messages. That it might, she realised with a start, even have been the person behind her disappearance.

"Detective Flanagan and Mr Evans told me to take the video down."

He didn't seem surprised. If anything, he looked like he'd been expecting it.

"I figured I'd let you know, just in case they pull you out of class to talk to you, too." Audrey leaned against the wall beside him, her eyes drifting to the lone reporter filming for some morning show outside. "Mr Evans wanted me to take it down right away, but Detective Flanagan said by the end of the day."

"How do you feel about that?" he asked. "I mean, after putting all that work into making it in the first place, now it's going to sit on a hard drive and do nothing. It feels like a giant waste of time, doesn't it?"

"It does," she agreed, "but Detective Flanagan says it's for our own good. He's worried that if someone took Jackie, they might still be out there watching the school, and they don't want to give them any reason to come after any more of the students."

Jackson nodded. "Putting your face on the investigation could make you a target, and the police wouldn't want that."

"Yeah, that's basically what he said." And now she'd potentially messaged whoever that person might be. Stupid, stupid, *stupid*.

"Well, do yourself a favour," Jackson said. "Leave the video up until the end of the day. Wait until the last possible moment before you take it down. That way, it still gives people the time to watch it and maybe get the word out before you have to remove it, and then it won't be a complete waste. You can go on knowing that you had the video up for as long as you could and you gave it the best possible chance."

Audrey nodded. She'd been willing to take the video down while she was at lunch, but Jackson was right. Why should she take it down ahead of its time? It deserved to have its chance to shine. And she deserved to feel like she'd done her part in trying to help, whether it painted a target on her back or not.

She'd keep it up until the end of the day. And with any luck, it would end up being her first success.

15

AUDREY VENTURED TOWARDS HER English class, which she was lucky enough—or *unlucky* enough—to share with all her friends. The closer she got to the classroom, the more her stomach began to do flips. She was already anticipating the things they were going to be saying to her and about her. *Oh, there's Little Miss YouTube. Go sit in the back with the rest of the losers, loser.*

And no doubt, the rest of the class would egg them on and take their side over everything. Typical.

Audrey sighed. She *really* didn't want to go to class. But what was the alternative? Speak to the counsellor she both did not want to speak to and who probably thought she was guilty of Jackie's disappearance? Skip class entirely? She knew she couldn't. Not only would her own mother flay her alive, but she needed to keep on the straight and narrow. Giving people any more reason to suspect her of any wrongdoing was the stupidest thing she could do right now. There was no other choice.

Christ, why was she thinking like someone who was guilty?

The second bell hadn't rung yet, and Ms Stanmore

hadn't arrived to open the door. Most of Audrey's classmates were milling around outside the room, waiting to be let in, their voices echoing as they jostled each other and laughed about their non-tumultuous lives. Audrey spotted her friends immediately, huddled in a little group closest to the door, Penny and Danielle chatting animatedly. She positioned herself as far from them as possible, behind Ophelia Andrews and Kane Leeland, and did her best to keep out of their sight. Lenore was a few steps away from the rest, her eyes on her shoes as she traced an invisible line in front of herself, but she couldn't risk signalling her without the others noticing.

Apparently, she needn't have bothered trying to avoid them. Penny's eyes caught Audrey's from her place by the door, and she straightened immediately. She must have been keeping an eye out for her because as soon as their eyes locked, she was storming down the short stretch of the hallway towards her, human shields be damned. Ophelia and Kane moved to the other side of the hall quickly, Ophelia almost tripping over her untied shoelace. Audrey couldn't blame them. Nobody wanted to be on the receiving end of Penny's wrath.

She frowned as her ex-friend approached, fully expecting the blonde to hit her, but the strike never came. At least not physically.

No. Penny's assault was verbal.

"What the *hell* do you think you're doing?!" she demanded. Pin-drop silence fell at once as the rest of the class stopped chatting to instead watch the drama unfold. "You know she didn't want you to post a video about her!

Are you seriously going to use her disappearance for some freaking fame?!"

That's rich, coming from someone who's probably been crying all over social media about it. But she'd never say that. Penny had the right to talk about Jackie all she wanted, even if she was doing it for sympathy and the extra following. But so did Audrey, especially when *her* reasons were the right ones.

"Of course she is." Danielle scoffed. She was still by the door, but her voice carried easily enough, projecting down the thankfully otherwise empty hallway. "That's the whole reason she made Jackie disappear in the first place. Why else would she have done it? She's probably going to come after the rest of us next. One at a time, so she gets the maximum number of subscribers and views for her channel. That's all she cares about these days. Her stupid YouTube career. She doesn't give a damn about any of us!"

"It's a good thing you told the police about her posting that video." Penny sneered. "Maybe now they'll find the evidence they need to arrest her!"

The class erupted. Several people started talking at once, each person trying to drown out the next. Audrey couldn't hear any of it. Her ears were ringing. Penny was in front of her, still screaming; Lenore had come to stand by Penny and was saying something to her angrily; Danielle was still yelling, and several of their classmates were yelling, too. Some of it was directed at Audrey, with looks of disgust and outrage on the faces of those behind it; others were yelling at Penny or Danielle. Delilah stood on the outskirts of it all, looking stricken.

Smack!

She hadn't seen Penny's hand coming, fast and strong and sure. The slap stung more than she'd ever expected one would. She raised a hand to her cheek, feeling the heat already beginning to grow. Was this how much a slap was supposed to hurt, or was it because it was coming from somebody she'd considered one of her best friends for years? Tears stung her eyes.

She looked back at Penny, wondering if she could see all of the hurt in her eyes. Wondering if she cared.

"You're a bitch." Penny spat at her feet. "I hope you take your YouTube fame and choke on it."

"*Hey!*"

Penny and Lenore jumped back, moving against the wall as Ms Stanmore rounded the corner. All of the yelling stopped.

Ms Stanmore looked furious. Audrey had never seen so much anger in the woman's eyes. She'd always been one of her favourite teachers, always been the approachable one. Now, she looked like she might shoot fire from her ears.

"That's enough of that," Ms Stanmore said fiercely. "My God, kids. You're supposed to be coming together in these times, not fighting with each other!"

"We're not supposed to be coming together for a murderer," Danielle muttered.

"There's no evidence to suggest that Jackie has been murdered." Ms Stanmore looked at each of them individually, holding their eyes a moment before moving to the next. Audrey looked to the floor before she could hold hers. "And even if there had, that isn't any reason to turn on your classmates. Leave the witch-hunting to the professionals. The next person to start a fight over this gets detention for the rest of the year!"

She unlocked the classroom door and pushed her way in with a huff. One by one, in complete silence, the class followed. Penny gave Audrey one last irritated look before she went in, Danielle trailing after her. Audrey let out a long, shaking breath as she watched them go. Her ex-friends. The people she'd thought she'd always be able to rely on. Her accusers.

Delilah remained. She stared at Audrey and Lenore, looking for a moment like she wanted to say something, but she kept her lips pressed firmly shut. Audrey stepped forward—to offer an olive branch, to ask her what it was that was on the tip of her tongue.

But Delilah turned and hurried into the classroom, her eyes back on her shoes.

A gentle hand fell on her shoulder. Lenore. "Are you okay?"

Audrey nodded, but before she could speak, someone else said, "Hey. Audrey?"

She turned to Malcolm Jasper warily. He wasn't the nicest guy at the best of times, and if he decided to kick her while she was down, she wouldn't know how she was going to hold the tears back. One blow was more than enough for the day. She braced herself for whatever he was about to throw at her.

"We just wanted you to know that none of us think you're guilty of anything," he said, gesturing to the boys still standing at his back. His buddies. Several from the soccer team, whom she knew casually as friends of Peter's. A couple of them nodded their agreement. "And actually, I think your channel's pretty cool. I haven't seen the video about Jackie, but I'll give it a watch later and share it on Facebook and stuff. Who knows, you might be right. Your video might be what helps the police find her, right?"

Audrey didn't want to burst his bubble by telling him that she was being forced to take the video down. Instead, she gave him the most genuine smile she could muster and said, "Yeah. Let's hope so. Thanks, guys."

The boys filed into class, several of them slapping her good-naturedly on the shoulder as they passed. Audrey's throat grew tight.

Lenore took her hand and gave it a squeeze. *I'm here for you, too.*

Audrey looked at her. At the only friend still on her side. At the girl she'd barely taken the time to check in with since all of this had started because she'd selfishly been so focused on herself. But Lenore had been enduring a lot of it with her. The hatred in the halls. The pressures of their teachers keeping a closer watch on them.

"Are *you* okay?"

"No," Lenore said simply. "But I'm dealing. Talking to Mrs Pillott has been helpful." Lenore gave her a pointed look and added, "She keeps asking me when you're coming to see her."

Audrey groaned. She'd been forced into sessions with her primary school counsellor after her father disappeared, and she had no intention of repeating the painfully boring experience. "I don't need to talk to her. I'm fine."

"You should go and see her. At least once." Lenore squeezed her hand again. "It might help, Auds. You're dealing with a lot more than the rest of us."

Her phone buzzed without warning, and she groaned again. Trust Penny to sit down in class and immediately get back to her verbal beat-down by texting it instead. There was chatter coming from the classroom again, which meant Ms Stanmore had begun making her notes on the whiteboard. She'd likely be out to drag them into class any second. It was a miracle she hadn't already.

Lenore saw Audrey's hand go to her pocket and frowned.

"Seriously?" she asked. "She's at it already?"

Audrey nodded and pulled out her phone. It was probably a dumb idea. She should ignore the message. Should just walk into class with her head held high, avoid looking at her *ex*-friends, and enjoy the lesson catching up with Lenore instead. Maybe they could get through the next hour acting like everything was right with the world.

She looked down at the screen.

Matt

> Have you checked your video lately???

Audrey was surprised to see Matt's name on her screen. They didn't often message during school hours, with the exception of the few he'd sent to check on her the week prior. He certainly never expected her to be checking her videos during class.

> I haven't looked at it since this morning. As soon as I got to school, I was practically ambushed. The principal wanted me to take it down. The detective said I had until the end of the day.

She stopped, looking back at his message. Why had he even asked her this? Her heart skipped a beat.

> Why? What's going on?

It seemed to take Matt an age to respond. The grey speech bubble popped up and disappeared several times, leaving Audrey practically holding her breath in the hallway. How long before Ms Stanmore yelled at her and Lenore to get their butts into class? She was tempted to navigate to YouTube on her own, but she couldn't make herself do it. Her hopes were already stupidly high. She didn't want to get there and be disappointed.

> Just go to your video and look at the comments. Ignore all the shitty ones. You'll know what I'm talking about when you see it. Take it straight to that detective you've been talking to. Do it NOW.

Audrey frowned. What on earth was he talking about?

Lenore gave her a curious look as she navigated away from Messenger and opened the YouTube app instead. She clicked through to her account, opened her latest video…

It was proving to be more popular than her videos usually were—already at three hundred and nineteen views—but it wasn't the viral sensation she'd been daring to hope for. She scrolled down to the comments, surprised to see that there were thirty-four of them. Usually, she was lucky if her videos gained two, and one was always Matt. A little thrill went through her, a smile crossing her face.

The smile didn't last long.

Most of the comments were from people she went to school with. They all had usernames that hid their identities, but who else would get onto her video about Jackie just to repeatedly tell her that she was trash, that she was a bitch, that she was responsible for Jackie's disappearance, and that this video had only been posted for fame. This must have been what Matt meant when he mentioned the shitty comments. So, what exactly was she supposed to be looking for?

She kept scrolling, reading them all despite knowing she shouldn't. With every new comment she read, she wanted to take the video down more and more. How many of these were from burner accounts created by Penny and Danielle, laughing to themselves as they put her work down, and how many were from people who legitimately thought she was trash? Some people really did think the worst of her. The only nice comment among them was from Matt, her knight in shining armour, her light in the darkest of places...

And then she saw it.

She almost dropped her phone. It was the fourth comment from the bottom, but the time stamp showed it was one of the newer ones—posted only an hour earlier. Audrey drew in a sharp breath. Beside her, Lenore's hands flew to cover her mouth. She understood what Matt was saying now. She knew without a doubt this was the comment he was talking about, and he was absolutely right. She needed to get this to Detective Flanagan *now*.

Ding, dong, the bitch is dead.
151 South Amberlain Street, East Drummond

16

"Miss Herringbone? ...Audrey?"

Lenore nudged her.

Audrey blinked and looked back at Detective Flanagan. He'd barely made it back to the station when she'd called for him the second time that day, this time so flustered she'd barely been able to get the words out. Lenore had needed to take the phone from her and explain the situation, her hands shaking but her voice steady as she relayed the information. He hadn't questioned her further when she'd read him the comment. He'd taken her word for what it was, told her he'd have officers dispatched immediately, and to *stay at school*. He'd all but demanded they both get to their principal's office and wait for him there.

He was sitting across from them now, making himself comfortable in Mr Evans's chair. Much like the first day they had met, there was a coffee in front of him, but this one remained untouched. Audrey wondered if it was another he'd been given by the school, which he'd accepted out of politeness but had absolutely no intention of drinking, or if he'd wised up and brought his own. It didn't matter. Nothing mattered right now.

Except for the comment somebody had left on her video.

She hadn't recognised the username—not that she got a lot of comments, anyway—and when she'd clicked through to view the account, she found that it was probably a burner. It had been created that same day, and none of the profile information had been filled out except the country: Australia. She'd shown all of this to Detective Flanagan when he'd arrived, but he hadn't commented on it.

"Audrey."

"Auds?"

She kept thinking about the address. She'd probably been down the street before, but she couldn't bring to mind a landmark or any notable feature to tell her what the area looked like. Was the message leading the police to a house? An abandoned building? Or worse, could it be a construction site or an empty lot? A lake? More importantly, were they really going to find Jackie there?

And even more important than that, what kind of condition were they going to find her in?

Was she finally ready to give up on the huge prank Audrey still desperately hoped she was playing? Was she hurt and in need of medical assistance? Or was the comment right? Audrey didn't want to think about it, but... it was a possibility. She shook her head. She didn't want that thought. Didn't want it taking up any space inside of her head. She shook it again, trying to dislodge the idea. *No, no, no, no...*

A pair of firm, strong hands landed on her shoulders, and Audrey looked up. Lenore was wide-eyed beside her. Detective Flanagan was standing in front of them now, half sitting on Mr Evans's desk as he practically leaned over her. Those were his hands on her shoulders, grounding her. Pulling her out of her spiralling thoughts.

"Calm down," he said gently. "Here. I want you to drink some of this."

He reached down to pull her water bottle from the outer pocket of her school bag and offered it to her. She took it from him with shaking hands but made no move to open it. How could she think about drinking water at a time like this? Her mouth was bone dry, but the thought of putting anything into her already roiling stomach made her nauseous.

"Come on, Miss Herringbone," he insisted. "Just a little. It will help."

Audrey popped the lid on the bottle and took a sip. It didn't help at all.

"Good." Detective Flanagan leaned away from her, straightening his back once again, but stayed where he was against Mr Evans's desk. She didn't know where Mr Evans himself had scurried off to. Didn't care either. "All right. Are you going to be okay if I ask you a couple of questions about this?"

Audrey looked up at him. She'd learned this lesson already. "Shouldn't I be calling a lawyer or something if you're going to be questioning me?"

"It's not that kind of questioning, but if you wish to have a lawyer present, that is your right." He looked to Lenore as well. "Your mothers are on their way, and I'm more than happy to wait for them to arrive so we can organise something for you. Of course, you're also free to refuse to answer any of these questions if you're uncomfortable. Do you understand?"

Audrey did. She nodded. "I'll answer what I can for you."

Lenore nodded as well, though she remained silent.

"Thank you." Detective Flanagan held out her phone to her. She knew behind the lock screen, it would still be open on the comment section of her latest video. Her head spun. "What else can you tell me about that comment? You said you didn't recognise the username or the account at all?"

"It's a new account," Audrey told him again. "It was created today, so my guess is somebody created it just to post that comment, and they probably won't ever bother to use it again. Like a burner phone, I guess, but with an account. It's easy. All you need to sign up is an email, and it's easy to create a million of those, too."

Detective Flanagan was nodding along. He probably knew all of this already, but Audrey was used to having to spell things out for her mother. It was something she really liked about him—that he seemed to have a grasp of technology and how it worked, so she didn't need to stop and explain the ins and outs of the Internet to him. The perks of being younger than thirty, she supposed.

"All right, that's fine," he said. "And what alerted you to the comment? Do you check the comments on your videos frequently? Did I hear you mention that a friend had pointed this one out to you?"

"Usually, I don't get very many," Audrey admitted, "but I do try to keep an eye out on the comment sections just in case I get any important comments like this. And yeah, my friend Matt told me it was there. He helps out a lot with monitoring the comment section of my channel. Kind of like a moderator, I guess. He told me the comment was there and that I should bring it straight to you."

Detective Flanagan nodded. "I'd like to speak with Matt, too, if that's okay. What class is he in?"

Audrey grimaced. "Matt doesn't actually go to this school. We're friends online."

Detective Flanagan raised an eyebrow. "Friends online? How do you know each other?"

Audrey hesitated. This was going to sound terrible. "Through the comments on my channel. Matt was my first real supporter. I covered a case that happened close to where he lives, just over the bridge, and he found me that way. He kept coming back to watch my other videos, we got to talking, and now he's one of my best friends."

Detective Flanagan gave her a hard look. "An online friend. One you've never met in person."

"I know how it sounds, but it's not what you think. Matt has never asked me for any personal information, and he's never tried to push the idea of us meeting in real life. We don't even have each other's phone numbers—we only message on Messenger. I'm being completely safe."

Lenore shifted in her seat. To anyone else, it might have looked natural, but Audrey knew better. She looked at her friend. Lenore was frowning deeply.

Detective Flanagan could read *that*, at least. "You don't

agree with Audrey's assessment?"

"No," Lenore said quietly. "I don't."

Audrey blinked. Lenore had known for a long while about her friendship with Matt—almost since the beginning, right before they'd started chatting frequently—and she'd never, not even *once*, given any indication that she didn't like it. This was completely out of left field.

"It just seems strange to me," she went on, looking sideways at Audrey now, "that you'd have all these videos where girls get tricked by people online, but you'll post them and go right back to talking to someone *you* only know online. You lecture the rest of us like a broken record about being safe and using fake names and not trusting anybody, but you use your real name with Matt, and he knows you live in West Drummond."

"And I know he lives just over the bridge in Kirawood."

"Do you?" Lenore turned to look at her fully. No hair in her face, no waver in her gaze. "Do you know that *for sure*, Audrey?"

Of course I do, she wanted to say, but... she didn't, did she? She believed it because that was what Matt had told her, and he'd never given her a reason not to believe him. But Lenore was right. As much as she wanted to trust Matt, the boy who'd always been her biggest supporter and whose moody little profile photo always made her smile, she never could. Not fully. Not really.

But she did.

As if Detective Flanagan hadn't heard a single word of this, he said, "I'm going to need to talk to him."

Audrey sighed. "All right. I'll tell him."

"No. You can give me his account information after we're done here." Detective Flanagan absently turned the Styrofoam cup on the table but still didn't make to take a sip of it at all. "The address mentioned in the message. Are you familiar with it at all? Can you think of any reason that Jacqueline might have been there?"

"I don't know what's at that address."

"Neither do I," Lenore said softly when Detective Flanagan turned his gaze on her.

He pulled out his own phone and typed something into it quickly. Maybe making more notes, or calling for back-up. Did he think she was lying again? Was she about to get into trouble? Was he finally going to have her arrested?

He held his phone out to her.

Audrey hesitated a moment before taking it, turning the screen so she and Lenore could look at the satellite image he'd pulled up on Google. It looked like a quiet, suburban area, with a string of little houses on one side of the street and a large park on the other. Its perimeter was thick with trees, like someone had planted them perfectly along the border and left the middle barren.

There was a small, empty canal running along the far side of it.

Audrey quickly offered Detective Flanagan his phone back. She didn't want to look at that. Didn't want to consider what could be at the site.

Lenore shook her head. "I don't know it."

"It doesn't look familiar," Audrey agreed. "And I don't

remember Jackie ever having mentioned anything like it, either." A sudden thought popped into her head. "What about Peter? Maybe he lives around there somewhere. She could have been going to see him that night and gotten into an accident or something."

Detective Flanagan shook his head. "Peter Fitzsimons doesn't live anywhere near this area. I went to his house to speak with him myself after you gave us his information."

"One of her family members, then? I don't know." Audrey shook her head. Her mind went back to that canal—a perfect place to dump a body if ever she'd seen one. "Maybe you were right about her talking to somebody online, and she went off to meet them or something. I just... I don't *know*. I don't know why she would do something that stupid and not at least *tell* me what she was doing or where she was going or who she was talking to or—"

"All right, all right." Detective Flanagan's hands were on her shoulders again, gently pushing her back down into a sitting position. Audrey hadn't realised she'd been rising to her feet. She was breathing hard. "Just calm down."

Audrey swallowed back the terror rising in her and nodded, closing her eyes for a blissful moment. *Breathe*, she willed herself. *In. Out. In. Out.* Lenore took her hand and squeezed. *I'm here with you.*

"Have you asked her parents?" she asked. Audrey opened her eyes. "Has... Has anybody told them about the comment? About the police heading out to check the address?"

"Officers were dispatched to their house," Detective

Flanagan assured her. "They'll keep both Mr and Mrs Chen updated on everything happening with the investigation. There are also officers here gathering up the rest of your friend group and Miss Chen's boyfriend to ask them many of the same questions that I just asked the two of you. Everything is under control."

Audrey nodded and let out a long, shaky breath. Everything was fine. Everything was going to be fine. The police weren't going to find a body at that address. They definitely weren't going to find *Jackie's* body there. Unless she was alive. Maybe she had posted the comment on Audrey's video herself as some final stage of her prank.

Lenore squeezed her hand again. Audrey squeezed back.

"So what do we do now?" she asked, her voice barely more than a whisper.

"Now," Detective Flanagan said, "we wait."

Audrey knew it was going to be the longest wait of their lives.

17

Lenore's mother showed up first, looking flustered and out of breath in her work uniform. Her usually neatly pressed pencil skirt and blouse were looking a little worse for wear today, sweat definitely pooling in the armpit that Audrey could see, and the curls she shared with Lenore were a frizzing mess atop her head. A clear sign that she'd hurried over, probably at a literal run. The real estate where she worked was only a couple of blocks away, and Audrey had no doubt the woman would make the trip at a sprint if she felt she needed to. Leanne Stevens was like Audrey's own mother in that way.

She was shown into the room by Mr Evans, who could barely contain her as she brushed past him and headed for her daughter. He gave Detective Flanagan an exasperated look before disappearing back down the hall to wherever he'd holed himself up, the door closing once more in his wake.

"What's going on?" Ms Stevens demanded. Her eyes had already run over Lenore quickly, assessing. She did the same to Audrey. "I got a call saying there was some kind of situation. Are you girls all right?"

"Ma'am." Detective Flanagan stepped forward, drawing the woman's attention to him. "If you'd like to step aside with me..."

No doubt to give her a rundown of what was going on. Audrey half expected Ms Stevens to argue, to insist that whatever Detective Flanagan wanted to tell her he could say in front of the girls, but she moved to the perimeter of the office with him without complaint. That was certainly a sign of the changing times.

Audrey listened to their hushed voices meekly. Lenore was silent beside her, doing the same. It felt like they'd been sitting there for hours, waiting for news. How long did it take to check a location? They had to be there by now.

She took another sip of water. It still didn't make her feel any better.

Ms Stevens returned. "Is your mother on her way, Audrey?"

"Yeah." Or at least, she assumed her mother was rushing over the same way Lenore's had. She prided herself on being independent, but if the police found a body at that address...

"Good. Let's go, Lennie. You don't need to be here for this."

Lenore froze. "But—"

"*No.* I don't want you around this. I'm sure Audrey can give you the updates when they come."

Lenore wanted to argue. Audrey could see it on the tip of her tongue. But she wouldn't. Not with her mother. She never did.

She stood with a sigh and picked up her bag. With one

last apologetic look over her shoulder, she and Ms Stevens were gone.

And then there were two.

Detective Flanagan returned to leaning against the desk, one foot crossed over the other, his palms braced on the wood behind him. Audrey kept her gaze on his boots. She could feel the weight of his stare on the top of her head. Probably judging her now that he knew about Matt. She could practically feel the incoming lecture. Her own personal lesson on why it was never a good idea to trust somebody you met online. How far would he take it? Would he give her homework on the subject? Ask her to block Matt while he watched?

The thought made her chest hurt. She couldn't block Matt. He was her rock. Her confidant. She needed—

"How are you feeling?"

She looked up. Detective Flanagan was indeed looking at her, but there was no judgement in his hazel eyes. She saw only concern there. It struck her for the first time that he really *was* young for a cop, maybe only ten years older than herself, and if she wasn't so worried about him arresting her, she might have called him a friend.

"I'm... okay," she said slowly. Even to her ears, it sounded like a lie.

"It's okay to not be okay, you know?" he said. The expression on his face, so much softer than she was used to, made him look more relaxed. It helped Audrey relax herself. "I know I wouldn't be okay in your shoes."

"Have you ever been in a situation like this?"

"I can't say I have."

She plucked at a loose thread on her navy skirt. "Have you ever been in a situation where you thought you were going to get arrested?"

Detective Flanagan chuckled. "Of course."

Audrey looked up, raising an eyebrow. "Really?"

"I was sixteen once, too, you know. And a bit of a rebel." He smiled fondly at whatever memory surfaced. "My buddies and I might have been pulled over a time or two for drinking and driving. Something I do *not* recommend, by the way. Especially when you're underage."

There were guys in her own class who did things like that. She couldn't see a single one of them ever making anything of themselves, let alone joining the police force. "How did you go from *that* to being a cop?"

"My father told me if I didn't get back on the straight and narrow, he'd kick my sorry butt onto the streets. It sounds like a great time until you realise none of your friends' parents will take you in, and earning a living wage isn't as easy as showing up at Macca's twice a week for a five-hour shift." He shrugged. "My uncle suggested the police academy. I never looked back."

Audrey couldn't imagine her mother even threatening to kick her out. But if she had, Audrey would have said with absolute certainty that any one of her friends would have invited her into their homes without question. But after all this... it seemed she and the detective had learned the same lesson in two very different ways.

"Is that what you're worried about?"

Audrey blinked. "What?"

"Getting arrested." Flanagan's smile was not unkind.

"You've been more distant since our first conversation about your YouTube channel."

She grimaced. Had she been that obvious? "I'm not stupid. I know I'm a suspect."

At this, Detective Flanagan raised an eyebrow. "You're not a suspect. You never have been."

"But you questioned me. About my channel. And about the argument me and Jackie had that day."

"Because," he said, "I was trying to determine whether your content may have made you a target for someone in the area, thereby making *Jacqueline* a target. I never suspected you of anything. I actually thought you might have been an intended victim."

A chill went down Audrey's spine. Jackie had sometimes said her videos could make her a target for the sorts of people behind the stories she was telling, but she'd never given it any serious thought. She did her part to keep safe, and that should have been that.

She hesitated a moment. "Do you still think that?"

Detective Flanagan was quiet for a time, assessing her. She listened to the clock on the far wall tick the seconds away until, at long last, quietly, he said, "I didn't. But the comment you received changes things."

Audrey's phone buzzed in her hands. Another message from Matt.

Matt

> I know the police are going to want
> to talk to me. Here.

It was followed by a string of ten digits—a mobile phone

number.

She turned her phone to show Flanagan. Without a word, he tugged his notepad from a pocket and jotted the information down.

Her mother showed up sometime around the time the end-of-day bell trilled. The ringing made Audrey jump. She hadn't clocked exactly how long they'd been sitting in Mr Evans's office, but she hadn't thought it was over an hour, even if it might have felt that way. Detective Flanagan pulled her mother aside before she could get to Audrey and gave her the same brief explanation he'd provided Lenore's mother, giving Audrey a moment to prepare herself. She watched the emotions dance across her mother's face—a mixture of anger, surprise, and then deep worry. She was past the man the second Detective Flanagan allowed it.

"Hey," she said by way of greeting, dropping into the chair Lenore had vacated earlier. "What's all this I'm hearing about a YouTube show or something?"

Her mother was still in scrubs. She'd obviously been pulled from the emergency room floor to be here. Audrey immediately felt the guilt rising in her. As much as she was grateful for her mother's presence, she hadn't wanted that. How much were they going to struggle to pay the bills this month if her mother kept missing work or leaving her shifts early? Were they going to be able to afford their rent? Maybe her mother would reconsider her offer to get a part-time job.

Audrey shook her head. "It's a YouTube channel. I've been doing it for a little while now."

"Doing what, exactly?"

Audrey hesitated. "I... I kind of do video reports on missing people from all over the world. I talk about the person, what they were like, what they were doing in the days before they disappeared, and anything people thought was suspicious, you know? And then I talk about the details surrounding their disappearances and basically ask people to keep an eye out for them and come forward if they think they might know anything about it."

She'd often thought about how she would tell her mother about the channel, but this had never been one of the scenarios she'd envisioned. She'd imagined sitting her mother down and showing her a video that had successfully brought somebody home. She'd even gone as far as to daydream about showing her mother a news article that said as much. But she hadn't known what to expect or how her mother would react when she finally found the courage to tell her. Would she be angry that Audrey was focusing her attention on something so trivial instead of school? Would she be angry that Audrey was, in a way, dragging up their messy past?

But her mother only sighed and said, "Is this because of your father?"

She should have expected *that*.

Detective Flanagan, who had returned to Mr Evans's chair after speaking with Audrey's mother, raised an eyebrow. "I'm sorry. I have to ask. What do you mean by that?"

Audrey's mother gave her a long, hard look before turning to Detective Flanagan. "When Audrey was a child, her father flew to Perth on business and never came home. The police never found any trace of him."

Detective Flanagan nodded, his expression neutral. A seasoned police officer's response. "I'm very sorry. I'm sure they did everything they could for you back then."

"No, actually," her mother said bluntly. "They didn't."

Audrey tried not to think about it too much—all of the distressed phone calls she'd overheard, all the nights her mother had cried herself to sleep, what all the kids at school had said to her when they had found out; what it had felt like to lose their house and end up in a tiny, dirty apartment until they could find and afford something better. And every night, no matter where they were, Audrey had gone to her window before going to bed and wished upon a star that her father would come back home, would sweep her and her mother up into his arms and make everything all right again. She'd go back to her old school with her old friends, and they'd live in their old house and be a family again.

But that had never happened. Her father had never come back, had never made any form of contact with them, and they had moved to West Drummond to start anew.

Audrey knew what the likelihood of ever finding her father alive was. Some days, she still held out hope, but others she was more realistic. She and her mother had never openly discussed it, but it was an accepted truth in their household that the man was dead. There was no way he would have left them otherwise. No way he wouldn't have at least sent a postcard. But despite this, and despite knowing that he was dead, and she would never get to see him again, she still felt that need to know. Her mother needed that closure, and Audrey needed those answers to prove to herself that these cases really could be closed. That not every long-term missing person was going to remain an unsolved mystery forever.

"When were you going to tell me about this?" her mother practically demanded of her.

Detective Flanagan was looking between them in silence. Could he sense the annoyance that was radiating off her mother the way that she could? Or was that something only children could detect from their parents?

"I don't know," she admitted, absently pulling at that loose thread on her skirt again. "I guess I was hoping at some point my channel would take off and get successful, you know? Tons of people on YouTube make a living out of making true crime videos, and I wanted to be able to do the same. Earn money to help out at home at the same time as I was helping to find missing people. I wanted to do something worthwhile. I wanted to make a difference to people. I never meant for any of *this* to happen."

"You wanted to make a career out of posting videos about missing people on the Internet?" Her mother gave her an incredulous look. "That doesn't sound like something reliable, Audrey. If you want to help look for missing persons, maybe you should think about working as a police officer and becoming a detective." She jerked her head at Detective Flanagan. "I'm sure the detective would be more than happy to talk to you about it. It might be the only good thing to come out of this."

"Always willing to talk to anybody who's interested in joining the force," Detective Flanagan said. "And I know you might not want to talk about it right now, but you have my number should you ever have questions. Feel free to give me a call any time."

Audrey nodded, but she didn't tell either of them that she didn't have any intentions of joining the police force. At least not at this point in time. She wanted to ask Detective Flanagan if he would extend that invitation to Matt, though. Surely, her friend would have a million and one questions he'd like to ask. But she wouldn't ask yet. The last thing she needed right now was her mother asking who Matt was and her having to explain that she was talking to some strange boy online. And one that she had met via her YouTube channel, no less.

Detective Flanagan's phone rang, making Audrey jump again. She really needed to get a handle on her nerves. He picked it up on the second ring, speaking into it quietly as he moved into the far corner of the room, glancing back briefly to meet Audrey's eyes where she sat watching him intently. Her hands gripped the arms of the chair a little too tight. Her mother looked almost as eager as Audrey felt. Was this the phone call they'd been waiting for? Had the police finally found Jackie?

"All right," Detective Flanagan said quietly. "I'll let them know."

He pressed the screen to end the call and slipped his phone back into a pocket, all the while moving back towards Mr Evans's desk. Audrey watched closely as he walked around to stand before her and her mother, half sitting on the desk again. He breathed a long, deep sigh through his nose.

"What is it?" Audrey demanded. "Did they find her? Is she in trouble? Are they going to arrest her for all of this crap? I'm sure she had a good reason for it. I don't know what it could be, but there must be *something*."

"Audrey..."

"She's always looking for attention, and I guess this was just the best thing that she could come up with. I'm pretty sure she never meant for it to go this far, and she probably didn't realise that her mother would call the police and she'd be causing such a big fuss with all the searches and stuff. She probably doesn't even know how bad it is to waste all those resources for a stupid prank."

Detective Flanagan's hand landed on Audrey's shoulder, squeezing gently, and she shut her mouth.

She knew what he was going to say.

Please, don't say it.

Her mother was tense beside her, and that made Audrey's stomach do a backflip. Detective Flanagan needed to spit the words out. Audrey held her breath, waiting. His face was impassive, but did she detect a hint of weariness behind those eyes?

Finally, he took a deep breath and said the words that Audrey had been dreading since the moment she'd learned her best friend was missing.

"They've found a body."

18

HER EARS HAD BEEN ringing for days.

Ever since Detective Flanagan had told her they'd found a body, she'd known. How could she not? There was no way it *couldn't* be Jackie. What would the point of the comment on her video have been, then? To give them all a scare by handing them a different corpse? No. This was somebody who knew what they were doing. Somebody who had wanted Jackie's body found, who wanted the world to know what they'd done. Why else would they have handed her the address? Why else would they have been taunting her?

She felt sick.

Why had they chosen to give that information to *her*? Why not anonymously send it to the police? The media? Jackie's parents? It made Audrey dwell on what Detective Flanagan had said—about thinking she might have been an intended victim. The thought now lived rent-free inside her head. Could it be true? Had Jackie been abducted as a second choice?

Should it have been Audrey's body discovered in that park instead?

She'd never been to a funeral before, so she wasn't sure what to expect. She looked her outfit over for the hundredth time. Was it too much? Not enough? She'd gone for a simple black dress with sheer black stockings underneath, but the only pair of black heels she owned had a spread of sequins across the back of them. Would people judge her for that? Should she have gone with a pair of flats instead? Were her ex-friends going to look at those heels and think she was celebrating rather than mourning Jackie's death?

She was twisting at the hem of her dress line too much. Her mother was giving her side eye from the driver's seat of the car. Audrey made herself stop.

She wished Matt was here.

He was the one she'd been confiding in since she'd found out. Her mother had taken a few days off work and told her she was there if Audrey wanted to talk, but Audrey didn't want to. It was much easier to pour her heart out into messages and send them off into the ether to a boy she'd never met and may not even be real. She'd felt somewhat ashamed of it after Lenore's admission of how she felt about her friendship with Matt, but real or not, he had been supportive, even answering her messages while she knew he was in class. He'd gone as far as to offer to come to Jackie's funeral to support her if it would make her feel better.

She'd seriously considered taking him up on the offer. Penny, Danielle, and Delilah still had her blocked on social media. She'd messaged Lenore once after the news had been confirmed, only to have her cousin Roxanne respond that Lenore wasn't taking things well and would reach out when she was ready. But apparently ready hadn't happened yet, leaving Matt as her sole support system.

But in the end, she had declined. She didn't want to think about the drama his showing up at the funeral would have caused. How would Jackie's parents have felt about her bringing some strange boy to their daughter's funeral? What would her friends have said? What would *Lenore* have said? She could only imagine the looks she would be getting from the police officers who were going to be in attendance, too. All this talk of keeping safe online, and she was going to come to the funeral with a boy she had met online but never met in person before?

But all of that would have paled in comparison to having to explain the entire thing to her mother. What a horror *that* would have been.

The car shuddered to a stop, and Audrey looked up.

Jackie's funeral was being held at one of the smaller chapels inside of a larger cemetery. There were a number of cars parked nearby already and several people milling around dressed entirely in black. Audrey scanned the faces, some familiar and some strange. She spotted several of her classmates, a couple of her teachers, Mr Evans making small talk with a police officer. A lot of the faces that she didn't recognise she took to be Jackie's family. She spotted a girl who looked like one of Jackie's cousins she'd met about a year ago, but she couldn't be sure. She couldn't think straight. She was too focused on what was about to happen.

Her breathing was coming in rapid little bursts. *Breathe,*

girl. Just breathe.

"Come on," her mother said gently. "We'd better get in there. Let's say our hellos to Mr and Mrs Chen and find our seats."

A couple of people turned to look her way as she climbed out of the car, but none of those eyes lingered. Good. She wanted to fly under the radar today. She let her mother wrap an arm around her shoulders and lead her into the sandstone building.

There were a lot of people inside already. Though their voices were hushed, the sound grew in the enclosed space to become something monstrous, looming overhead like a dark cloud threatening to descend. Audrey immediately wanted to leave. Breathing outside had been hard—breathing inside was impossible. She'd never been claustrophobic before, but she imagined this was what it felt like. This feeling that there was too much around her, that there wasn't enough space for her to *breathe*.

Her mother spotted Jackie's parents right up the front of the room and pointed them out. They'd both clearly been crying, stood arm-in-arm, and were talking to a priest who held a series of small white cards in his hands. Jackie's grandmother was close by, her withered face grave.

"Oh, look," her mother said suddenly. "There are the girls. Do you want to sit with them?"

Audrey looked to where her mother was gesturing. Her friends were sitting together in a row close to the front of the chapel, their backs thankfully to her. In the row behind them sat a couple of their parents; Danielle's mother was off to the side of the room, talking quietly into her phone.

Audrey grimaced at the sight of them all. Lenore was with them, her cousin by her side, but there was a noticeable gap between her and the others. Once upon a time, she would have jumped at the chance to sit with them. But now she could barely stomach the thought.

"No," she said, and she hoped it hadn't been too quick. Her mother didn't seem to notice there was anything wrong, so she guessed she had been successful. "I don't want to sit up there. Can we just sit here instead?"

She slipped into an aisle before her mother could say anything. Thankfully, her mother remained silent and slipped in beside her.

Audrey's gaze went to the front of the room—to the white casket that was taking centre stage, to the smiling photographs of Jackie everywhere. There were a couple of photos in there that Jackie would have approved of, though Audrey was surprised her parents had known the photos even existed. That probably meant one of her friends had been speaking with Mr and Mrs Chen in the days since the police had found Jackie's body. Maybe they all had. Had Mr and Mrs Chen wondered about her absence? What had her friends been telling them about her? She hadn't felt up to calling them, but maybe that had been a bad idea. Why hadn't she mustered up the strength to make at least one phone call to the pair of grieving parents? It wouldn't have killed her.

But them thinking she was a murderer might.

She spotted Peter sitting several rows in front of her. Did Jackie's parents know he'd been her boyfriend? Audrey supposed they were probably learning a lot about their daughter now that she was gone, which would make a difficult situation worse for them. She frowned. There had to be something that she could do for them.

"Audrey. Mrs Herringbone."

Audrey looked up with a start. There was Detective Flanagan, wearing his usual blues and a gentle smile as he looked down at her. She couldn't help but smile back, albeit weakly.

"Detective Flanagan," she greeted him in return. "I'm glad you came today."

"Of course. We're here to show our support for the family."

And to watch out for anybody who might be acting strange, Audrey was sure. She knew it was a possibility the killer might show up to take in all of the misery they'd caused. She couldn't imagine ever being that twisted.

"Thank you for coming, Detective Flanagan," Audrey's mother said. "I'm sure Jackie's parents appreciate it."

"Thank you, Mrs Herringbone." Detective Flanagan rested a hand on Audrey's shoulder and gave it a quick, gentle squeeze. "I'm afraid I can't stay, but I'll be around if either of you need anything at all. Please don't hesitate to ask."

Audrey nodded. "Thank you."

Detective Flanagan gave her one last smile before he walked away. As he stepped out of her line of sight, Audrey's eyes fell on the door where Jackson had just entered the chapel. They hadn't been in touch in the days since Jackie had been found, so she hadn't known whether he would be attending the funeral, but of course he would. For Peter's benefit, if for no other reason. He looked different in all black when she was so used to seeing him in their school's uniform. He caught her eye and gave her a two-fingered salute. She smiled back as best as she could and raised a hand to wave him over to join herself and her mother. This boy she could explain easily enough.

But before she could gesture to him, she heard, "What the hell is *she* doing here?!"

She turned back towards the source of the voice. Her heart sank right down into her stomach when she saw that Penny had not only stood up from her place in the aisle but was also now storming towards her. Every pair of eyes in the room had turned to see what was going on. Audrey's mother had stilled in surprise beside her. Audrey herself stood up, hands raised in defence, prepared to have Penny hit her again.

But instead, the girl only snarled, "Outside. *Now.*"

Several people hissed, "*Penelope!*" Behind her, Audrey's mother was one of them. Penny's own father had done it, and Audrey was sure she'd heard Roxanne's voice mixed in there, too. But she didn't dare turn her head to look at any of them, not wanting to take her eyes away from Penny's. No way was she making that mistake again. She'd be safer turning her back on a viper. She nodded, slipped out of the aisle, and waited for Penny to start her march outside before she followed.

If Penny's aim for going outside was to avoid making a scene, she'd made the wrong call. While the most important people were inside the chapel, outside, there were *more* people present. Audrey opened her mouth to suggest they go around the side to talk, where there were fewer prying eyes and much less ears, but Penny rounded on her right there on the chapel steps, the sunlight gleaming down on them.

"I can't believe you had the nerve to show your goddamn face today!"

Audrey stared at her. They'd really expected her to skip the funeral.

"Is this a joke?" she asked, keeping her voice low. Penny had drawn the attention of several people already, but Audrey wanted to avoid drawing the attention of any more. "Why wouldn't I come, Pen? Jackie was my best friend. There's no way in hell I wouldn't be here for her. And for her parents. This is going to be the hardest day of their lives."

"Oh, shut the hell up with that bullshit!" Penny was practically shouting. She tossed her hair over her shoulder in annoyance. "There you go again, always making shit about yourself. Obviously, she wasn't your best friend if you chose to kill her, and her parents sure as hell don't need you for support. They have Jackie's *real* friends here to help them. You're only here to get more material for your goddamn YouTube channel!"

She gaped at Penny. "What are you *talking* about? Are you ma—"

Penny held up a hand to silence her. "No. You know what? If it's fame you want to get out of this, then fine. You're going to get it."

She turned to face the crowd that was unashamedly watching them. Audrey could feel the weight of many of their eyes on her.

What she hadn't immediately noticed was the media standing among the mourners.

And it was the media that Penny addressed, her head held high, the perfect picture of a grieving friend. She thrust a finger at Audrey, pointing her out for all to see as a couple of cameras flashed.

"This girl," Penny snarled, "is a murderer! She pretended to be Jackie's friend for years so she could get close to our group because she wanted to use our popularity to help her stupid YouTube channel gain views! But she never liked that none of us agreed with the stuff she was posting. She talks about missing people and murder, so I guess if anybody knows how to make their best friend disappear, it's her! Look her up, everybody! Audrey Herringbone! Go on her YouTube channel and give it the attention that it *really* deserves!" Penny turned hard eyes on her once more. "Let's let the whole world know what a horrible, disgusting person she is for murdering her 'best friend' for a little bit of fame!"

Audrey's head spun. Her ears were muffled. She barely noticed when somebody grabbed her arm and began dragging her down the stairs of the chapel. It was finally happening. She was finally being arrested. She looked up to see her mother, expression grim, dragging her back towards their car. Behind them, people were shouting questions. She glanced back, hating that there were at least two reporters following them while the others stayed filming and taking photographs of Penny, who was lapping up the attention with Danielle now by her side.

Lenore was running after Audrey and her mother.

Audrey regained her senses long enough to clamber into the car and slam the door shut before either of those reporters could ask her any questions. As Lenore opened the back door of the car to climb in, Audrey could hear her mother yelling at the reporters to leave them alone and that they didn't have anything to say about these disgusting accusations. Audrey sunk down deeper into her seat. How had today gone so horribly wrong? Never in any of her wildest imaginings had she thought that this would be the end result of showing up for her best friend's funeral. Maybe she should have stayed home after all.

"I'm sorry."

Audrey turned her head, looking at Lenore behind her. The girl looked broken. It was clear she'd been crying most of the morning, if not most of the week, and there were fresh tears in her eyes now. Audrey was too numb to cry. Too much had happened in such a short period of time. Too much was *still* happening.

Her mother climbed into the car and started it. Without a word, she backed out of their parking space, made a right turn back into the main road of the cemetery, and made a beeline for the exit. Her lips were pursed tightly, and her knuckles were nearly white on the steering wheel.

"Would one of you care to explain what just happened?"

Audrey rubbed her eyes. "I think it was pretty obvious what was going on there, Mum."

"Maybe," her mother said, "but I'd like to hear it from you, Audrey."

Audrey didn't want to talk about any of this right now, but there would be no getting out of this conversation, especially when she was going to be trapped in the car with her mother until they made it home.

"It's the girls' fault," Lenore spoke up. Audrey's mother glanced at the brunette in the rearview mirror, and Lenore took that as an invitation to go on. "After Jackie disappeared, Penny and Danielle kept saying that Audrey had probably done something to her because Jackie's always being rude about her channel. They argued about it on Friday, and then Jackie went missing that night, so I guess in their minds, it made sense." She took a breath. "Penny and Danielle are convinced that Audrey did all of this because she wants her YouTube channel to get popular. They even think she posted the comment on her own video that led the police to Jackie's body."

Audrey's mother glanced left at her. "Why didn't you tell me any of this was going on? You've been dealing with all this on your own? I thought you and your friends were supporting each other through this!"

"No," Audrey admitted. And then, since her mother was finding everything else out today, she decided to add, "I've been getting support from a friend I have online."

Her mother didn't bother to react to the news. She was probably at her limit with everything already.

"Well, what are we doing now?" she asked. "Do you girls want to go somewhere to eat, or do you want to go back home? Because there's no way in hell we're going back to that funeral."

Audrey didn't care. So long as she didn't have to face the

mess Penny had created, she was happy to go anywhere.

19

Her mother took them home. Neither Audrey nor Lenore had felt like going anywhere else, least of all a public space with eyes on them, so it had been the only logical choice. She'd worried briefly that her mother would change her mind and want to take them back to the funeral, insisting they should fix things with the girls like friends were *supposed* to do, so she was extra glad when their old Toyota turned onto their street, and their ugly apartment complex came into view. She'd never been so glad to see the monstrosity. To see *home*.

Her mother had the foresight to busy herself in the kitchen while Audrey and Lenore headed into Audrey's room and shut the door. Audrey breathed a deep sigh, letting the tension go out of her shoulders. Lenore settled onto the bed, sinking into the mess of blankets, looking as exhausted as Audrey felt. She kicked off her heels and settled in comfortably beside her friend, falling back against the pillows. And to think, she'd thought her shoes were going to be the thing to cause her the most pain that day.

There was silence between them for a long while.

Lenore's gaze was on the window, on the sunshine outside, on the world that carried on as if there wasn't a funeral happening a few suburbs away for a sixteen-year-old girl.

For Jackie.

A breath shuddered out of Audrey. She hadn't been at the chapel long, but it had been long enough. She could still feel the space pressing in on her, the room feeling far too small for the occasion. Could still see the casket sitting up the front, a beautiful thing of white wood and gold accents, beautiful enough she was sure it would have fit even Jackie's standards to house her body.

Jackie's body.

The blood rushed from her head. Bile rose in her throat. The same thing had happened when she'd first heard those words from Detective Flanagan: *They've found a body.* She'd thrown up then, right there on the floor of Mr Evans's office, had gotten the contents of her stomach all over her hands and school skirt as she'd tried to escape the room, and her knees had given way.

She had no desire to repeat the scene. She squeezed her eyes shut, taking deep, slow breaths like her mother had told her to on the floor in that office. *In. Out.* She was fine. Everything was fine.

Lenore's weight shifted on the bed to lie beside her. A moment later, she was squeezing Audrey's hand. "You okay?"

Audrey nodded.

It was a lie.

"So Matt's been your person, huh?"

She opened her eyes and turned her head enough to look

at Lenore, whose blue eyes were shining with unshed tears. She was pale, but at least she looked more put together than Audrey felt. And she was offering a lifeline. A way out of the dark.

"Yeah." She swallowed. "We text every day. He's always checking in. Always responds quickly." She smiled softly. "He even texted back at two in the morning the other night."

"You sound like you're in love with him."

Her face warmed. "We've never even met in person."

Lenore shrugged. "You don't have to meet someone to fall in love with them." After a moment of consideration, she added, "You don't respond at two in the morning if you don't care, either."

"Is that you saying that maybe Matt isn't so bad?"

Lenore shifted her gaze to the ceiling. "It's just an observation. I'm glad you had someone to talk to." She frowned at the peeling paint. "I'm sorry it wasn't me."

"It's okay." Audrey squeezed her hand back. "You needed time, too. I'm glad you had Roxanne to talk to."

Lenore nodded. "Me too."

"Where is Rox?"

"She stayed back at the funeral to deal with Penny," Lenore said. "But she's on your side, too. You know what she's like. Thinks the others are all air-headed bitches. You're the only one of my friends she actually likes."

Audrey managed a small smile. Good old Roxanne.

They lapsed into a comfortable silence, Lenore again staring out Audrey's bedroom window. The sheer curtain fluttered on a light breeze, birdsong floated in. It was such a beautiful day out that it was hard to believe the morning's events had taken place in the same universe. Audrey's attention went to the photos she still had plastered all over her wall—the ones of all of her friends, the ones of their group hanging out together at various places.

The ones of Jackie alone.

She wondered how the funeral was going. Were people giving speeches yet? What was being said about Jackie? Were her parents telling everybody about how she'd been a perfect daughter who always made them proud? Was Danielle shocking the family by telling them what Jackie had *really* been like? Audrey frowned. She didn't care how her friends were doing at the funeral. All she really wanted was to be there for Jackie's parents—for Mrs Chen, who had always been a second mother to her, and for Mr Chen, who had done his best to step away from being the typical, strict Chinese father and allow his daughter at least a little more freedom, even if it was never as much as Jackie had wanted.

Audrey's phone chimed, making both her and Lenore jump.

Lenore gave her a wary look. "You don't think that might be the girls messaging, do you?"

"I doubt it," Audrey said, though she was unsure herself. "They'd have to unblock me first, and I can't see them going to the effort when they still think I'm a criminal."

Lenore looked surprised. "They actually *blocked* you?"

Audrey nodded as she dug into her clutch purse for her phone. She pulled it out easily and flipped it over.

It wasn't any of the girls.

Matt

> So I guess the funeral didn't go well, huh?

How could Matt have known that? She hadn't messaged him about the funeral yet, and none of the girls would have interacted with him. Her heart gave a jolt. Had Matt turned up at the chapel even when she'd told him she didn't need him to come? Was he going to turn out to be one of those weird Internet stalkers after all? Christ, had he been the one to kidnap and murder Jackie?

She brought that line of thinking to a screeching halt. Now was not the time to let other peoples' thoughts take root in her mind.

Lenore read the message over her shoulder and then watched her carefully. Audrey unlocked her phone and typed back a response.

Audrey

> How did you know that?

She expected a longer wait for a response—for Matt to take his time in crafting some elaborate story about how he knew what had happened at the funeral. Maybe that he'd been in the area and had decided to stop by after all. Or maybe he would backtrack and say that he was just *assuming* it hadn't gone well because it was her best friend's funeral, and how could that ever have gone well?

But the response was lightning fast. She hadn't needed to wait at all before Matt had sent her the link to an article on some local news site. And she didn't need to open the article to know what it was about. The headline loaded along with the link.

Killed By Best Friend for Internet Fame?

"Oh," Lenore breathed. "Oh, *no*."

Audrey knew she shouldn't click on the link. She *knew* she should put her phone down and walk away. There wasn't going to be a single good thing about her in that article. But she had to open it. She needed to know how bad it was. She had to know what the media were going to be saying about her, so she knew what kind of hate to expect whenever she decided to show her face in public again. Her thumb hovered over the link, hesitant. How bad could it possibly be? The worst that could happen was it would call her a murderer. Right?

She pressed on the link.

It was as bad as she'd expected.

As a minor, she knew the media couldn't name her, but apparently, they had no problem with sharing her face on video. The article opened with actual footage of Penny on the chapel steps, starting with her giving the speech full of outlandish claims she'd made about Audrey and ending with the visual of Audrey, her mother, and Lenore climbing into their car and fleeing the cemetery. Audrey grimaced. That definitely made them look bad. But it hadn't been like that at all!

The text was worse.

Sixteen-year-old West Drummond High School student Jacqueline Chen was laid to rest today at Northmeadows Necropolis. She was accompanied by friends and family, teachers and classmates, and the girl we suspect police are looking at to be her killer.

Jacqueline's best friend, Penelope Masters (17), stood on the steps of Northmeadows Chapel and opened up about how their former friend was the most likely culprit behind Jacqueline's untimely end. Her motive? YouTube fame.

The article talked about her YouTube channel crassly. The journalist had obviously only done some very quick research on it and not bothered to watch any of the videos because they accused Audrey of being an obsessed, true crime nutter who would know the ins and outs of how to cover up a murder because she'd been so fascinated by them for so long. Again, not true, but there was nothing to be done about it now.

Her channel was linked in the article, alongside the quote of Penny essentially asking people to get onto YouTube and attack her online. Great. She could only imagine the kinds of trolls that would come out of the woodwork now.

The article finished up with the journalist clutching at straws. There was talk about the argument she and Jackie had on the Friday before she vanished; there was mention of how the police had spoken to Audrey several times, including at her own home earlier on in the investigation. Audrey wanted to reach through the screen and say *of course* they had—she was Jackie's best friend, and Jackie had been using her as a cover. The police had to have spoken to her. It was literally a part of the investigation!

The worst part of the article was the final section, though—where the journalist said that Jackie's official cause of death had been ruled as ligature strangulation, which was a crime of passion and right within the realms of something that Audrey would have been capable of.

Audrey's stomach roiled. She closed the article immediately.

Had Jackie's cause of death been strangulation? Audrey hadn't bothered to ask any of the police officers or her mother, and she'd been avoiding any news reports about Jackie ever since her body had been found. Wasn't it still too early for the coroner to have made a ruling on that? Did things really work that fast in these cases?

No kidding.

Lenore was painfully still beside Audrey. She knew her friend had read the article too, had seen absolutely everything it said about her. For a moment, she wondered if Lenore was about to change her mind. What if she decided Audrey was guilty after all and decided to take off? Audrey couldn't blame her, she supposed. It would suck, but Lenore had to put her own safety first.

But as if she could hear Audrey's thoughts, Lenore was shaking her head.

"You should tell your mum about this," she said quietly. "Isn't it illegal for them to imply you're a suspect? And show your face on video? Maybe the police can do something about it."

Audrey nodded. Maybe. She didn't want to stress her mother out more, but she knew that it would be much better for the woman to hear about this coming from her own daughter rather than seeing it on the news later. She sighed and stood, Lenore standing with her.

"Let's get this over with," she said.

20

Within five minutes of her mother calling for him, Detective Flanagan was standing on their doorstep. Audrey's mother invited him in quickly, no doubt wanting to hide the fact that he was here from the media and nosy neighbours alike, but Audrey knew better than to even try. Nosy Nellies were going to get their information, no matter what. It was more about managing the aftermath than preventing the problem at this point.

Detective Flanagan had come directly from the funeral. Audrey, Lenore, and her mother were still dressed in their black attire, too, not having had the energy or the care to change, but not one of them mentioned what had happened there as they gathered in the tiny living room and sat across the two old couches. Audrey and Lenore occupied one; the two adults sat on the other, a mug of fresh coffee in front of each of them. Detective Flanagan took a slow sip from his before setting it down carefully on a coaster that had, like the rest of their belongings, seen better days.

"So," he started, "I assume I'm here so we can talk about what happened at the funeral today?"

"Not quite," Audrey's mother said. She nodded to Audrey, and Audrey unlocked her phone until she was once more staring at the article Matt had linked her to. She offered the device to Detective Flanagan, keeping her hand as steady as possible. No need to let her mother or the detective see she was shaken. She wanted to hear what he had to say about it before she let herself descend into a panic. And even then, it would be in the privacy of her bedroom.

He took the phone from her in silence and spent the next minute or so reading the article, his face impassive as he scrolled. Audrey listened to her mother sip at her own coffee—something she knew the woman was doing to keep her own hands steady. Lenore was quiet as they waited.

Audrey wondered what Detective Flanagan was thinking. Probably that she deserved this. She was the one with the questionable YouTube channel, after all. How could she run something like that and not expect some backlash from it? Maybe it was time to find a happier topic to talk about. Maybe it was time to shut the channel down altogether.

Absolutely not. She shook that thought from her head almost as soon as she had it. She'd worked too long and too hard on her channel to simply shut it down because of some bad publicity. Calling it quits now would be a mistake. What about all the missing persons she still had on her list to cover? What about her father's case? She couldn't abandon all of those people now. *Somebody* had to speak up for them. Somebody had to show their families there was still hope. And she would be that person for as long as she could, no matter the consequences. She vowed it.

Detective Flanagan looked up from the screen. "Has there been any action on your YouTube channel since this article was posted?"

"I don't know," Audrey said carefully. Truthfully, she'd been too afraid to check. "But the article's only been up for like half an hour, so…"

Detective Flanagan was already on his feet, stepping out of the living room and tugging his own phone from a pocket. Audrey's mother watched with pursed lips as he made his call to somebody at the station by the sounds of things. Lenore bounced a leg nervously beside Audrey. Audrey tried to give her a reassuring look, but it fell flat.

She would have to get in touch with Jackson, too. Let him know people might be watching their video and have a few choice things to say to him. Had he made it out of the funeral unscathed? For his sake, Audrey hoped the hate only focused on her, Jackie's supposed killer. Jackson didn't deserve it. He'd only wanted to help her get that video out. The last thing she wanted was to get innocent people mixed up in her madness. She was no better than Jackie's killer then.

Jackie's killer. Now there was something she needed to think about.

"Okay." Detective Flanagan stepped back into the living room and offered Audrey her phone back. She took it and placed it flat against one of her knees, screen down. She didn't want to look at it anymore. "I've contacted one of my superiors, and they're going to see what we can do about at least having the video's link removed from the article. We're going to do our best to keep on top of this for you, but I can't make any promises. The media are a difficult beast to tame, and they know where they can blur the line between immoral and illegal."

"They're vultures," Lenore grumbled.

"Thank you for doing what you can, Detective." Audrey's mother said. "It's very much appreciated."

Detective Flanagan nodded. "We take these matters very seriously, particularly when a minor is involved. Especially when we worry this minor might be one of many that may become a target for our perpetrator."

"What?" Lenore asked in surprise, at the same time that Audrey said, "You're still looking into that theory, then?"

"We are," Detective Flanagan confirmed. "So I want to know immediately if you start getting any strange messages or if you see anything that you think is out of the ordinary. I don't care what it is or how innocent it might seem. You get anything that feels even a little bit weird, you call me. Day or night. Do I make myself clear?"

Audrey nodded. "Crystal, sir."

"That goes for you too, Miss Stevens."

Lenore nodded. "I understand, Detective."

Detective Flanagan nodded. "For now, try not to worry about that article. If we're lucky, we'll have it down before too many people get wind of it."

Audrey hoped so, but she knew how the Internet worked. Once something was on there, it was on there forever. It was incredibly unlikely that Matt had been the only one to spy the article. In fact, if he had seen it so quickly, it was likely the link had already been posted on some public forum to spread the word quickly. She should have asked him. Maybe she would later.

"What happened at the funeral after we left?" her mother asked. "I was going to call Suzy later to apologise. I can't believe Penelope had the nerve to pull a stunt like that at her friend's *funeral*."

"It got worse." Detective Flanagan glanced at Audrey. "Penelope went on talking to the media until an officer asked her to step back inside, and once she was there, she and her parents were asked to leave."

Audrey winced. She could only imagine what had happened after that.

"She threw quite a fit," Detective Flanagan went on, confirming Audrey's assumption. "Started screaming about how this was her best friend's funeral and she wasn't going to miss it, that it would have been disrespectful to Jacqueline if she was evicted. She didn't stop yelling about it until Jacqueline's father screamed at her to leave. Both he and his wife were already in tears by that point. I think that shocked the girl. She hadn't taken much notice of them before that."

Audrey's heart sank. Yes, that sounded just like Penny—always wanting to make things about herself and forgetting that she wasn't the main character of every scene. How could she have done that to Mr and Mrs Chen? Jackie's parents were already mourning the loss of their only child, and Penny had just gone and completely ruined her funeral. The last memory those parents would have of their daughter was forever marred.

"I think Mrs Chen intends to drop in to see you a little later," Detective Flanagan said gently, his eyes back on Audrey and Lenore. "I think she felt bad that you'd left. She really wanted the two of you to be at the funeral, and she's very sorry that you had to miss it because of one bad egg. That's a direct quote."

That only made Audrey feel worse. To think that she and Lenore had added to Mr and Mrs Chen's pain today, even in a small, indirect way, was terrible to think about.

"Are we able to press charges?"

Audrey was stunned to hear the words come out of her mother's mouth. Lenore looked just as surprised.

"What?!" Audrey demanded. "Mum, *why?*"

"Because the accusations that Penny was making are extremely damaging to your character," her mother said. Her lips were pursed so tightly they were barely visible. It was obvious she was still seething on the inside from the way she was holding her coffee mug just a fraction too tightly, but she was doing her best to keep cool and collected in front of Detective Flanagan. Audrey would probably hear the full extent of her outrage later when the two of them were alone. "Those are the sorts of accusations that could cost you future job opportunities, especially if you want to go down the criminal justice route."

A chill ran down Audrey's spine. "It's that serious?"

"If it sticks," her mother said.

"But Audrey didn't do anything," Lenore said, looking between Audrey's mother and Detective Flanagan.

"Something like that would only stick if it was actually her, and it wasn't. The police will find the real killer, and all of this will go away for Audrey."

"Ah," Detective Flanagan said, drawing their attention to him. He had the decency to look apologetic. "That may not be entirely true. Even if we caught the person behind this and publicly declared that Audrey was in no way involved in the disappearance or murder, there would probably still be sceptics out there who would go to the grave believing that she was the mastermind behind it all." He sipped his coffee. "And you're forgetting that there's always a chance we may never find who was behind this, leaving Audrey as the main suspect in many people's eyes." He gave her the tiniest of smiles as he added, "Not mine, of course."

Audrey's heart sank further into her stomach. "What do you mean you might never find them? They could get away with abducting and murdering a teenage girl?"

Detective Flanagan gave her a sad smile. "It's always a possibility, with any case. We have to be realistic about things. You know that."

"Is it true that she died by strangulation?" Lenore practically whispered.

Detective Flanagan shared a look with Audrey's mother. The woman looked highly reluctant at first but eventually nodded her consent.

"Yes," Detective Flanagan finally admitted. "She did. And that's all I can share, I'm afraid. Now that this is a homicide investigation, I'm technically not even on the case anymore."

Audrey was still reeling from the thought that Jackie's murder investigation might never meet its end. She knew that some cases went cold, of course, and that not every murder was solved—but to think that her own best friend's murder might never make it to that point? To think that Jackie's parents might never have closure? It was unacceptable. As unacceptable as Audrey herself never getting her closure over what had happened to her father. She was not going to allow those wonderful parents to go through the rest of their lives not knowing what happened to their daughter.

And there was one way she knew how to help. The *only* way she'd ever known how. Forget looking for happier topics. Maybe it was time to think about her YouTube channel branching out from only covering missing persons.

21

THE CHEN HOUSEHOLD WAS darker than Audrey had ever seen it, but at least somebody had taken the time to fix the garden stones so they were orderly once more. She looked them over carefully as she walked up the path, but every stone was back in place as though they'd never been disturbed at all. She wondered if it had been Mrs Chen, and whether the woman had found the burst of energy before or after Jackie's body had been located. Probably before. The house had looked relatively normal from the outside then. Now, the curtains were all drawn instead of flung wide, and Mr Chen's daily newspaper sat uncollected on the front porch. Audrey picked it up as she reached the door. Then, she noticed the previous day's edition kicked carelessly to the side.

Mrs Chen said little as she opened the door to her and led her into the house. The kitchen was empty and looked like it hadn't been used or cleaned since Audrey herself had washed those few dishes, and Mr Chen's stack of newspapers had grown. She dumped the two she'd picked up outside with the rest.

Audrey had never understood the term "thick with

grief" until that moment. The atmosphere inside was noticeably heavy, particularly in the living room, which was apparently no longer a place for the living. As upset as she'd been over Jackie's passing, she knew her emotions could never compare to those Jackie's parents must have been experiencing. To have lost their only daughter—their only *child*—and having to live with that for the rest of their lives was going to be a tough pill to swallow. She couldn't begin to imagine. It was a fate she wouldn't have wished upon her worst enemy, let alone the people she thought of as her second family.

She ventured a guess that Mr and Mrs Chen had barely left their bed since hearing that Jackie's body had been found, but Mrs Chen had made an effort to make herself presentable when Audrey had called to say she was going to be swinging by, if that was okay. Of course it was okay, Jackie's mother had said. Audrey was always welcome in their home, and she had wanted to speak to her, too. That had startled Audrey, making her heart flutter with worry. What was it Mrs Chen wanted to talk to her about? Had she decided she was on Penny's side of the argument? That was doubtful, given she'd said Audrey was still welcome at the house any time, but what did she want to talk about if not that?

The thoughts had stirred in her head relentlessly as she made her way to the house, and they were stirring again now that she was sitting in Jackie's parents' living room. Mrs Chen was in the kitchen for what must have been the first time in days, preparing tea as she had done every other time Audrey had come to visit over the years. She would usually have turned the offer of a drink down, but Mrs Chen seemed to need the task to keep her hands and mind occupied. And so she let the woman work.

When Mrs Chen finally sat down opposite her, she looked absolutely exhausted. Her dark hair was done up in its usual bun, but it was messier than usual. She was barefoot instead of wearing her house slippers, and there was little to no make-up on her face. She looked pallid without it, as lifeless as Jackie probably looked now, six feet underground. But at least Mrs Chen was up and moving around, doing her best. Not letting her grief win. She was trying.

The same way, a lifetime ago, Audrey's mother had powered on after her father had disappeared.

Mrs Chen held out a cup and saucer to Audrey with shaking hands, the porcelain rattling gently. Audrey accepted the tea the woman offered her out of kindness and said thank you, bowing her head. Mrs Chen nodded gratefully and sat opposite her with her own cup.

There was silence between them for so long that Audrey wasn't sure if it was safe to speak. She kept a hold of her tea carefully, eyeing Mrs Chen over the rim of the cup. Despite the effort, she looked like hell. Her eyes were distant as she sipped, looking but not seeing, like a doll that had been on display too long. She looked frail. Like one little gust of wind would knock her down and break her.

Proceed with caution.

"Mrs Chen," Audrey began gently, her heart pounding in her ears, "I wanted to apologise for what happened at the funeral the other day."

She'd been rehearsing the apology in her head all night, agonising over the right words to say, but before she'd even gotten a start on it, Mrs Chen was brushing it aside, shaking her head no. Audrey's heart sank. The cup and saucer in her hands clattered. So maybe this was about the funeral after all. Her best friend's mother was not even going to let her apologise for what had happened.

But then said was saying, "No, Audrey, it's fine. Everything is fine. We know it wasn't your fault. Penelope should never have said the things she did. I wanted you to know that no matter what anybody is saying, we don't think you had anything to do with what happened to Jacqueline. We know you would never do such a thing. We know that you were a true friend to our daughter." Mrs Chen gave her a sad, puffy-eyed smile. "I wish you and Lenore would have stayed. Jacqueline would have wanted you there."

Audrey swallowed back the lump in her throat. Would she? Or would she have chosen Penny over her primary school bestie? "I wish we would have stayed too, Mrs Chen. I'm very sorry that we didn't at least say goodbye first."

"All is well," Mrs Chen said, waving her apology away again. She sniffled. "The nice policeman explained to us afterwards what happened with you and Penelope. He said it was better that you and your mother left before the reporters could call in extra people. I am very glad that you got away from the harassment."

Audrey nodded. She didn't have the heart to correct her.

"Your videos online," the woman went on. "Are people attacking you there, too?"

Audrey hesitated, but she didn't want to lie to the woman. She respected her too much for that. She'd checked her channel very briefly before she'd gone to bed the night before. Only long enough to see that, yes, people were visiting her channel—and yes, it was bad. "Yeah. But it's okay. They're just comments on a video from people who don't even know me. I can handle them." She hesitated again before adding, "Actually, I kind of wanted to talk to you about my YouTube channel..."

"You wanted to ask if it was okay to keep talking about Jacqueline in your videos."

Audrey wasn't surprised the woman had correctly guessed her intentions. It wasn't a far stretch, after all. "Yes."

Mrs Chen didn't hesitate. "Of course, Audrey. Actually, I would like it if you did. Jacqueline's father and I... we want answers. We want to know what happened to our daughter. And we wish for people to remember her. If you can help us with that, I would like for you to do so."

"I feel obliged to mention," Audrey said, "that Jackie didn't really approve of my channel. And she did say she'd never want me to film videos about her. So... that might change your opinion on the matter, I guess."

"Oh, sweetheart." Mrs Chen gave her a sad smile. There were tears glimmering in her dark eyes, so like Jackie's. "Jacqueline may not have been the biggest fan of the things you talk about, but she was always proud of you for putting yourself out there like you do. She would have come around on the matter eventually, and she would have supported you no matter what you chose to keep making videos about."

Audrey swallowed again. Oh, how she wished that were true. "No, I doubt that very much."

"You can doubt it if you want, but it's true. She was proud of the woman that you're becoming. And you should be, too."

Audrey smiled a little. She didn't know how true any of that was, but she desperately wanted to believe in what Mrs Chen was saying. To have Jackie be accepting of her work, to have her best friend on her side... that was all she had ever wanted. Never Jackie's approval—only her acceptance.

She wondered what her best friend would have said now, with her truly being gone and Audrey fighting to figure out what had happened to her. Would she have stuck to her word and hated being put on display in such a way? Or would she be grateful for Audrey's attempting to bring more attention to her case? Would she be smiling down on her if Audrey managed to figure out who was behind her disappearance and death?

I hope I'm doing right by you, Jackie.

"Make the videos," Mrs Chen insisted. "Ignore what all of those disgusting people are saying. Keep doing your good work, Audrey. Please. Please, help find my daughter's k-killer."

Audrey nodded. "I'll do my best, Mrs Chen."

And she would.

"We're going to have a vigil. Some of..." Mrs Chen

swallowed. Steadied her shaking hands. "Some of her cousins are putting it together. It's going to be on Friday, at the park where…"

She paused to take a deep breath. Audrey had to take one, too. It was getting harder to breathe around that lump in her throat.

"Will you come?" Mrs Chen asked. "You and Lenore? And help spread the word?" There were tears glistening in her eyes. They made Audrey's own eyes burn. "I want my girl to know how loved she is."

Audrey swallowed hard. "Of course, Mrs Chen. I'll definitely be there. Nobody could stop me."

Mrs Chen dabbed at her eyes, but the smile she gave Audrey was genuine. "You've grown up to be such a beautiful young woman. I just know you're going to do amazing things one day."

Audrey's cheeks warmed. "Thank you, Mrs Chen."

Mrs Chen reached out to cup her cheek, her eyes still shining. "Well. I'd best let you go. Call me when you get home so I know you made it safe."

"I will. I promise."

"Good girl."

She reached up to brush strands of hair away from Audrey's eyes, the way she'd often done with Jackie. The lump in Audrey's throat grew larger, but she kept still, standing her ground. Let Mrs Chen have her moment for as long as she needed. It wasn't quite the moment she wanted, but it was the closest she would ever get again. Her hand lingered a long while before she finally pulled away.

Audrey cleared her throat. Blinked away the stinging in

her eyes. She would *not* cry in front of this already grieving woman. "Send me the information for the vigil when you have it all. I'll spread the word at school and get as many people as I can to come." She thought about it a moment, then added, "I don't think I could stop Penny and the others from showing up..."

Another wave from Mrs Chen before she used that same hand to brush a lone tear from her cheek. "I'll be speaking with their mothers, don't you worry. We won't be having any repeats of the other day. If they do choose to come, they'll need to be on their best behaviour."

Audrey didn't want to tell her that the best behaviour from Penny and Danielle seemed non-existent lately. Let her speak to their parents. Maybe it would open their eyes, show them how wrong their actions had been lately. It was time they realised this wasn't a game of numbers.

And besides, they must have been due a miracle by now.

22

Her YouTube channel was exploding.

The phrase *be careful what you wish for* came to mind. It was what she'd always wanted, but not like this—thousands of views, hundreds of comments, and a dozen or so new subscribers who probably didn't have any actual interest in her content. Just the drama. She'd had to stop reading the comments after the twentieth person had accused her of being a murderer, but she couldn't bring herself to shut the channel down. Not when she had wanted to keep it going, to branch out, to put out the word on more cases, more people, more crime.

To figure out what had happened to Jackie.

She was counting her lucky stars the universe had brought her to Jackson. Suddenly, she was eager to know everything he did about forensic psychology, to know what could have been running through the killer's head when they had targeted her friend. What kind of person were they? Why had they done it? Would they attempt to do it again?

"Are you ready for this?" Jackson had asked her. "We're going to have to do some heavy research, and that includes finding out as much as we can about what happened to Jackie. *Exactly* what happened to her. Every detail is important in a murder case."

Audrey had nodded. She wasn't going to like it, but she knew it was necessary. For Jackie.

Jackson and Matt had both offered to do the lion's share of the research into the murder. Audrey had considered it. It would have been easier to let them read all the news, all the articles, all the press conferences. But she couldn't do that. She couldn't back down on this now, not when she owed it to Jackie. And she owed it to Jackie's parents to help to give them closure.

She had braced herself for the worst that first day, typed Jackie's name into Google, and hit search.

The results had been disappointing. Audrey had anticipated finding some long, detailed article that would give her every gruesome detail of her best friend's murder, but she didn't find that at all. Instead, she found a whole lot of articles stating that strangulation had been the cause of death, but the police had not confirmed anything else yet. Part of her was relieved that she wasn't being confronted with the details, but the other part of her was... disappointed. How were they supposed to help with this investigation if the police weren't being forthcoming with their information?

"Maybe we can ask Detective Flanagan?" Lenore had suggested. "If he knew it was so we could try to help the police out, maybe he might be willing to share a few more details than what they're telling the media?"

But that had been a dead end. Detective Flanagan was

unwilling to tell them *anything* the media hadn't already gotten wind of. He had cited a number of reasons to them—their young age, not being allowed to discuss the specifics of an ongoing investigation, and not needing to ever know those details. Audrey had understood, but that didn't make it any easier to know they were currently at a standstill with their own investigation. They were going to have to wait for details the same as everybody else.

But Audrey didn't know how long she could wait before updating her YouTube channel again. Because, bad publicity or not, she was getting a lot of views on her page and videos, and not *all* of those people were bad. Some of them were genuinely watching her content and posting worthwhile comments, interacting in positive ways. Most of the hate was on the video she had done for Jackie—every reaction on her other videos appeared to be of a better sort. Hope bloomed in her chest. Just a shred, but it was there.

They planned the next video quickly.

She'd never realised how much more intense plotting out her content could be when she had a team working with her. Jackson dove headfirst into researching what he thought the killer might be like. Matt helped, too, gaining whatever information he could about Jackie's case from whatever sources he already had or could successfully find and verify. Lenore and Audrey planned and wrote out the script, piecing everything together and giving it structure. Audrey was glad for the help and for the fresh perspective that Lenore was able to provide with her non-criminally orientated mind. It was great to finally have one of her friends not only on board with what she was doing with her channel but to also be actively, willingly helping her.

"You're sure about doing this video?" Lenore asked. "I know the police haven't told you not to post any more of them, but aren't you scared about what people are going to keep saying about you?"

"No," Audrey said, surprising herself. "I'm more worried about finding the person that did this to Jackie. And all those people leaving those comments are just more people that are watching my videos. Maybe with this one, we can actually get through to them and get them to help us instead of insulting me and calling me a murderer."

"By admitting that you're Jackie's best friend?" Lenore clarified.

Audrey nodded. That was the plan. It was time to remove the mask she'd been hiding behind and tell the world the truth.

They chose to do the video at Jackson's house again. Audrey had liked the clean, professional set-up that his living room had provided. It was the sort of area she would someday set up for herself. One day, when she had the space to be able to do it. But for now, she was confined to her tiny bedroom. Jackson had also been kind enough to offer the use of all of his equipment again—the DSLR camera, his faster computer set-up, his mother's lights. Audrey had already started window shopping around to see how much money she would have to save to score herself anything of half the quality.

She and Jackson sat down on his dark leather couch in front of the camera. Lenore sat behind it, opting to be their director for the day. Audrey gave her a thumbs-up, indicating they were ready to go, and Lenore started the recording. It was now or never. Audrey took a deep breath and began.

"Hi again, everybody," she said. "For those of you who are new here, my name is Audrey Herringbone, and you've stumbled across my channel where I've been doing a video series that I like to call *In the Days Before*, detailing the lives and investigations of missing persons all around the world. Today, I'm going to be stepping a little outside of that theme, so I hope that's okay with my regular viewers.

"A lot of you are new here, and a lot of you have found my channel because of the disappearance and murder of Jacqueline Chen here in Sydney. Instead of stepping back and letting the rumours run wild, I decided to come on here and clarify a few things.

"First of all, yes—it's true that Jackie is..." Audrey paused. "Or rather, she *was* my best friend. We'd known each other since primary school—elementary school, for my American viewers. Her family is a second family to me, and I know she felt the same about my mother. I could sit here and talk about Jackie for hours, but that's not what any of you are here for, not really. A lot of you are here because you think that I killed her. And you know what? That's okay.

"I acknowledge that the situation looks suspicious, and I'm not going to hide anything. If you have questions for me, feel free to post them in the comments below, and I'll do my best to answer them. But to answer a few that I know people have already...

"Yes, it's true Jackie and I had an argument the same day

she disappeared. I had just posted the Amanda Mulgrave video using our school's computers. She wanted me to finish up faster so we could get to lunch, and by the time we finally left the computer lab, she was annoyed. She always made it abundantly clear that she wasn't a fan of my channel or anything that I posted. She herself wanted to be an influencer—as I'm sure a few of you have discovered since you're looking into everything online—and she would often insist that I stop with my missing persons series and do videos on make-up instead. Or tie the two together, like some other YouTubers do. Things got heated, and yes, I asked how she would feel if *she* was the one to go missing. Wouldn't she want me to post about it here and bring attention to her case? She was very adamant that she wouldn't want that. And yes, I went against her wishes and did it anyway because that's what friends do. You do what's best for each other, even when they might not like it.

"Another question I get is why I didn't raise the alarm when Jackie didn't show up for our sleepover. That's a simple one: we never actually planned a sleepover. Jackie often used that as a cover story whenever she was planning to do something her parents didn't approve of, like going to a party or sneaking off to see her boyfriend. Usually, if I wasn't involved in whatever her plans were, she would give me a heads up so I knew what to say in case her parents called to speak to her. I like to think she told me what she was doing, too, because she knew it was safer to let somebody know. But that Friday night, she didn't tell me or any of our other friends anything at all. As far as any of us were aware, she was going to be staying home that night. It was a huge surprise when her mother called me the next day to ask if Jackie had left my house, because I'd never known she was supposed to be there. It's as simple as that."

She looked to Jackson. He nodded.

"Jackson and I have decided to take this video in a different direction today," she went on, turning her attention back to the camera. "I would first like to clarify that any information we have is freely available to the public, and the police are not offering up any additional information in regard to Jackie's case just because we're her friends. That said, from now on, I am going to be posting regular video updates on my channel in regard to the Jacqueline Chen murder investigation. I understand I'm a suspect in many of your eyes, and again, that's fine. But we're going to be looking into other theories and analysing the evidence that we do have. I'll be looking at the investigation from Jackie's side, while Jackson will be looking at things from the killer's perspective.

"For those of you who don't know, Jackson is a classmate of mine who intends to study criminology and forensic psychology after we graduate. As such, he has a completely different perspective on things from what I am used to hearing, so I'm hoping you'll find what he has to say interesting. I know I will."

"I promise not to get too dark," Jackson said with a light-hearted grin. "But without further ado, should we jump into things and get this investigation rolling?"

It was hard not to sound like a broken record, given she'd

already done one video on her best friend, but Audrey tried as she talked about the Jackie she'd known. She veered more to the side of speculation, talking about how the police wanted to use Jackie's social media accounts to determine if she might have been speaking to someone online. How they would have done already, had they known her passwords or had access to—

Audrey's heart gave a jolt. *Jackie's phone.* Had the police found it with her body? She couldn't remember reading it anywhere, but maybe it was something they were keeping quiet. But she needed to know. She needed to call Detective Flanagan to find out. Maybe, just maybe, she could help more than he realised. The thought buzzed around in her mind as she threw the video over to Jackson, barely able to sit still.

Jackson spoke as though he were a seasoned detective on a late-night investigative show, talking about the way a killer's mind worked. He spoke about how sophisticated this killer must be to be able to kidnap a smart, Internet-savvy teenage girl, potentially keep her for several days, and then dump her body and not immediately have it discovered. He talked about how daring this person had to be in order to post a comment to Audrey's own YouTube video with the location of the body and how smart they must have been to do so in a way that the police had not been able to trace. He said something about VPNs and how it was likely the killer had used one of these to avoid his comment being traced back to him. She knew every word of it was true. As much as she wanted to think of Jackie's killer as being some scumbag fool the police would catch within the week, she knew that wasn't the case. The person they were looking for was educated in the ways of committing a crime.

"That's all that we have for now," Audrey said to finish up their video. "I know this is no longer a missing persons investigation, but the same warnings still stand: please be careful out there, and if you have any information at all in regards to what happened to Jackie, please don't hesitate to contact the West Drummond Police Force or call Crime Stoppers on one eight hundred, triple three, triple zero. Thanks, guys, and we'll see you again soon!"

"What is it?" Lenore asked as she and Audrey stepped aside, leaving the equipment to Jackson. He and Audrey had both agreed he was the quickest and most proficient at editing the videos. She would only get in his way trying to work with software she had no experience in. "You had a look during the video when you were talking about Jackie. You thought of something, didn't you?"

"We need to go and see Detective Flanagan," Audrey said eagerly. "I want to ask him if they found Jackie's phone when they found her body. Nore, if they did, I can get into it! I know her lock code!"

"And…" It took Lenore a second, but then her face was lighting up, too. "Oh my God. And then they'll be able to look at her messages and see if she was talking to anybody we didn't know about!"

Audrey nodded. She was buzzing. As soon as they were done here, as soon as the video was posted, they would call the police station. Maybe this would be it. Maybe this would crack the case. Her heart did a flip at the thought.

Maybe, just maybe, this would be the end of the case, and they could try to get on with their lives. Mr and Mrs Chen would get their closure. Penny, Danielle, and Delilah could eat their words. It was a lot to hope for, but...

A girl could dream.

23

It ended up being another dead end. Detective Flanagan had picked up on the second ring and had told Audrey to slow down twice before she'd managed to get him to understand what she was saying—that if he could grant her access to Jackie's phone, she could get him into those social media accounts, no password required!

But Jackie's phone hadn't been located with her body. Nor had it been found anywhere within the park she'd been discovered in or the canal that ran along the back of it. Yes, they'd been searched thoroughly by several officers and a K9 police dog. Yes, he was sure. The triumphant feeling in Audrey's heart faded immediately after hearing the words. No phone meant they were still stuck at square one, still completely in the dark. She'd been so sure they were going to have their answer that she could taste it.

Now, all she tasted was defeat.

She kept her head down and her nose clean the rest of the week, counting down the hours until the Friday night vigil Jackie's cousins had quickly pulled together. It was set to start at seven, so Audrey, Lenore, and Jackson set off at six-thirty sharp, unsure what to expect but preparing for the worst. Audrey's mother had initially agreed to join them, but a nursing shortage in the emergency room had Jackson stepping in to be their chauffeur instead. He'd told Audrey's mother that he didn't mind and assured her at least three times that he would drive safe, had never caused an accident, and hadn't lost any demerits on his licence. Audrey had to fight the urge to groan as her mother gave Jackson the third degree and fought it harder when the woman turned to give her *the look* when Jackson had turned his back. That look of *are you interested in this boy?* It was a small blessing her mother had needed to leave. She was already dreading having to have the rest of the conversation later.

There were dozens of people milling about by the time they'd managed to find parking in an adjacent street and make their way to the park. Audrey swallowed her unease as they approached. Despite the warm spring breeze, Lenore shivered beside her. Jackson swung an arm around each of them—not in a way that bragged to the gathered crowd that he was with both of them, but in a way that was meant to comfort. Audrey forced herself to relax. Even Lenore looked thankful for the gesture.

She took in the location where Jackie's body had been found—overgrown, yes, but beautiful all the same. The area was practically a shrine to her best friend now, an explosion of beautiful bouquets, stuffed animals with sparkling eyes, photographs and signs of every kind. She couldn't count on one hand how many *I love you* declarations there were. Probably not nearly as many as there were *Gone But Never Forgotten*.

It was easy to see how she'd gone so long without being discovered. The trees around the perimeter were thick, their trunks close enough together that Jackson, with his broad shoulders, would have to turn sideways to slip through them comfortably. In the dark, they would form an impenetrable barrier, difficult to climb between and even more impossible to see through. Jackie had been found on the other side, in the park that looked like it hadn't been tended to in months. Dumped like trash in the long, flowering weeds.

How could the site of something so horrible look so tranquil?

Lit by the setting sun and flickering candles, it was hard to believe this had been a place of such tragedy. She could see where a path had been cut through the trees for ease of access and where the grass had been trampled by who knew how many police footsteps, all of it leading to a patch of ground where the grass was flattened and browning. Where a body had laid undiscovered for days. Where *Jackie* had been all that time, just waiting to be found.

It was Audrey's turn to shiver.

"Keep close," Jackson said, his hand gentle on her elbow. Was he warm, or was her own skin cold? "You probably don't want to hear this, but the killer will probably show up tonight to—"

"To enjoy all the misery they've caused," Audrey finished for him with a grimace. She knew. It was something Matt had taught her once when exactly that had happened on a case she'd covered. The thought had horrified her. "You really think they will?"

"I practically guarantee it."

"The police are here," Lenore observed, nodding towards the gathering of people, "so my guess is they agree."

Audrey followed her gaze. She was right. Half a dozen police officers were posted around the area, some making light-hearted conversation with people and others walking the crowd, observing. Their cruisers were parked close by, and at least one of them still had a pair of officers seated inside. Ready to go should anything happen, she guessed.

She spotted Detective Flanagan among them, in his police blues as always, chatting easily with a trio of boys she hadn't seen around before. There were a lot of people attending she didn't recognise—kids from other schools in nearby areas; families with children as young as seven or eight with light-up shoes and innocence printed across their coloured t-shirts; girls who looked like they might be Jackie's family, handing out pamphlets and bowing their heads to people in thanks. So many people. So many faces. How could the police keep track of them all?

There were familiar faces among them, too. She counted every teacher from their school, right down to Mrs Balford and Mrs Pillott. There were students from every year, whether they'd known Jackie or not. Most of her own class appeared to be in attendance, though she didn't immediately see Penny, Danielle, or Delilah's faces among them. Fashionably late? Or would they forgo the event entirely? Maybe Mrs Chen calling their parents had done some good after all. Or maybe they felt they were too good for such a *morbid* event.

She looked around for the Chens, knowing they couldn't be far. And they weren't. She spotted them last, dressed in outfits similar to those they'd worn to the funeral, Lenore's cousin Roxanne standing close by as they spoke to...

Audrey's eyebrows rose at the sight. "Peter's with the Chens."

He was clearly making an effort, too. His black button-up shirt might have been casual on anyone else, but on him, it was definitely dressing up. His blond hair was gelled neat and flat, rather than all over the place like he usually wore it, as if running his fingers through it once or twice was a styling method. Even more surprising was the hand Mr Chen placed on his shoulder. The gentle smile Jackie's father wore as they talked.

"He introduced himself at the funeral," Jackson said. "He never liked that Jackie kept him a secret, and he knew the police told her parents about him once they found out. He didn't want them to think he was some thug or that he was hiding." Jackson eyed his friend. "It's a shame, really. Her father seems to like him."

They made their way over to the crowd, stopping to accept lit candles and pamphlets with Jackie's smiling face on them from the girls who must have been her cousins. Audrey did her best to smile, trying to ignore the eyes she knew were falling on her. People were pointing her out. Whispering things to their friends. Was it her imagination, or was the crowd pressing in tighter around her?

"Audrey! Lenore!"

Mrs Chen had spotted them and was waving for them to

join her and her husband, whose expression wilted slightly at the sight of them. Two reminders of his daughter he couldn't escape. Was that why she hadn't seen him the two times she'd stopped by their house? Not because he'd been bedridden, but because he'd been hiding?

"Oh, girls." Mrs Chen beamed at both of them, brushing gentle fingers over their cheeks when they came into reach. "I'm so glad you could make it. Roxanne said you were on your way, but I wasn't sure…"

Roxanne nodded once in greeting. Next to Peter and the Chens, she looked entirely out of place in her heavily-worn Docs and dark make-up. But that was her way. She wasn't about to change it for Jackie, who'd never had a nice word for her anyway.

She flung an arm around Lenore, replacing Jackson, who had moved on to clap Peter on the shoulder. "Hey, Audrey. It's been a while. Been a little busy being accused of murder?"

Audrey gave a start. "I—"

"I've totally been there," Roxanne went on, ignoring her stunned expression. "Don't worry. People will get over it."

Audrey gave her a pointed once-over. Black skinny jeans. Ripped band shirt. She dressed in a way Audrey's mother would have deeply frowned upon. It was shocking that the Chens weren't giving her cautious glances. "I guess it kind of comes with the territory for you, huh?"

"Oh, yeah. I'm a regular Manson."

"*Rox*," Lenore hissed, but Audrey smiled.

"I hope people are being kinder to you now," Mrs Chen said. She clasped Audrey's hands in both of her own, soft and warm and familiar. Her second home. "We saw your new video. With you and your friend." She beamed at Jackson, too, who nodded to her politely. "Thank you both for putting it out. Many people called the police after they saw it."

Audrey blinked. "They did? Did it help?"

"The police are following up on a few of the calls, but nothing solid yet. But we hope…"

She could have bounced for joy, but the setting didn't feel appropriate. Instead, she beamed back at Mrs Chen, shared a triumphant look with Jackson, and let herself enjoy the moment. Finally. *Finally*, her videos were doing what she'd intended. Maybe the headlines would name her the hero of this story, not the villain. Maybe the articles would turn in her favour, and the comments would be positive.

Maybe all her hard work would finally be worth it.

Mrs Chen was saying something else, but Audrey had been too lost in her daydreams to hear it. "You're just so good at it; I thought you'd be the best person for it."

"Sorry," Audrey said, truly apologetic. "The best person for what?"

"To give a speech. To tell the crowd about our Jackie."

Audrey froze. Mrs Chen wanted her to speak *publicly*?

"I…" She swallowed. "Mrs Chen, I usually read from a script. I don't…"

"You don't need a script for this. Just speak from the heart, dear."

Audrey grimaced. She didn't *do* speaking from the heart. Too much could go wrong. What if she said something and it got taken the wrong way? What if she stumbled over her words or she couldn't think of what to say next? The thought of fumbling with all those eyes on her—

All those eyes! She was used to speaking to her phone, or the lens of Jackson's camera. How was she supposed to address a real-life crowd of living, breathing people? Some of whom *wanted* her to fail?

A hand squeezed her shoulder. She expected Jackson, or maybe Mr Chen, but when she looked up, it was Peter. "I'll stand with you. They've asked me to speak, too. We can do it together."

She looked at Jackie's parents. Mrs Chen beamed even brighter, if that were possible. Mr Chen nodded. "I think that would be wonderful."

There was no stage, no podium for them to stand behind. There was no microphone to amplify their voices, but someone had had the foresight to bring a megaphone for the occasion. Peter held it tightly in one hand, his burning candle in the other, as he and Audrey made their way to the little section where the trees had been cut away, the site that had come to fall somewhere in the middle of the gathering. Audrey glanced over her shoulder as they stood there. She looked to the place where her best friend had laid not long ago. To the flowers. The photos.

The sun was setting now, bathing them in darkness. She looked out to a sea of faces illuminated by candlelight. Was it ethereal, or was this a horror story about to unfold? The eyes of the crowd all looked dark and hollow above their candles, their faces vacant of expression as they focused on her and Peter. Her heart pounded against her ribcage. Was there a monster among them?

She clutched her candle tighter. Focused on her friends, standing off to the side with the Chens. Forced herself to breathe slowly.

Peter raised the megaphone. Unlike Mr Evans, who was lost somewhere in the crowd, he didn't need to fight for quiet. "Good evening, everyone, and thank you for coming tonight. And a big thank you to Jessica and Kristine for pulling this all together for us. You've done a spectacular job, guys."

There was a smattering of applause as the two girls who'd been handing out pamphlets and candles gave a little wave of acknowledgment. Audrey tried to smile at them, but she wasn't sure she was wearing it right. It felt too forced, too uneasy.

"It goes without saying why we're here," Peter went on. "Whether big or small, Jackie played a part in all our lives. She was our friend, our classmate, the girl we followed online, or the girl we only heard about after she went missing. No matter why you're here, I think we can all agree—"

"He's got a knife!"

The crowd erupted. Audrey's eyes darted to Peter instantly, but there was no knife in his hands—just his candle and the megaphone, which he quickly lowered, looking startled. His gaze shot right to where people were darting away from the treeline, closer to the road, many of them screaming. But there was one person running faster than the others. Running towards where she and Peter stood.

He was almost impossible to make out in the darkness. Black pants. Black shirt. Black mask over his face, leaving nothing but his eyes open to the crowd. Eyes that, in the darkness, looked as black as the outfit he wore.

She caught the flash of the knife as he came barrelling towards her.

24

Everything happened in slow motion.

Jackson grabbed her by the arm and yanked her back out of the line of attack. He caught her as she stumbled, Peter only half a step behind, his face white as a sheet. She couldn't hear what they were saying over the pounding in her ears, the shouting of the crowd, the sudden scream of police sirens as their lights came to life. Lenore was at her side in an instant, Roxanne with her, both of them wide-eyed as they watched the chaos unfold. Mr Chen darted past them, Detective Flanagan hot on his heels.

"Go home!" His voice was loud, even with the noise engulfing them. "I want all of you out of here, *now!*"

Nobody stopped to ask questions. Audrey let Jackson and Lenore lead her away from the trees, back towards the road, in the direction of Jackson's parked car. She forced herself to breathe through her nose, long and slow. What had just happened? A glance back told her nothing—the police were converging, Mr Chen was yelling, and people were stopping to stare as officers motioned them back, back, away from whatever was unfolding.

"Audrey!"

The sound of her own name brought reality snapping back into place. Lenore's grip was tight around her wrist; Peter was lamenting about how he'd frozen instead of jumping into action like he thought he should have. There were people shouting behind them. The wailing of police sirens would be the soundtrack to her nightmares.

Delilah was rushing towards them.

She looked paler than Peter, and when she drew close enough, Audrey could see there were tears brimming in her eyes. She only had a moment to consider what that meant before Delilah was flinging her arms around her, engulfing her. For the second time in as many minutes, Jackson caught her as she stumbled back.

"Oh my *God*," Delilah breathed into her shoulder. "Are you *okay?!*"

Audrey blinked in surprise. "Well, yeah. Why wouldn't I be?"

Roxanne laughed. Outright *laughed*. Delilah pulled back quickly, looking aghast. Strands of her auburn hair were clinging to her cheeks. "He was coming right at you! I thought he was coming *for* you!"

Audrey glanced back over her shoulder in the direction of the *he*. There were two officers actively dragging the black-clad figure to a cruiser now, while a third and fourth did their best to hold back an irate Mr Chen, who was yelling in Chinese loudly enough that she could hear him from their position almost a block away now. Had the figure been coming for her? He'd definitely been coming in their direction, but for her specifically?

Peter blew out a breath. "I think he was just trying to

make a scene."

"I thought the same as Delilah," Lenore countered.

"I'm more concerned with whether he's Jackie's killer and he was going for suicide by cop."

This from Jackson. Roxanne was nodding her agreement, looking back in the direction they'd come from. "If that's true, he failed. They didn't shoot him."

"Well, of course not. This isn't America."

Delilah was silent, trembling in front of Audrey. In shock? She reached out, grasping Delilah's forearms firmly. "Hey. It's okay. Everything's fine. They caught the guy before he could hurt anybody." *Anybody else, anyway.* As an afterthought, she added, "Are Penny and Danielle here? Do you need a ride home?"

Delilah shook her head, brushing tears and hair from her cheeks. She let out a shaky breath. "They're not here." She hesitated. "I came here hoping to find you, actually, because... I need to tell you something about them."

"She's already worked out they're fake bitches," Roxanne said. "No need to tell her that."

Lenore swatted her cousin's arm, but nobody contradicted the statement. Not even Delilah, who kept her eyes solely on Audrey.

Well, it couldn't hurt to hear what she had to say. "What is it, Del?"

"Penny has the laptop."

The words practically fell out of her mouth. Audrey stared at her, letting her mind pick them up off the ground one at a time. Penny... had...

Lenore got it first. Her eyes went hard in a way Audrey

had only seen once—their first day back at school after Jackie's disappearance, when she'd stood up to Danielle. "She has *Jackie's* laptop?!"

Her voice was a screech by the end of the sentence. Delilah winced and glanced over their shoulders, back over to where the police were probably carting off their man by now. They should turn around and find an officer. They should go back and get Detective Flanagan. They should—

"We're going to get it from her," Audrey said. "Right now."

The police were busy. And if they already had their man, getting the laptop to them wasn't of the utmost importance anymore. It might give them the evidence they needed to convict their suspect, but they had enough to hold him for now. Possession of a deadly weapon had to count for something, after all. They could deal with him.

Audrey wanted to deal with Penny.

Nobody argued.

They split into two, Peter taking Lenore and Roxanne back to his car while Audrey and Delilah followed Jackson to his. Both girls were quiet, Delilah still shaking and Audrey seething.

Penny had had the laptop *this whole time?*

How long had Delilah known? Did Danielle know, too? How long had they *hidden* it? And, more importantly, why? They had to know it was wrong. They all knew the police were actively looking to get into Jackie's social media accounts, so *why hide the laptop?* She wanted to pull her hair out at the thought. It was crazy!

"You were going to tell me," she realised, looking back at Delilah. "That day, we were in Jackie's room. Weren't you?"

"I should have," Delilah said. She grasped the handle of the back passenger side door, her expression stricken. "If that guy had gotten to you, and I hadn't ever said anything…"

Audrey wanted to say that, yes, she'd been stupid not to tell somebody about this—specifically the police—but there was no use in kicking her while she was already down. Audrey just got into the car.

The trip was silent, Jackson following Peter's car closely as they weaved their way into East Drummond and down the immaculate street Penny lived on. The closer they got, the tighter Audrey's chest grew. It was one thing for Penny to have turned on her. It was another entirely for her to have concealed evidence from the police. Why? *Why* would she have kept it hidden? What did she possibly stand to gain from that?

She stopped breathing as it occurred to her. "Do you think Penny did it?"

Jackson glanced left at her from the driver's seat, the streetlights reflecting in his eyes and highlighting his hair. "Did what?"

"Killed Jackie."

"*What?!*" Delilah shrieked from the back seat. It was the first sound she'd made since entering the car. "Penny? Are you *crazy?!* They just caught the guy!"

"They caught *a* guy," Jackson said.

"She has Jackie's laptop," Audrey added.

"Because Jackie gave it to her after school that day," Delilah insisted. "Penny said Jackie'd given it to her so she wouldn't have to double back home for it on Saturday morning after she'd been wherever."

"But she's kept it hidden from the police." Audrey sounded hollow even to herself. "And she's been doing everything she can to make people think it was *me*. Where was *she* that night?"

There was silence in the car for a long minute. Audrey waited. She needed that minute as much as Delilah apparently did.

"She said she was home," her friend practically whispered. "But..."

Jackson raised an eyebrow, glancing at her in the rearview. "But?"

"But she and Jackie were supposed to meet up on Saturday morning. To work on stuff for their socials."

An appointment Jackie would have taken her laptop to. An appointment she would have taken her *charger* to.

Audrey's head spun. It was possible. *It was possible.* Maybe Penny hadn't been home after all. Or maybe she and Jackie had met up that night. Or maybe Jackie hadn't gone missing on Friday at all. Maybe it had been Saturday all along. Penny's parents worked a lot and barely paid attention to their children, even when they were home. Maybe Jackie had stayed at Penny's that night. She thought back, trying to remember if she'd seen or been told anything about the time of death...

Jackson parked. A short distance from them, Peter, Lenore, and Roxanne were climbing out of Peter's Ford.

They'd arrived at their destination.

Jackson looked at her. "How do you want to play this?"

She didn't want to play at all. She was tired of this game. She wanted to get off this ride.

She rubbed her eyes with the palms of her hands. They should call the police. It was the right thing to do. But she had to know. *Needed* to know.

She unbuckled her belt and stepped out of the car.

Penny's father answered the door. He looked agitated, probably at having a bunch of teenagers show up on his doorstep at the late hour, but waved them on through as he carried on with the phone call he seemed to be in the middle of. There was a barrage of noise coming from the living room, from whatever shooter game Penny's younger brother was playing, and there was music playing from upstairs. How anybody could live among so much noise, Audrey would never understand. She longed for the silence of her own apartment even as she pushed through and made her way up the stairs.

Even if she'd been in a knocking mood, there wouldn't have been any point to it. Penny's room was the source of the music, and it was blaring loudly enough there was no way anyone in that room could hear themselves think. Audrey braced herself and shoved the door open.

Penny and Danielle both looked up from where they were sprawled on the bed, Danielle flipping through a magazine, Penny scrolling on her phone. They were in pyjamas, loose shorts and tank tops, make-up free and hair messy. Jackson and Peter were probably in for the shock of their lives, seeing them in such a state.

Penny's expression went from surprised to annoyed in an instant. "I'm sorry, who invited you to this slumber party, *loser?*"

This wasn't what a killer was supposed to look like.

Killers were dark and disturbed. They were grizzled old men with terrifying eyes or strung-out guys in their thirties. They weren't teenage girls obsessed with social media, hanging out in their pyjamas on a Friday night. They weren't the girls she went to school with.

Criminals come in all shapes and sizes, Matt had once told her. But did they come in a size ten bottle-blonde?

Penny was already on her feet by the time Audrey managed to blurt out the words, "Did you kill Jackie?"

Penny's eyes were wild. "Get the hell out of my house!"

Danielle scrambled for the stereo and spun the volume knob down. Jackson gripped Audrey's shoulder and pulled her back, slotting himself between her and the girls. Peter slipped up beside her.

From somewhere behind her, Roxanne said, "Did we miss something?"

"What the hell is this?" Penny growled. "Get *out!*"

"We know you have Jackie's laptop," Jackson said calmly. "Hand it over, Penelope."

For a long moment, Penny only stared at him, the growl still on her lips. Behind her, Danielle had gone wide-eyed and was looking between Penny and the rest of them like she might try to flee the scene. Not that she could, with Lenore and Roxanne blocking the door.

Penny looked past them all, her eyes seeking one face in particular. She found it, and her eyes narrowed.

"I knew it." She scowled. "I *knew* you wouldn't keep your mouth shut!"

Out in the hallway, against the far wall, Delilah flinched.

Audrey saw red. "Are you kidding, Penelope? You're lucky she covered for you as long as she did, because *I* would have thrown you to the police without needing to think twice! Now give us the goddamn computer. And so help me, if I find out you did this to Jackie—"

"Oh, get off your high horse!" Penny snapped. "*I'm* not the killer here!"

"Then why do you have her laptop? Why did you never turn it in?"

"Because there's nothing important on it," Danielle cut in. "Jackie wasn't messaging any creeps or meeting up with randoms. We looked. So the cops don't need it."

"I think we'd better let them decide that," Peter said. His jaw was clenched. "Don't you think?"

"Why do you even have it?" Audrey asked. "Did you rush to the Chens' to steal it the second you realised she was missing? Or was Jackie here before you—"

"Jackie left it with me before she went out that night," Penny spat, "so she wouldn't have to double back for it the next day. And I kept it for the *content*, you psycho bitch. Not because I killed her!"

"Hand it over."

"Or we can call the police and have them pick it up from here," Jackson suggested. "I'm sure your father would love that. He's a lawyer, right?"

If there hadn't been murder in Penny's eyes before, there certainly was now.

"Well, you've certainly found your crowd, haven't you, Horrorbone?"

Penny took three long strides across her room to the walk-in closet, almost the size of Audrey's room, and dug under a stack of clothes on one of the shelves. Out came Jackie's laptop case, the charging cable sticking out the top, the zipper only pulled halfway closed.

"Here." Penny *threw* the case at her. Audrey barely managed to catch it as it slammed into her stomach. "Take the stupid thing, and *get the hell out!*"

"What's going on up here?"

Lenore and Roxanne stepped out of the doorway, allowing Penny's father to take their place. He was off the phone now but still looked annoyed.

"I told you to keep the noise down up here." He narrowed his eyes in much the same fashion as Penny had done to Delilah. "And you know the rules, Penelope. No boys in the bedrooms."

"Don't worry, Dad," Penny said, her glare falling back on Audrey. "They were all just about to leave."

Yes, they were. Audrey clutched the laptop to her chest and gestured for the boys to step out of the room before her. Peter went first, with a quick apology to Penny's father as he went. Jackson raised an eyebrow at Audrey but followed his friend without a word. Audrey didn't bother looking back at Penny or Danielle before she trailed them out and made a beeline for the stairs, suddenly eager to be out of the house.

To be long gone before Penny realised that if she'd told her lawyer father about whose laptop they were taking from her, he might have done everything in his power to stop them.

25

The police station was nowhere near as chaotic as Audrey had expected. In the movies, there were always police running everywhere, endless stacks of paper threatening to spill onto the floor, and stale cups of coffee abandoned all over. But the station at West Drummond was surprisingly quiet, even after what had happened at the vigil. When she'd told the receptionist that she and Lenore were there to see Detective Flanagan, the woman had instructed them to wait in the lobby and said he would be right out.

They'd waited, just the two of them, not wanting to overwhelm the detective with six teens showing up on the station's doorstep. Audrey knew it had been the right choice when she spotted him.

Detective Flanagan looked tired as he stepped out from the back and was clearly surprised to see them. No doubt he'd expected them to do as he'd asked and go home. But without question, he ushered them to follow him into the squad room. They did so in silence, taking in their surroundings as a whole as they followed him back to his desk on the far side of the room, stepping around other officers who were on phone calls or pouring over reports.

His desk was one of the messiest, and Audrey was unsurprised to find a half-drunk cup of coffee that was likely cold and stale.

"Girls." He gestured for them to pull up the two chairs in front of his workstation. "I wasn't expecting to see either of you again tonight. Was there a reason you came?" He stopped in his tracks for a moment. "If you're here to ask for details about what happened tonight, I'm afraid you're going to be disappointed. You know that I cannot and will not provide you with any more information. *Especially* if you're here without your parents' knowledge." He gave them both a stern look. "Do your parents know you're here?"

"No," Audrey admitted, "but it's okay because we're not here to get details about anything. We actually have something for you."

Detective Flanagan raised an eyebrow. "You have something for me?"

Audrey carefully unslung the laptop bag from her shoulder and set it on the desk before them. Detective Flanagan looked over the dark floral print as she tugged the zipper open and extracted the MacBook.

"Girls," he said, "I'm sure you've been doing some wonderful online sleuthing, but you know I can't talk to you about your friend's case. It's still an ongoing investigation."

Lenore paused. "So the guy you caught tonight...?"

"We don't know anything for certain. But I doubt it. He claims he did it on a dare."

"We haven't been online sleuthing," Audrey cut in. "This is Jackie's laptop."

Detective Flanagan's eyebrows rose so high they were in danger of disappearing into his hairline. "Excuse me?"

"Penny had it." Lenore's voice was dripping with shame. "I'm sorry. We didn't know. But the second we found out—"

"We can get into it," Audrey cut in. "You can look through her social media."

And hopefully, teach Penny a lesson she'll never forget.

Detective Flanagan slipped into his own seat carefully. "I assume you've looked through it already."

Audrey bristled. "No. I wanted to, but..."

"We knew it was better to bring it straight to you," Lenore finished. "Penny and Danielle said they'd looked, and there was nothing suspicious. But I wouldn't take their word for it."

"Neither would I," Audrey mumbled.

Detective Flanagan considered them for a moment, blue eyes moving from one girl to the other and back again. "All right. Let's take a look."

Lenore handed the laptop over. Audrey watched it exchange hands, gripping the edge of her seat as Detective Flanagan cleared away a mess of papers to set it on his desk. A moment later, he was booting it up, and her knee was bouncing with anticipation.

"Password?"

"Exclamation mark, hydrangea with a capital H, one-six-six," Audrey supplied quickly. When Detective Flanagan raised an eyebrow, she said, "The sixteenth of

June is her anniversary with Peter, and hydrangeas are her favourite flower."

"And she didn't use the same password for her social media accounts?"

"No. I guess she didn't trust us not to hack in and steal all her followers."

He nodded and typed it all in.

Even Lenore leaned forward at this, but Detective Flanagan held up a hand to halt them both and tilted the screen closer to himself. Audrey watched eagerly as he manoeuvred the cursor, clicking a few things open. He had not yet thanked them and asked them to leave. That had to be a good sign, right? Would he maybe tell them if he found anything?

The clock ticked on as he read through messages, his eyes scanning lines almost as quick as his fingers could move through them. Every now and then, he would glance up at Audrey and Lenore, as if to make sure they were still sitting there, and then his eyes would return to the screen. On and on it went until, at long last, he leaned back in his chair.

And then he turned the laptop around and slid it across the table towards them. But his hand remained firmly on the top of the screen, keeping it just out of their reach.

"I want you both to take a look through her messages," he said calmly, "and let me know if there are any names you don't recognise or anything you feel is out of the ordinary. Can you do that for me?"

It was more than they could have asked for. They both nodded their agreement, and Detective Flanagan slid the laptop the rest of the way towards them and then released it.

Jackie's long list of messages was already open before them. The first several were exactly what Audrey had expected to see: messages from her, messages from Lenore, messages from each of the other girls, all of them asking where she was and what was going on. It looked as though Penny had been using Messenger to vent to Jackie every day, even after knowing she wasn't around anymore. They dated back to the day they'd learned of Jackie's disappearance, and there was one as recent as that morning. Lenore had given Audrey a sympathetic look as they had opened them only to see all the hate Penny had been pouring onto the absent Jackie, telling her even in death how terrible of a friend she thought Audrey was and how there had been all of these signs that the girls had missed over the years. How they should have known Audrey would do something like this. How she had turned stupid, gullible Lenore against the rest of the group. If she had been an outsider to the situation, Audrey might have felt bad for Penny and the other girls. But seeing what her ex-friend was saying about her hurt.

But at least it meant Penny wasn't a killer. Maybe she'd jumped the gun on that.

Lenore pulled them out of that particular message so they could go on looking at the rest. They took their time, certain they'd be able to pick up on suspicious behaviour in a way Detective Flanagan couldn't, in a way that Penny and Danielle would have been too careless to see if they'd really checked at all. They knew the messages from

Peter were completely normal. They knew that Jackie not responding to her cousins was normal, too, and that she didn't use messages to keep in touch with her parents, who always insisted that a phone call was quicker and easier for everybody.

Audrey gave a start when she saw a familiar name. She knew that Jackie texting Jackson was *not* normal.

Lenore spotted it at the same time she did and looked just as surprised. She pressed the message to open it, and they both leaned a little closer to the screen to read the interaction between the pair. Audrey breathed a small sigh of relief when she saw the messages were just about an assignment the pair had been doing together for their history class several weeks back. Nothing unusual. Just two classmates being paired up by a teacher who didn't approve of friends working together.

More messages with her cousins. Another to an old classmate detailing another assignment. For all her focus on beauty and make-up, Jackie really had been focused on her studies. Her parents could be proud of that at least—

"Isn't that *your* Matt?" Lenore squeaked.

Audrey's eyes travelled down to where Lenore was pointing to a message with a name that shocked her to her core. *Matthew Callaghan.* Yes, that *was* her Matt, with his moody little profile photo. Matt, whom Audrey had met through the YouTube channel that Jackie hated so much. Matt, who had always been her number-one supporter. Matt, who had openly disliked Jackie from the moment Audrey had first mentioned her name.

Matt had never mentioned exchanging any messages

with Jackie, and Audrey's face must have betrayed that. Lenore gave her a mildly horrified look. Across the desk, Detective Flanagan wordlessly jotted something down in his notepad.

She couldn't take the suspense anymore. She clicked the thread open.

The messages were from almost a month ago. She scrolled right back to the start of them to see the exact date. It looked like they'd all been sent on the same afternoon, and Jackie had been the one to start them.

Jackie

> Hey, is this the Matt that Audrey always talks to?

Jackie

> The one from her YouTube channel?

She'd likely found him through Audrey's own account. No way would she have trawled through the millions of Matts in the search results. It had taken Matt almost half an hour to respond to that message, which was an usually long time for him, especially when it was an hour after school. If she scrolled back through her own messages, she imagined she'd probably find messages between the two of them from the same day and time, with no time gap between. What had taken him so long here?

Matt

> Yeah, it is. You must be Jackie, the best friend.

Jackie

> I am. And as her best friend, it's my job to watch out for her. So I'm gonna need you to stop texting her, you fucking creep.

Whoa. *What?*

Lenore's mouth formed an "O". Detective Flanagan was watching them closely. Audrey's heart was pounding as she looked at the messages. She imagined Matt had to have been surprised by the message, too, because he had not responded to it. Twenty minutes later, Jackie had sent him another.

Jackie

> Don't try to play this game with me. I know all about your kind.

Jackie

> You get behind your keyboard and your stupid computer monitor, and you go online and look for innocent girls like Audrey. I'll bet you think you're real smart too, don't you? Choosing somebody like her. She knows all about creeps like you and being safe on the Internet, and you've still got her fooled. Well, you can fuck right off with your act, or I'm gonna be calling the cops on you, pervert!

Matt

Whoa! Listen, I get where you're coming from, trying to protect your friend. But I am NOT some forty-year-old creep living out of his mum's basement trying to lure teenage girls off to be my sex slaves or whatever. I am REALLY just a sixteen-year-old guy who lives in Sydney. Look, I'll accept you as a friend so you have access to my account. My school's listed in my info. You can call them up, and they'll confirm that I really am a student there. Or you can call the police and let them do it. Whatever you want, but you need to stop harassing me, or I'm going to block you.

There was a half hour of silence in which Audrey imagined Matt and Jackie must have become Facebook friends, where Jackie would have proceeded to look through his profile. Audrey knew what she would have seen, and it wasn't much. Matt was a private person. There were very few photos of him on his profile, and the ones he did have were full of artistically placed shadows or hands that covered identifying details. He was an aspiring police officer who dreamed of a side gig photographing creative portraits, he'd told her. She had seen a lot of his work on Instagram. He was good at it.

Aside from this, he kept his friend list quite small, at only a hundred and fifty or so people. Most of them were his friends or family, and the remainder were made up of classmates that he had added only to keep in the loop of things at school. He had once told Audrey that she was literally the only person on his friends list whom he had never met in real life. She hadn't thought anything of it at the time, but... maybe it was suspicious that his friends list was so short. She would have been wary if he had only had less than twenty friends on there, but... he had likely known that. Known and taken steps to make sure his account didn't look suspicious to her.

No. What was she *thinking?* This was Matt they were talking about. Matt, who she trusted completely.

...didn't she?

There were no more messages after that. It looked like Matt had blocked her.

Lenore looked up at Detective Flanagan. "Did Jackie

ever file a police complaint against Matt Callaghan?"

"I don't believe so," Detective Flanagan said, "but I'll look into it."

Audrey knew he'd be looking into something else, too. Some*one* else.

"I need you to look through any other sites she may have messages on," Detective Flanagan went on, albeit a little apologetically. "Anywhere she might have been talking to people. Can you do that for me?"

"Of course," Lenore said.

Audrey only nodded. But her mind couldn't focus on the task at hand anymore. Now, all she could focus on was the fact that Jackie had gone out of her way to contact Matt and confront him about being an Internet stalker, and less than a month later, she was dead.

And not once had Matt ever mentioned to her that he had spoken to Jackie.

26

"I FEEL LIKE SUCH an idiot."

Lenore was silent beside her. She'd been quiet since they'd arrived back at Jackson's house, but the look Roxanne had given Audrey when they'd arrived said she had at least explained to her and Peter what they'd discovered on the laptop. Audrey had done the same with Jackson and Delilah. Delilah hadn't said anything except to ask if they would drop her off at her own house, which Jackson had obliged without question. He'd been quiet the rest of the journey to his own house, most likely lost in his own thoughts.

He set a glass of water down in front of her. Audrey took it gratefully and downed half of it in one shot, wishing for the first time that she was old enough to drink something harder. The thought of whiskey burning down her throat, punishing her for her stupidity, sounded amazing. Jackson dropped onto the couch across from her, next to Peter, with his feet already on the coffee table. She wondered if his parents knew how he treated their furniture.

"You shouldn't feel like an idiot." His tone was gentle, his eyes soft. If there'd been one good thing to come out of any of this, it was him. "If Matt really is one of those guys who prey on girls online, then he's probably had a lot of time to perfect what he's doing. You're probably not even the first girl he's fooled."

"That doesn't make me feel any better," Audrey said bitterly. She glared down at the papers strewn across the table. Their research on Jackie's case. Research that all this time had been pointing to *Matt*. Matt, who'd been asking her for updates. Who knew enough to at least guess where she went to school. Who was always telling her that Jackie was a terrible friend.

God, she'd been so *stupid*.

"My point is," Jackson went on, "these kinds of people make a living out of this. That's why so many Internet predators are successful at luring kids away from their homes and families." He picked up a pen and spun it between his fingers absently. "But if *this* makes you feel any better, I don't think Matt is some creepy old man preying on young girls."

Audrey raised her head in surprise. "You don't?"

"I don't," Jackson said. "At least, I don't think he's a *creepy old man*. I can basically confirm it. You said that detective spoke to him after the comment showed up on the video we did for Jackie, right? You don't think he would have told you if your online friend was actually some old guy?"

Audrey had no doubt Detective Flanagan would have been on the phone with her mother immediately if that had been the case. And she wouldn't have been attending the vigil because she'd have been grounded for life.

She hated herself for it even before she said, "I just thought he was different, you know? He was smart, and he was nice, and he made me feel like I wasn't a freak for filming my videos. I told him practically everything. I *trusted* him."

I imagined a future with him.

"It's not like it matters," Roxanne said from the other side of Lenore. She was bouncing one booted foot. "Murderers come in all shapes and sizes. Even the serial kind. I'm pretty sure you could Google it and find a story about a sweet little girl who killed her family. And people get killed by their partners all the time. Or what about those girls in the States who tried to kill their friend to get in good with some fictional monster?"

Lenore snapped her head to her cousin. "That did *not* happen."

"Did too."

Jackson shrugged. "Just because people think somebody's nice or charming or whatever, doesn't mean they can't also be a killer. Look at Ted Bundy. Look at Charles Manson. Some of the greatest minds the world has ever seen have been serial killers. People adore them, and people fall right into their traps. And even after they were caught and the world found out what they'd done, people still found it hard to believe. People still wanted to like them. People still *did* like them. Now that... that's the mark of true genius, that is."

"True evil, more like it," Lenore said with a shudder. "Nobody should be allowed to be that charismatic and likeable and then also be a sadistic serial killer."

Unfortunately, that was the way of the world. It was a cruel twist of fate that some of mankind's greatest traits had been gifted to some of the world's worst.

Audrey shook the thoughts from her head. She didn't want to think about Matt right now. Let the police think about him instead. "Can we talk about something else? Please."

"All right," Jackson said. "What do you want to talk about?"

"I don't know. Are you going to the formal this weekend?"

Jackson raised an eyebrow. "I hadn't been planning on it. Why? Are you asking me?"

Oh, no. Lenore looked at her in surprise; Peter grinned and nudged his buddy. Roxanne barked out a laugh. Audrey grimaced. Now, she looked like she'd been fishing for a date. That had not been her intention *at all*, but would he believe her if she said that?

"Actually, I'd been planning on giving it a miss, too."

"So had I," Lenore said, giving her a subtle nudge, "but I think Jackie would have wanted us to go."

That was definitely true. "The formal was one of the last things we talked about that day, you know? She was bugging me about finding a date, so I didn't show up alone like a total weirdo. She wouldn't listen when I kept saying that I didn't need a date. That I'd rather go alone or not go at all." Audrey shook her head. "And now it's her that doesn't get to go. She's probably spinning in her grave."

It felt strange to say that.

"Well, let's not disappoint her entirely," Jackson said

gently. "Come to the formal with me. I'll be your date, so that way Jackie gets at least one of her final wishes. You're not going to the formal alone."

Audrey's face felt hot. Was she *blushing?*

"Well, I won't be outdone on this," Peter said. He turned his gaze on Lenore and Roxanne. "Ladies. Would you allow me the honour of escorting you to the ball?"

Roxanne snorted. "Only if I can show up in jeans and a band tee."

Audrey found Jackson's eyes still on her. Waiting for an answer?

When she didn't reply immediately, Jackson said, "It's a standing offer. And I'm being completely serious when I say that you can literally call me five minutes before the formal starts and tell me that you want to go, and I'll make it happen. I'll even come with you in jeans and a t-shirt. How does that sound?"

Audrey smiled a little. "That sounds really great, actually. I guess I'll let you know."

Jackson nodded. "You do that."

"No jeans and shirts," Lenore said between the two girls. "We should go dress shopping this weekend. The three of us. I guarantee it'll be more fun than going with Penny and Danielle." She gave Audrey a pointed look. "And we can go to the places we can actually afford. Roxy's basically a thrifting expert."

She let herself imagine it—showing up at the formal in a cheap but still beautiful dress, feeling like royalty, with her friends by her side and a boy on her arm. If she was being honest with herself, there'd been a number of times she'd daydreamed about showing up at the formal with Matt. It was easy enough to imagine there was a handsome, charming boy behind all of those obscure photos he posted, especially when he'd always been such a great friend to her. The thought made her sick now. He was the *last* person she would ever consider taking.

Audrey waited until Jackson and Peter stepped out to get them something to eat, and Lenore and Roxanne were deep in conversation about the best thrift stores to go to before she pulled out her phone and opened her messages with Matt.

Audrey

> Why did you never tell me that Jackie had messaged you?

She couldn't take the not knowing.

Although it was their usual time to be chatting on a Friday night, Matt took a strangely delayed amount of time to respond. It took almost half an hour before the message's status changed to *read*, by which time their little group was twenty minutes into a movie and eating pizza and chicken strips the boys had managed to dig out of the freezer. It took another fifteen minutes after that before Matt finally responded.

Matt

> It wasn't anything I couldn't handle. You were already having trouble with her.

I didn't want to add to the drama
or come between you and your best
friend.

A likely story. Audrey typed back furiously, praying her thumbs weren't audible with her barely concealed fury.

I don't believe that for a second,
Matthew.

You and me have been friends for
over a year now, and we've always
been totally honest with each other.
Or at least I THOUGHT we were. The
Matt that I know would never have
kept that from me. He would have
told me so I could have dealt with it!

I am the Matt you know, and I just
told you why I didn't tell you.

Had this still been her long-time friend, Audrey might have read exhaustion in his tone. But this was now a stranger with wholly different intentions towards her, and all she was reading was frustration. She wouldn't be his would-be victim any longer.

I'm sure you could have handled it on your own, but I was able to handle it on my own, too. She was a bitch to me, called me all sorts of crazy things, and when she wouldn't stop, I blocked her. It was as simple as that.

As she was reading, she saw another speech bubble pop up to indicate that Matt was still writing. She waited until the next message showed.

And it wasn't like this message was her saying anything you didn't already know about. You told me the minute you told your friends that you and I talk, Jackie started saying I was probably some old guy trying to lure you into his sex dungeon or something. The only difference here is that she brought her opinion straight to me instead of saying it through you.

Audrey shook her head. She wasn't having any of this.

You should have told me about these messages.

Audrey

Especially after she disappeared!

Audrey

Did you deliberately not tell me about them so I wouldn't take them to the police?

Matt

Audi, I took them to the police myself. When they asked to speak to me after the message showed up with the address on your channel. They came out to my house to talk to me and my parents, and while they were there, they asked me if I knew Jackie at all. I told them I mostly only knew her through you but that she had messaged me once. I showed them the messages. They've known about them the whole time. So don't you think if there was anything to this, they would have brought me in already?

Could that be true? Had the police known about Matt's messages with Jackie practically from the beginning of the investigation? If she thought back, Detective Flanagan hadn't looked all that surprised, but he *had* made notes about it. Maybe he had just been keeping his face straight as he always did when they were talking about the investigation.

Or maybe Matt was just working off the fact that she had always trusted him before, without question. God, she'd been such an idiot. Here she was, telling the Internet about all of these people who had gone missing, girls just like her who had put their faith in the wrong person and landed themselves in some serious hot water because of it. Girls who had wound up murdered, like Jackie had been. And almost worse, girls who had vanished without a trace with only theories left in their wake—were they dead, or was their fate something worse?

What had Matt been planning for her?

Before he could spin another lie, she blocked him.

27

IT WAS HARD TO wake up on a Saturday morning and not immediately text Matt.

Audrey didn't realise how ingrained he'd become as part of her life until she'd blocked him. It felt like she'd cut off a hand. Like there was some important piece of her missing, left at Jackson's house to rot behind the couch. She'd still woken up to the sun and the birds, still found her legs tangled in her sheets, still found herself rolling over and reaching for her phone... but then stopped. Because who was she texting at this hour, if not Matt or Jackie?

Her phone dinged.

For a brief moment, everything was the way it had been a month ago. Matt was messaging to ask if she'd seen the news about the latest victim to be found alive and well. Jackie was texting to see if she was up for a day of mani-pedis with the girls. The world was bright and beautiful, and bad things didn't happen in West Drummond. Bad things didn't happen to *her*. Hadn't since she was eight.

She picked up her phone. Read the message displayed on the screen.

Lenore

Still on for dress shopping today?
Roxy's excited.

It wasn't Matt, and it wasn't Jackie, but the world was still bright and beautiful. And even though bad things *did* happen in West Drummond, even though they *did* happen to her, there were good things, too.

She smiled as she opened the message.

Audrey

Meet you outside the mall at ten-thirty?

Ten minutes later, she was out the door.

Roxanne had a giant smile on her face when Audrey stepped off the bus outside their local shopping complex. She looked like a rockstar donned in black tights and a loose, ripped shirt, her eyes behind a huge pair of sunglasses and her hair in a messy-but-still-stylish bun atop her head. She was effortlessly cool in a way Penny and Danielle could only dream of being.

"Glad you could join us," Roxanne said earnestly as Lenore jumped up from her seat behind her, stuffing a flimsy paperback into her bag. "Should we get this party started or what?"

Audrey had dress-shopped with her friends before, a year ago—all of them together, preparing for their tenth-grade formal like it was the event of their lifetimes. Jackie and Penny had dragged them to what must have been every high-end boutique in Sydney, trying on dresses that cost more than Audrey's mother earned in a week, acting like prima donnas the entire time. She distinctly remembered thinking they were going to be nightmares to deal with when their future weddings came around, and she still wasn't over the shame of having to find her own dress at a discount department store. It hadn't been a fun experience. It was likely why she hadn't wanted a repeat for their year eleven formal. Why did they even need a formal this year? There was nothing impressive about graduating the eleventh grade.

Shopping with Lenore and Roxanne was the opposite. The two of them were in similar financial situations to Audrey, so they all had the same idea about what they were looking for. Lenore knew a few inexpensive boutiques they could visit along the main street; Roxanne knew where all the best op shops and thrift stores were hidden.

Audrey was happy to let them lead. Memories of the year before had made her doubt how successful the day was going to be, but by noon, she was pleasantly surprised. Lenore was an entirely different person around her cousin, out of the shadows of the rest of their group, laughing and chatting and blossoming between worn-once wedding gowns and second-hand books. She had a moment to regret that she and Lenore had never bothered to spend one-on-one time together, her too caught up in her old friendship with Jackie and Lenore stuck in hers with Penny, but that was all in the past. The future was looking brighter.

Even with Roxanne insisting that everything she wore needed to be some shade of black or grey.

They'd all walked out of Vinnies with dresses they both loved and could comfortably afford. Lenore had managed to find a pair of cute kitten heels to match, but Audrey had decided not to bother looking for a pair of shoes to go with her dress. She would be much more comfortable in a pair of old sneakers, and it wasn't like anybody was going to be looking at her or her feet.

And it wasn't like she needed to impress anybody. She already had a date.

They went into the complex for lunch. Lunch with Jackie and the girls usually meant finding some bougie café or upscale restaurant where the food was as bland as it was expensive. Lunch with Lenore and Roxanne was fun—they grabbed greasy fried chicken, soggy chips, and full-fat shakes and sat at a bench together, not caring how they looked or who saw them or what they talked about. Roxanne even had the nerve to bring up the events of the vigil the night before.

"There was an article online this morning," she told them. "Police released the guy. He was just an idiot fifteen-year-old. Said his friends dared him to do it."

"That's so dangerous," Lenore said. She frowned deeply. "I mean, if any one of those cops had been trigger-happy, he'd be dead. He probably *should* be, the way he was running for you and Peter."

Audrey shook her head. "I think he's lucky the crowd didn't attack him before the police got to him. Or Mr Chen."

Roxanne snorted. "Would have been a good lesson for him."

"Jackson said the same thing."

Lenore looked to Audrey, a smile in her eyes. "Speaking of Jackson…"

Audrey took a long, slow drink of her chocolate shake, raising both eyebrows at Lenore over her straw. *What?* her expression asked. But she knew Lenore wouldn't ask. Knew she was too shy, too uninterested in—

She asked. "Is there something going on between the two of you?"

Audrey removed the straw from her mouth before she could choke on it. "No. Of course not."

From Lenore's other side, Roxanne crooned, "Do you *want* there to be?"

Audrey's cheeks warmed. In all the time she'd been hanging out with Jackson, she'd never seriously considered it. He was attractive, sure. She'd have to be blind not to see that. But the thought of there being something between them—something more than making videos and talking about crime together—felt somehow forbidden. She'd never let herself dwell on it.

Until last night, when they'd discussed the formal.

"Can I say something that might come across as… kinda mean?" Lenore asked hesitantly.

Audrey blinked, surprised. "Yeah. Of course. Friends are honest with each other, right?"

"Right." Lenore took a deep breath. "I think you've been dodging guys for a long time. I know Nathan Vellani asked you out a while back, and I know you turned him down, and even back then, I thought… I thought maybe it was because of Matt. Because you were talking to this guy online, and you really liked him, and it would feel like a betrayal to him if you went out with another guy."

Audrey frowned. "Me and Matt are ju—*were* just friends."

"Yes," Lenore said, "but you wanted to be more."

Audrey opened her mouth to disagree, but... Lenore was right. The longer she'd known Matt, the more they talked, the closer they'd grown, and she'd let her imagination wander. To a future where their interactions weren't limited to a screen. To a future where they were working together. To a future where maybe, if he liked her too, there might be something more personal between them.

She'd never wanted to admit it, even to herself, but she'd been falling for him.

And losing him hurt in more ways than one.

"It's okay." Lenore was smiling gently, her eyes a little sad when Audrey turned to look at her. "I'm sorry you're going through this, but it's for the best, right?"

Audrey swallowed. "Yeah. Yeah, it is." Better she found out he was a creep now than when she finally had the guts to ask him to meet face to face. Or before he'd asked her.

"You should give Jackson a shot," her friend went on. "He's a nice guy. You have similar interests. And I think he likes you, too."

Audrey definitely blushed this time. "He does not."

"He absolutely does," Roxanne snorted, shovelling a bunch of fries into her mouth. "I saw the videos you did together. No guy helps a girl that much if he's not interested."

Lenore was beaming. "Audrey and Jackson, sitting in a… cemetery?"

This, Audrey decided, was what friendship was supposed to feel like. Comfortable. Easy. Not like she was stepping on eggshells, trying not to say the wrong thing. Not like she was terrified of being dropped from the group at any moment for being too poor, too uncool, too *morbid*. And even though Audrey would have hated being faced with Jackie's expensive tastes and overbearing attitude, she dearly wished Jackie had been there, too. To experience this. To maybe get back to the way they'd been when they were younger.

She was lighter than air when she got home after four, reading the quick note her mother had left on the fridge and dumping her shopping bags on the floor in the corner of her room. Just to complete the teen movie aspect of the scene, she fell back onto her bed with a sigh and stared at the ceiling. Dwelling on the day. Dwelling on the turn her life was taking.

Her phone was digging painfully into her hip in her pocket. She tugged it out and opened her messages out of habit—but instead of navigating to Matt, she went straight to Jackson.

Audrey

I found a dress.

He read her message immediately and was responding just as fast.

Jackson

So I guess that's a yes to the formal?

Lenore and Roxanne might be right. Maybe Jackson *was* interested. Would he have responded this quickly if he wasn't?

Could he fill that gap in her dreams Matt had left in his wake?

He ended his message with a wink.

By the time Audrey fell back into bed that evening, she was finally satisfied that things would only get better from then on.

28

Audrey deliberately left her phone out of reach as she got ready for the formal, even though it felt like cutting off her right hand. What if she had a sudden thought for one of her videos? What if a case came to mind, and she wanted to jot down a few notes? Google was always right there in the palm of her hand with all the information she needed; Matt was always available to bounce ideas off and give her a clearer perspective on what she wanted to say.

But Matt wasn't welcome in her life anymore.

His absence still hurt, especially so soon after having lost Jackie. But if he'd been the one to hurt her, to *kill* her, how could Audrey, in good faith, keep their friendship alive? The police hadn't arrested him yet, and Detective Flanagan had refused to comment on the "active investigation" when Audrey had called, but she knew. It was only a matter of time before they got their ducks in a row and descended on him, and she didn't want to be caught in the crosshairs when the time came. She couldn't take that chance. Not for herself, and especially not after everything Jackie had sacrificed for her. If only Jackie had told her before it had all been too late.

Although, Audrey had to admit, she never would have believed her. Not about this.

Her gaze caught on one of the photographs hanging from the corner of her mirror, an old Instax photograph of her and Jackie at a party. They were young in the photo—ten, or maybe eleven—and it was one of Audrey's favourites because it had always summed up their friendship so well. They were both grinning wildly, Jackie slightly in front of Audrey, sequined top bouncing the light from the camera's flash right back at the lens. The photograph was blurry, an absolute mess just like they had always been. Back then, before they'd hit high school, it had been the two of them against the world. They hadn't even discovered social media yet.

Audrey plucked it from the mirror and held it in her palm. Jackie may not have been able to attend the formal in person, but Audrey would bring her along in her own little way. At least then, her best friend wouldn't be missing out entirely.

"You'll get your perfect formal," she told the photograph. She probably looked like an idiot speaking to it, but what did she care? "I even got a date, just to shut you up."

She could practically see her best friend's eyes sparkling with victory as she tucked the photograph into her little purse.

She knew Jackie would have never let her hear the end of it if she hadn't done her hair and make-up properly, so she took her time in front of the mirror to go through a routine that Jackie had insisted she learn. It was a simple look, something that would go nicely with her simple dress. It took her less than twenty minutes to get her face done, and she spent another half hour on her hair, painstakingly making sure that every strand she curled was perfectly in place and not about to make her look like a fool. She took a cursory glance in the mirror and deemed herself ready. Hopefully, Jackie would have been proud of her attempt. It wasn't straight off the cover of a magazine, but it worked well enough for her.

Jackie most definitely would not have approved of the tattered pink sneakers she pulled on to complete her outfit. At least they matched the colour of her chiffon dress! Audrey giggled to herself as she imagined Jackie rolling her eyes before gesturing for Audrey to follow her out of the room. She grabbed her bag and did so, following the ghost of her best friend as she slapped off the light switch.

Her mother was waiting for her with a camera in the living room, beaming and demanding pictures before Audrey was allowed to leave the apartment. Audrey rolled her eyes but complied with the request, knowing there would be absolutely no arguing with her mother on this point. Her mother would have wanted these pictures regardless, but they were even more important now after all of these opportunities had been stolen from Jackie. Audrey tried not to let her smile slip as she realised the formal wasn't the only thing Jackie would be missing. That there were a million other life events she was never going to experience. Graduation, a wedding, having children, succeeding in her influencer career. Jackie would get none of that. All of her dreams were dead now, buried in the ground with their dreamer like so many other dreamers before.

Hopefully, she'd been Matt's only victim. She would certainly be his last.

Her mother must have sensed the switch in her mood because she tucked the camera away quickly. She was already dressed in her scrubs, ready to start her shift shortly after she dropped Audrey off at the function centre where the formal was being held.

"All right," she conceded. "Are you ready to go? What time are Lenore and Roxanne meeting you there?"

"We agreed on a quarter to seven."

"Uh-huh." The corner of her mother's lip twitched up almost into a smile. "And what time did that boy say he would be there?"

Audrey rolled her eyes for real this time. "Same time, Mum. Can we go now? We're both going to be late if we don't."

They drove in comfortable silence, Audrey watching the sun set over West Drummond in the distance. In a lot of ways, the night was beginning to feel like an ending of sorts. This formal was marking the end of the eleventh grade for her and her friends. It was the last solid plan she'd made with Jackie, and it felt more like a goodbye than her brief time at the funeral had. She knew she, Jackie, her friends, and the Chen family were going to be getting their closure any day now when the police circled in and finally arrested Matt, and then it would be time to move on. If they were lucky, everything would come to a close that night. Her throat grew tight at the thought. She clutched her bag in her lap.

And with endings, of course, came new beginnings. University was right around the corner, only a year away, and with it, the beginning of the rest of their lives. Maybe tonight would be the start of that brilliant new partnership with Jackson. Or maybe, she dared to hope, it could be the beginning of a tentative new relationship between the pair of them. They hadn't mentioned the formal much over the week, but he'd definitely been smiling at her more, touching her hand more. She could almost see it as being Jackie's final gift to her, making sure she got a boyfriend, even in death. It was exactly the sort of thing that her best friend would have done. Jackie was probably sitting in the back seat of the car right now, screaming, "I told you so!" into the night. The thought made Audrey smile.

There were already a number of people standing outside the function centre when Audrey's mother pulled up in front of it, and Audrey was downhearted to see that a news van also sat not too far away. She spotted the crew almost immediately, a cameraman and sound guy filming a dark-haired woman dressed boldly in red as she gestured wildly towards the venue. Audrey gritted her teeth.

"We can leave, if you want," her mother offered immediately. "You can call your friends, and I can take you somewhere else."

"No," Audrey said, shaking her head. Jackie had wanted her here, and she was staying. "Soon everybody will know the truth anyway, and nothing the media said about me will mean anything. I just have to make it until then." She took a deep breath. "And I've already had enough things ruined in my life. I'm not going to let some shitty journalists ruin tonight, too."

Her mother gave her a gentle smile and didn't bother to scold her for the language. "All right. Get on in there, then. And *call me* when you're heading back to Lenore's. Don't text. If I haven't heard from you by midnight, I'll be sending in a search party."

It felt like the wrong time to roll her eyes and complain. "I'll call you. Have a good night at work, Mum." Almost as an afterthought, she added, "I love you."

"I love you too, Audrey."

Lenore must have spotted Audrey's mother's car because she and Roxanne had come down to the street to meet her as she climbed out of the front passenger seat. They were both looking stunning in their thrifted outfits, Lenore in the kitten heels she'd scored and Roxanne in her usual combat boots. Roxanne threw a leather jacket over Audrey's head and hurried her up to the doorway of the venue, helping her bypass the media like a publicist might have helped a celebrity. Lenore was laughing at the silliness of it the entire time, and Audrey couldn't help but laugh along with her. Maybe tonight was going to be a blast after all. How bad could it be with her friends by her side?

And with Jackson waiting for her just outside the doors.

Roxanne led her right to the boy, and Audrey's cheeks flushed when she caught sight of him. She had known he would look good—after all, he always did—but she'd been entirely unprepared for what the sight of him in a pressed, dark suit would do to her. Somehow, he managed to look sophisticated and casual all at once, and when he smiled at her, she forgot all about the media and all of her classmates standing behind her. All that existed for her that night were Jackson and her friends, and that was all she was ever going to need. The media couldn't ruin that for her. Penny and Danielle couldn't ruin that for her. This was her life, her story, and she was going to make sure that from here on out, it was a good one.

"Ladies," Jackson greeted them with a wink. "Shall we?"

Inside wasn't the stuff of dreams. She'd pictured a large, open dance floor with fairy lights strung above it, glimmering stars and streamers dancing down from a high ceiling, and a long table with an assortment of snacks and a large punch bowl for them to drink from. Maybe that would come next year, with their final school formal, not for this in-between. Or maybe she'd just seen one too many American high school movies.

Instead, what they got was a mostly dark room, lit only by dim round lights in a ceiling that was far too low to be hanging anything spectacular from. There was a dance floor, but it was small and situated at the far end of the room, in front of a small stage that was clearly not going to be utilised by their party. There was a table for snack foods, but small menus on each table indicated that their three-course meal was going to be provided for them throughout the night.

It was like a low-budget wedding. But despite this, it was enough. She was with her friends, loved and cared for and safe, and that was what truly mattered.

The round tables scattered throughout the room held a host of name cards on them. She had a vague recollection of filling out a form months ago, an attempt by the school to determine who wanted to sit with whom so they could arrange a seating chart, and they'd obviously done their best to make it happen. One long table sat with names that she recognised. Her own card glimmered in gold right beside Penny's.

Before she could say anything, Roxanne had walked right up to the table and gathered up all three of their names. The school had at least seated her next to Lenore, who had, in turn, been placed next to Danielle. After a moment of consideration, she plucked Delilah's from the tabletop, too.

"How about we find Jackson and Peter's names too," she suggested, "and find ourselves an empty table somewhere?"

Yes. That was a great idea. She gave her newest friend a thankful smile. Tonight, she was not going to stress at all. Tonight was going to be all about fun.

Before they left the table, Lenore gathered up one last name with a grimace.

"I guess the school never bothered to update the venue on what happened," she said as she flipped the name around.

Jacqueline's name glimmered back at them, perfectly printed in gold glitter. She would have loved it. Audrey pressed a hand to her purse.

"Bring it with us," she said without hesitation. "After everything Penny and Danielle have done lately, there's no way Jackie would still choose to sit with them. She can come and sit with us."

"I kind of brought a photo of her so she could sit with us anyway," Lenore said sheepishly. "I know it sounds weird, but. I felt like I needed to do something."

Audrey blinked. "So did I!"

Jackson chuckled. "Wow. You girls really are all like-minded. And it turns out sometimes that's a good thing."

They found and stole Jackson and Peter's name cards easily enough, then found themselves a table closer to the back of the room, tucked into a dark little corner. It might have seemed strange to some, and Audrey was sure the venue had actually put the table there to keep it out of the way, but she found it to be quite cosy. The dim lighting worked better here, and they had a nice view of the entire room and its exits.

She especially appreciated the table when Penny and Danielle strolled in looking like movie stars, decked out in their stiletto heels and long, flowing gowns—and didn't look twice at the table in the corner.

"Good riddance," Roxanne muttered to herself. "How are they ever going to outdo themselves for the red carpet?"

"They won't be wearing dresses," Jackson said. "They'll just roll themselves in glitter."

Lenore choked into her water. Jackson chuckled.

Both sounds were music to Audrey's ears.

29

THEY HAD TO WAVE Peter over when he finally arrived. He'd walked into the room, looked it over twice, and still not spotted them until Jackson got up to motion him over. Peter looked surprised for a moment but weaved his way through the other tables quickly.

"Are we being punished?" he asked, only half joking. "I mean, this table isn't anywhere near anybody else. I don't know whether to complain or thank people."

"You can thank us," Roxanne replied. "We chose this table ourselves. Come on, sit down."

"You guys see the reporters outside?" Peter asked as he sat. "I heard someone say Penny and Danielle were planning some kind of memorial. You think they're here for that or something?"

"Or something," Jackson said, glancing at Audrey briefly. "I think they might be hoping for a little drama."

At the mention of drama, Audrey found her eyes drifting across the room to where her ex-friends were sitting. They both had guys with them, but even so, their table was still noticeably empty. Penny crossed her leg, letting it show through the long slit in her dress, and rubbed it against her seemingly on-again boyfriend, who grinned right back at her. Danielle was fawning all over the senior she'd managed to score as her date. The group laughed loudly—*too* loudly. It had to be for show. It had to be to draw attention, and it was working. Audrey grimaced. Tonight was supposed to be about everybody, and whatever memorial they'd planned should have been about Jackie. But she had a feeling Penny was going to try to make the entire evening about herself, just as she had done at the funeral.

She knew the rest of her table was having the same thoughts.

Lenore rested her hand over Audrey's and gave it a light squeeze. "Don't worry. You've got people on your side now. If the girls try to stir anything up, or if their guys try to start anything, we'll speak up for you. And I'm sure others will, too. People did after the funeral. They'll do it tonight, too."

"Thanks," Audrey said with a small smile. "But honestly, I'd rather we make it through the night with no drama at all. I don't want anything to ruin tonight."

By seven o'clock, the rest of their classmates had finally made their way indoors and settled into their seats so the venue could serve them their first meal of the night. Audrey did her best to relax and enjoy herself, eating and laughing with her friends, dancing when the music started to play, and trying not to look in the direction of the girls that she had once called her friends. The weight of Jackie's photo was heavy in her bag, but it was a comforting weight.

A weight that grew heavier when the music stopped and

the lights in the tiny function centre grew brighter.

Penny took the stage at the front of the room. Audrey hated the sight of her up there, stiletto heels clacking across the wooden floor and a huge smile on her overly made-up face. She must have spent *hours* on her hair, a mountain of elaborate curls that tumbled over both of her shoulders. She had the nerve to wink and wave at a few people as she moved towards the microphone and took it in both hands like a pop star.

"Christ," Roxanne swore under her breath. "She's not going to start singing, is she?"

"Thank you all for coming tonight," Penny said instead, looking around at everybody gathering around the stage. Her eyes narrowed slightly when she caught sight of Audrey, Lenore, and Roxanne, but she said nothing to them and looked instead at the people who *weren't* getting closer to the stage. "Ex*cuse* me. Patterson? Bellini? Can't you see we're starting the memorial up here? Everybody needs to get over here!"

"*Look at me, look at me!*" Roxanne mimed flicking long hair over her shoulder. Several people laughed.

Audrey sighed. Of course Penny was going to take the opportunity to make sure all of the attention was on her. God forbid some people not be interested in watching the memorial. Audrey felt for them. But much to her surprise, the boys she'd called out grumbled and complied with Penny's request for them to come closer to the stage and pay attention.

"Much better." Penny flipped her perfectly curled hair over one shoulder and beamed around at everybody.

"Now. The school and the local council came together and decided they wanted to do something for Jackie after all of this *awfulness*, and Mr Evans decided that I would be the best person to make the announcement."

Audrey didn't doubt that for a second. Penny was charismatic, attention-demanding—and, of course, had never publicly been considered a person of interest in either Jackie's disappearance or her murder. It didn't matter in the slightest that Audrey had always been Jackie's best friend or that Mr and Mrs Chen would have asked that Audrey be the one to make this announcement. Penny was an innocent face in this scenario, whereas Audrey's reputation was forever going to be marred because of it.

Penny turned dramatically to the back of the stage, where thick curtains blocked their view of whatever lay behind it. Everybody's gaze was drawn that way when Penny waved a hand at somebody off to the side of the stage, motioning for them to pull the curtains open. Audrey watched on as the curtains were drawn, revealing a series of images on large easels.

"This is the memorial park that the council are going to be setting up for Jackie," Penny explained, gesturing wide to the pictures. "It's going to be set up right where they found her body. That park is going to be cleared of most of the trees and the shrubs, and they're going to add in more overhead lights to make it safer and more well-lit at night. There's going to be seating, a fountain, and a walking trail. They want it to be a place where we can all go sit and think about Jackie and also a place where you can go to be safe. It's going to be totally beautiful, and they're going to rename the park for her. Isn't it just perfect, guys? Me and Danielle came up with it ourselves!"

It was definitely something, Audrey had to admit. Jackie most likely would have loved it, and that was what mattered.

But there was something about the whole thing that was off-putting to her. Putting up a memorial that was meant for gatherings and sitting quietly to reflect in an area where a young woman had been found murdered? If it had taken the killer—if it had taken *Matt*, she corrected herself—dumping the address into their laps for Jackie's body to be found in the first place, then the area couldn't have been that safe. A couple of extra streetlights and some cleared trees were not going to make a change when it came to that.

Danielle was up on the stage now, too, having her moment in the spotlight. Audrey thought she was imagining the camera flashes that were sparkling off hers and Penny's dresses, but when she turned, she found that there were indeed a couple of photographers in the building taking photos of everything, and there was the reporter from earlier, her cameraman filming everything as Penny and Danielle tried to raise the excitement level of the small crowd gathered in front of them.

People were turning to glance at Audrey, Peter, and their friends. Were those looks of sympathy she was getting today in place of blame? Of course her classmates would know it should be her up there, making the announcement with the appropriate amount of sorrow, without any fanfare. The fact that her two ex-friends had taken it as yet another opportunity to put themselves in the spotlight made her feel sick to her stomach. Roxanne was grimacing. Lenore just looked sad. Peter looked almost angry, his jaw set tightly. Audrey didn't need to be a mind reader to know that he was dying to say something to the two girls. She'd wished she'd done as Delilah had clearly decided and not bothered to show up for the formal at all. This had been a mistake.

"I need some air," she choked out.

"I'll come with you," Jackson offered. "Come on. There's a side door we can slip out so the media won't see you leaving and decide they want to follow you."

Audrey let him lead her that way, his arm a gentle guide around her shoulders. His hand was warm against her bare skin, and she gave an involuntary shudder at the contact as his fingers brushed against her. This was hardly the time to be thinking about his skin against hers—and yet, at that moment, she wanted to think of nothing else. It was easier than thinking about what was happening at that stage.

The side door led them to the small alley at the side of the function centre, and Jackson immediately began leading her back to the light of the main street. Safety. She let him lead without complaint, not caring where they went so long as it was far away from Penny and Danielle and their circus. How could they even *think* about using this opportunity to make a name for themselves? They were taking everything away from Jackie. How must Mr and Mrs Chen be feeling about this? It hurt Audrey's heart to think about.

"Let's walk awhile," Jackson suggested. "You seem tense. Maybe it'll help you calm down."

Audrey nodded. Taking a walk sounded like a great idea.

And it was a good night for it, too. There was a nice breeze in the air that chased away the heat the day had left behind, and an almost full moon provided enough light for them to see by, even when they stepped into darker areas. Jackson led her slowly away from the main shopping strip, away from the crowds of people that she didn't want to be anywhere near. She would have to thank him for it later. How could he know her so well already when they had only been hanging out for such a short period of time?

"Talk to me," Jackson said gently. "What are you thinking about?"

"All sorts of things," Audrey admitted. "I'm thinking about Jackie. The memorial. How Penny and Danielle have been using this whole crazy situation for their fifteen minutes of fame. I don't understand how they can do all of that and not feel even a little bit bad. Jackie literally *died*, but all they care about is getting their stupid faces in front of those stupid cameras." She laughed bitterly. "It's funny that they think I'm the one who's using Jackie's death to seek attention by posting my videos when it's really them taking advantage of everything."

"Honestly, it sounds to me like they've been jealous this whole time," Jackson said calmly. "Jackie was, too. Jealous that even though they were getting more followers than you, you were the only one who was posting anything worthwhile. Their accounts are all about clothes and make-up and gossip, and trying to get as many people to follow them as possible by flashing their tits and showing off their asses. Yours is about helping people, and because of that, you get better comments than any of them ever do."

Only because of Matt.

Audrey doubted any of the girls really cared about that, but it was nice to hear Jackson say so. No. She knew the other girls only cared about the total number of followers they had and not the quality of the feedback they got. It was all about looks for them. All about the bragging rights. It had never mattered to them when Audrey had been excited over getting her first true viewer—Matt, who had made long, thoughtful comments on every video and made an effort to engage with her. Jackie had never been able to boast a regular who interacted with her. All she got were girls who talked about either how much they wanted to be her or how much they hated her and guys who talked about the things that they would do to her if they ever managed to get their hands on her.

It was frightening that Audrey had always considered those men the true danger here and not the person she had thought she could trust.

The light, chiffon skirt of her dress danced in the wind as they walked along, and Audrey thanked her lucky stars that she'd chosen to wear sneakers instead of a ridiculous pair of heels. Perhaps Jackie was still looking out for her from the other side after all. Had she gone as far as to lead Jackson to her that day in the library, too? Sneaky bitch, still playing matchmaker from the other side.

The sounds of the main street grew almost non-existent

as Jackson walked along with her. At some point, his hand had come down to encircle hers, and now they walked hand in hand down quiet streets under the twinkling night sky. Audrey let all of her anxious thoughts fade away as they strolled. Penny and Danielle making a spectacle of themselves? Forgotten. The reporters implying she was guilty? Soon, they wouldn't be a problem anymore. Matt spending months fooling her into believing that he was a true friend and supporter? Well, that one was going to take some time, but for now, she could push those thoughts to the back of her mind and pretend like he didn't exist. And in this moment, he didn't. It was just her and Jackson, his presence warm beside her.

Audrey came back to her senses when she realised that she was walking in long, damp grass. It was so overgrown that it had no trouble at all reaching up over her high-topped sneakers and brushing at her calves. She looked down at it, only able to make it out by the light of the moon. She looked up at the rest of her surroundings—long grass, clusters of trees, and blissful silence. Jackson came to a stop and turned to face her fully.

Their location hit her at once. "What are we doing here?"

He was so close to her now, barely half a step away. She could feel the heat from his body; his lips were parted ever so slightly.

Jackson reached up to brush a few strands of hair out of her face, and his hand came to rest just below her chin. "I thought we could make this spot something more important before those bitches come in and ruin it with their memorial garden."

His hand on her face was so soft, so warm. Everything around her faded away. He was all she could see. "And what did you have in mind?"

He smiled at her—a genuine smile that lit up his face, a sparkle in his eyes. "I thought you might like to know what it was like."

Audrey's heart was pounding in her chest. She moved half an inch closer to him. Another two inches and their lips would be touching. Was he going to kiss her?

She had to force herself to breathe. "What what was like?"

Jackson's other hand came up, both of them gently cupping her chin. This was it. It was really going to happen. Audrey's eyes fluttered closed. She felt rather than seeing Jackson lean in that little bit closer, his warmth spreading all over her. She heard his lips part further, heard his voice barely louder than the night breeze...

"What it was like when I strangled Jacqueline in this very spot."

30

Audrey didn't have time to react. One minute, she was on gently trembling legs, her hands resting softly on the rolled-up sleeves of Jackson's dress shirt, certain she was about to be kissed for the first time.

The next, she was cold and damp, lying in wet grass with a heavy weight on top of her, unable to get any air into her lungs.

Jackson loomed over her like a dark shadow, his size suddenly intimidating rather than a comfort. At first, she'd thought it was his weight on her chest preventing her from drawing a breath, but a fresh new wave of shock rolled over her when she realised it had nothing to do with him pressing against her body and everything to do with whatever it was that he had wrapped around her throat.

In a panic, she scrambled to grab whatever it was and pulled.

But Jackson was pulling tighter. He had a better grip on whatever it was; he was in a much better position to be hurting her than she was to be helping herself. She twisted beneath him and kicked her legs out in a desperate frenzy, but he was well out of their way where he sat, straddling her waist. She couldn't manoeuvre her legs around far enough to get them in front of him and kick him off. She could bring her knees up to hit the back of him, but that only brought him closer to her.

Her fingers gripped his, desperately trying to loosen whatever he'd wrapped around her throat. It was thin, but it was strong, and she couldn't get her fingers beneath it. She had no leverage. She had no *chance*.

When she looked up at him, dark eyes stared back at her. Jackson's pupils had grown so big they seemed to entirely take over his irises.

"You have no idea," he breathed, "how long I've been waiting for this moment."

Audrey's heart thundered in her chest, in her ears, in her throat. She needed to *stay calm*. She knew that. But how was she supposed to stay calm when Jackson had something wrapped around her throat, and he was pulling, pulling, *pulling,* and nobody knew where she was because she was stupid, stupid, *stupid* and hadn't bothered to tell anybody. Lenore, Roxanne, and Peter knew she'd left the venue with Jackson, but they wouldn't know where they'd gone. Wouldn't know anything was wrong. And by the time they realised something wasn't right and raised the alarm, it would already be far too late for her. Her vision was already growing spotty. Her head was spinning.

Was this how Jackie had felt?

Had she been lying in this exact spot, with this same boy on top of her, his weapon wrapped around her throat? Had she fought back? Had she managed to land a blow?

Without warning, Jackson released the pressure around Audrey's throat—just enough for her to cough for a moment, get a long, deep breath in, and then he was tightening his weapon again. She never even had time to scream.

"Killing Jackie was definitely something," Jackson went on, his voice low in the night. Audrey pushed at his chest and tugged at his hands, but he didn't falter. "That bitch has had it coming for *years*. Always walking around acting like she was better than everyone else. I don't know why you ever bothered hanging with her. Especially with how she treated you."

Audrey tried to kick at him again, though she had even less success than she'd had previously. A twisted little grin crossed Jackson's face.

"You always thought you were so smart, didn't you?" he asked. It was almost like they were having a completely casual conversation, minus the fact that Audrey was fighting for her life. "Honestly, I thought it would be a lot harder to get you out here alone, but you fell even easier than your idiot of a best friend did. It took me ages to convince her to forget that stupid assignment and follow me. Had to say Peter wanted to surprise her. *That* got her moving. I thought it would have been a lot harder to get you to turn against your buddy Matt, too, but you went right ahead and blocked him, didn't you? You got one little whiff of thinking he was guilty, and it was game over for the poor schmuck. Oh, Audrey." Jackson pulled his weapon tighter around her throat. Panic raced through her. She blinked tears from her eyes. "Didn't I tell you?

If you're going to have any success with that channel of yours, you're going to have to broaden your horizons. It's not just about knowing the person that went missing. It's about knowing the person who *took* them." He leered down at her. "You're welcome, by the way. For posting the comment with the location of the body. You can attribute that to how your channel ended up on the map."

Audrey wanted to ask why any of this mattered now. Her channel was done whether she liked it or not because, in a matter of minutes, she was going to be *dead*. She could feel the wet leaves and twigs twisting up in her hair, which was no doubt a mess now, even after all the time she'd spent on it. Instead of reporting on a new missing persons case this weekend, people would be reporting on her instead, talking about her murder. Would they be speaking about it as an unsolved crime? Was Jackson going to get away with this?

Audrey steeled herself. He most likely would—just like he'd flown under the radar on Jackie's case.

Unless *she* made sure he didn't.

She let go of his hands and went for his face instead, reaching for his eyes with both of her thumbs. A trick Matt had described to her long ago. Jackson jerked his head back too quickly for her to reach them, so she went for his bare arms instead, digging her short nails in and scratching down the length of them, leaving red marks on both and drawing blood with just one of her nails. Jackson jerked back with a hiss, and for a moment, the pressure around her throat was loosened. She sucked in a sharp breath and took the opportunity to slip her fingers beneath her noose, trying to pull it off. Definitely thin and cord-like, she determined. If she had to make a guess based on its texture, she would have wagered that this was a shoelace. Was that what Jackie had been murdered with?

She gave a cry of pain as the shoelace tightened around her throat again, trapping her fingers with it this time.

"Clever, clever," Jackson said with a chuckle. "But there's no need for any of that, Audrey. I have no intention of killing you tonight. I mean, really. Where would all the fun be in that?"

"What do you want?" she managed to choke out, trying and failing to fight back the tears that were rolling freely now. Her head spins were making her nauseous; she was freezing, and everything was beginning to hurt. "Why are you doing this?"

"Exposure." Jackson's eyes were wild. "I want you to tell my story, Audrey. It's already begun. Just think of all the views you're going to get when people find out the boy who helped you cover your best friend's murder case was the one who killed her all along. And nobody ever suspected a thing."

Audrey's head spun with his words. It hadn't been Matt at all. It hadn't been some random stalker from Jackie's Instagram. It hadn't been a stranger, a sex offender, or any of the people Audrey believed would have done this. All along, it had been this boy who had stepped right up to help her, who had inserted himself into her investigation at the earliest possible moment. She should have known. *She should have known!*

But how could she have? How could she have known

that the one person who was on her side would be the one who had committed the crime? Jackson had never come across as a killer to her. He had done his best to help her, providing his insights into the minds of serial killers and other criminals, teaching her about their methods and the way they would think. He had been the perfect addition to her YouTube channel, helping her prepare and record and adding that extra dimension to her videos. And all along, he'd been working on his own story. Giving the world a glimpse of a sociopath in the days before he was set to really make his mark on the world.

Audrey felt cold all over, and it had nothing to do with the weather.

"Our story will be one for the ages," Jackson promised her. "Your name will be bigger than Sherlock Holmes, and my name will always be right there beside yours. The only question left to answer now is which of us is going to win in the end." He leaned down and planted a kiss on her forehead, and she jerked her head to the side to get away from him. He chuckled. "And that's why I won't be killing you, Herringbone. Because every villain needs a hero, and I want you to be mine."

He was insane. Audrey couldn't believe what she was hearing. He wanted her to be a hero? Did he know heroes always won in the end? She tried desperately to remove the shoelace from her throat again, but Jackson pulled it tighter once more.

"Just give in," he practically whispered. "Our story can't begin until we've gone our separate ways."

Audrey struggled desperately. She didn't want *anything*

to begin, least of all some continuing story that he had imagined happening between them. How could he be doing this to her? How was it possible that even though this was all happening to her right now, she still didn't look at Jackson and see a killer? He was her classmate. Her research companion. Her date to the formal. He was the boy who had been on her side right from the beginning, when everybody else had taken their stance and decided she was guilty of kidnapping, of hurting her best friend, of *murder*. But, she supposed, it was easy to stand by somebody and assure them that you knew they weren't guilty when you knew who the real culprit was. When the real culprit was *you*.

Her heels kicked at the ground in frustration. His grip on the tie around her throat was too strong. *He* was too strong. She was in too much of a bad position to be able to throw him off, and her head was spinning too much for her to be able to see straight. Even if she'd decided to take a swing at him and try to fight him off, her strength was draining at an alarming rate. She would never be able to fight him. She was going to die right here, right now, with wet grass itching at her bare upper back and the chiffon of her dress's skirt riding up. She hated the thought of being found like this. She hated the thought of her life ending this way.

She hated the thought of her life ending at all. She'd had so much left that she wanted to do. Her YouTube channel was finally starting to gain a following. She was almost done with high school. What came after that, she had never been sure, but that didn't mean she wanted to miss out on it. And what about her mother? She had never truly recovered after Audrey's father's disappearance. How would she take this? How would Audrey's friends take it?

And Matt. She so desperately wanted to apologise to him for ever thinking that he could have been a bad guy. She hoped against all odds that when he heard about her death on the news, he knew how sorry she was. She hoped he would know the truth of what had really happened and that he might be able to help the police solve the case. She hoped that maybe he might carry her memory with him, think about her from time to time, and use it as fuel to help him through his training to become a police officer.

She hoped she wouldn't be forgotten. She hoped she wouldn't become a statistic. She wanted people to remember her as somebody who had tried to make a difference in the world and not just another victim of some twisted sociopath.

"Just close your eyes," Jackson whispered, "and it will all be over before you know it."

Was it her imagination, or were there sirens in the distance? It didn't matter either way. They were getting quieter the longer she struggled to hear them, so even if by some miracle they were coming for her, they would never make it in time. Nobody in the houses across the street could hear her struggles; none of the passing cars could see her in the dark. She could hear a motorcycle getting closer, but unless the rider drove it right into the park, they would not be able to help her either.

Jackson was right. There really was no point in her struggling.

Her bag was still a weight at her side, and inside of it she remembered Jackie's picture. It was practically vibrating against her leg. She wished she could look at it one last time, to tell her best friend that she would be seeing her again soon. She stopped trying to free her hands to remove the shoelace, letting Jackson strangle her without a struggle.

See you soon, Jackie.

Audrey closed her eyes and let the darkness take her.

31

She came up gasping for air.

Her body flailed as she scrambled for purchase, her arms flying out towards Jackson again. How could she have thought about giving up? She had to keep fighting. She *had* to. She couldn't let this bastard win, couldn't let him get away with this, couldn't let him—

Somebody was holding her down, but it wasn't Jackson.

She knew it by the feel of the hands. Jackson's hands had been soft in hers when they'd been walking and strangely absent while he had been committing his crime. These hands were calloused and rough against her arms, larger and stronger but also somehow... gentler.

"*Audrey*," he was saying, his voice soft and familiar. "*I need you to open your eyes.*"

For a brief moment, Audrey was reminded of her father—speaking to her quietly, calming her after a nightmare. Maybe this *was* her father, having been waiting for her all these years on the other side. The thought of it hurt her head and her heart all at once. She'd long accepted her father was dead, but even now, she would have given anything for it not to be true.

But if she was dead, why was everything so loud and chaotic? Death was supposed to be quiet and peaceful... wasn't it?

She was sure it was also supposed to be dark, but when she peeled her eyes open, it was very much the opposite. Bright lights rained down from above her, making it difficult to keep her eyes open. She turned her head to the side, and something pulled at her nose.

"Whoa there," Detective Flanagan said, a hand moving to her shoulder instead. "Be careful, all right? You've got an oxygen tube up your nose."

The emergency room. She was in the emergency room, Audrey suddenly realised. There was Detective Flanagan standing over her, removing his hands and taking a step back to give her some space. There was her mother, in full nurse mode, in her scrubs and latex gloves, as she rushed over to check that Audrey was okay. She could see other nurses and doctors rushing past the little cubicle she was in, their voices carrying all through the little department. Of course they were busy. It was a Friday night, and her mother always said that was when all the loonies of the world came out to play. The fact that it was almost a full moon probably didn't help.

"Oh my God," her mother was saying over and over, her hands fluttering around Audrey. "Are you all right? When they brought you in and told me what happened, I thought... Oh my God..."

"Do you remember what happened?" Detective Flanagan asked gently, at the same time that her almost hysterical mother asked, "Did that boy *touch* you?"

Audrey's throat felt tight. She forced herself to swallow before she tried to speak. It hurt like hell.

"No, Mum," she said quietly. "He didn't touch me. And yes, I remember what happened."

She remembered *everything*. Every moment of Jackson leaning over her was ingrained in her brain. She could still see his eyes, the pupils so large they made his eyes look black; she could still feel his weight on top of her, pushing her into the wet grass as his hands tugged at the tie around her neck. She raised a hand to her throat now, to the mark that was no doubt there...

"Did you catch him?" she practically whispered.

"We were too late," Detective Flanagan said apologetically. "Your friends beat us to the scene, and even when they got there, Mr Miranda was already gone." Detective Flanagan patted her shoulder gently. "You gave them all quite the fright."

"Oh, yeah," her mother agreed with a humourless laugh. "They're out in the waiting room right now. Do you want to see them?"

Audrey did. She nodded, and Detective Flanagan left her alone for a moment with her mother as he went to retrieve her friends. Her mother grasped one of her hands and squeezed gently, the lines around her eyes seemingly deeper than ever.

"I'm glad you're all right," she said softly. "I don't know what I would have done if..."

Audrey nodded. They didn't need to talk about that right now.

"I'm still supposed to be on shift for another few hours,"

her mother went on, "but I'm going to speak to my supervisor in a while, as soon as they say you're safe to go home. I think we should both take a couple of days to recover after this, huh?"

"Sounds great," Audrey said. But nothing sounded great at that moment. Not when her entire world was crashing down all around her. Not when she was now second-guessing literally everything that she knew.

Lenore was the first to enter the room, her cheeks traced with tears. Audrey felt terrible at the sight of them, at knowing that she was the cause of them. Roxanne looked more put together but still frazzled. Peter came along with her, giving Audrey a short nod that told her everything she needed to know from her old best friend's boyfriend. He was glad that she was safe.

"We should never have let you go off with him alone," Lenore was moaning as she absently smoothed down the blankets that covered Audrey. "We should have known better. After everything that's happened lately especially, we should have known!"

"It's okay," Audrey said. "Really. None of us could have known." Which made her wonder... "How did you know where to find me?"

"We didn't," Roxanne said evenly. "Honestly, we weren't even worried about you and Jackson being gone until *he* showed up and started asking questions."

Audrey frowned. "Until who showed up?"

Roxanne jerked her head towards the direction they'd entered, and Peter stepped away from the end of her bed, giving her an unobstructed view of the opening of the curtains, where a boy she did not recognise was standing. He was watching her, too, completely silent as he stood there in a leather jacket with a motorcycle helmet tucked neatly under one arm. The more Audrey stared at him, the more he began to look familiar to her. That dark hair, those eyes... Hadn't she seen those in photographs before?

With a start, she gasped, "Matt?"

The boy smiled back at her softly. "Hey, Audi."

She pushed herself into a sitting position. Her head spun dangerously, but she forced herself to continue staring at him. He looked nothing like how she'd imagined he would, and yet, somehow, he was also entirely familiar to her. His eyes were tired but alert, his smile timid but warm.

And he was here. Actually *here*, standing right in front of her.

"You have him to thank for us finding you in time," Lenore said with a sad little laugh. "If he hadn't shown up asking where you were and then guessed at where you probably went..."

Audrey blinked. "I... What?"

Matt took a few hesitant steps forward, coming to stand closer to the bed. Closer to Audrey. He seemed to be looking her over the same way she was him, taking in her injuries like she was taking in his face. She supposed it was a little different for him. He'd seen her unobstructed face in photographs on Facebook dozens of times, but this was the first time that she had seen his.

"I remembered you saying that your formal was tonight," he said quietly. His voice was gentle but strong, nothing at all like the boy she'd imagined. "I've also been trying to get in touch with you all week, but you sort of made that difficult when you blocked me." Audrey opened her mouth to apologise for that, but Matt was already shaking his head. "You don't need to apologise. You did the right thing. Or at least, you thought it was the right thing. It would have been the right thing if you'd been right about me."

"I should have known I wasn't," Audrey cut in. "I'm sorry, Matt. I should have trusted you. But you were asking for updates, and you didn't tell me you'd messaged her, and Jackson always seemed so innocent..."

Her mother put a firm hand on her shoulder. She was getting worked up. She forced herself to let out a breath and relax.

"Yeah, about that," Matt said, rubbing the back of his neck. "Turns out I go to school with his cousin. I'd been watching your videos with him, and he was giving weird vibes, so I spoke to her and, well... She's sort of the reason that I made it my mission to find you tonight."

"Why don't you explain what happened, Mr Callaghan?" Detective Flanagan said. "Starting at the beginning, if you please."

"His cousin, Maxine, said she never really interacted with him because he gave her the creeps. Their dads are brothers, but they barely speak to each other, and the only reason she and Jackson even have each other on Facebook is in case of a family emergency or something. She said he was obsessed with serial killers. Which isn't totally weird," he added, offering Audrey a small smile, "but when I rewatched those videos and really listened to the way he talked about killers and how smart they are… I mean, he wasn't *wrong*, but the way he said it…"

"It made your arachnid senses tingle," Roxanne offered. Matt accepted the explanation with a shrug and a nod.

"I figured there was a good chance you might end up going to your formal with him, and I knew it would probably be the only time I'd be able to find you and speak to you. So I…" Matt grimaced and had the nerve to look ashamed as he said, "I decided to do basically exactly what your friend had been accusing me of in the first place. I got onto Facebook and I started to track you down."

"But how?" Lenore asked, looking confused. "Audrey said she blocked you almost a week ago, and everything on her profile is set to private. There's no way you could have seen anything on there."

"I still had Jackie on my account," he said with a shrug. "All I had to do was unblock her."

"But she never posted anything about the formal," Audrey said. "How could you have figured anything out from her account when nothing's been posted since…?"

She didn't need to finish. Everybody in her little cubical knew exactly what had happened to Jackie.

"You might keep all of your posts on social media private, Audi," Matt said, "but I can't say the same for your other friend, Penelope. I found her through Jackie's account, and every bit of information I needed was right there out in the open. She posted about when the formal started, where it was happening—everything. She even posted a picture of her invitation so I could alter it, print it out, and walk in like I was a student at your school." He glanced at Detective Flanagan sheepishly. "I hope you're not going to arrest me for that."

Detective Flanagan gave him a half smile. "I think we can let it slide this once, Mr Callaghan, seeing as you're being so forthcoming and cooperative."

Matt nodded. "Well. I took all of that information, jumped on my motorcycle, and headed for the function centre. When I didn't see Audi anywhere, I used the photos from Penelope's account to figure out who Lenore was and asked where Audi—where *Audrey* was. And when they told me she'd gone off to get some air with Jackson, and we went outside and couldn't find either of them anywhere..."

"What made you think they'd have gone to that particular park?" Audrey's mother asked suspiciously. "Such a strange thought to have, don't you think?"

"Not necessarily. I know you're going to think this is strange, Mrs Herringbone, but I have somewhat of a fascination with criminals. My plan after graduation is to go on to the police academy. So trying to think like these sorts of people do is almost a hobby of mine." Matt took a deep breath. "I figured that if Jackson was what I thought he was, it was likely he'd been the one to murder Jackie. And if he was the one who did that to her, then there was a big chance he was going to take Audrey there, too." He nodded to Lenore, Roxanne, and Peter. "I told them exactly what I was thinking, asked them to call the police, and got back on my bike. Lenore insisted on coming with me, and we rode to the park as quickly as we could."

"It was terrifying," Lenore said. "At first, we thought that we'd gone to the wrong place because we couldn't see or hear anything. We were calling out for you, Audrey, but nobody was calling back. Matt was starting to worry, thinking that he'd led us and the police in the wrong direction, but then we saw you lying in the grass." Lenore's lower lip trembled, and she took a deep, shaking breath. "We thought you were dead. You were so pale, and your lips were turning blue..."

"It's okay," Audrey said, and she was surprised that the words were coming out of her own mouth. "As weird as it sounds, I don't think I was ever really in any danger. Jackson said..."

Everybody was silent. Detective Flanagan was standing as poised as ever, his eyes hard.

"He said what?" he asked. "Do you remember exactly?"

Audrey nodded. "He said that he had no intention of killing me. At least not yet. Because... he wanted me to keep telling his story."

"His story," Detective Flanagan repeated. When Audrey nodded, he added, "On your YouTube channel? And what story is that exactly?"

"I'm not entirely sure," Audrey admitted. "I guess... maybe the story of what he did to Jackie? Maybe he wanted the whole world to know what he did and that he got away with it?"

"I think," Matt said slowly, "that he wants to make a name for himself. Your channel is all about what happens to people 'in the days before' their lives are changed forever. Maybe that's what he was hoping you'd be doing for him, too. Maybe he wanted you to show him and tell his story from the days before he became whatever it is that he's about to become."

"And what do you think that's going to be?" Audrey's mother asked. Her nails dug into Audrey's shoulder.

Matt grimaced. "Best case scenario, this will be the end of his crimes. He'll have had a taste for it and be done. Better yet, the police will find him and lock him up."

"And the worst-case scenario?"

Matt glanced at Audrey before looking back at the group at large. "I think Jackson Miranda might be an aspiring serial killer."

32

Audrey was a local celebrity.

She was all over the news again, though this time not as the girl who'd potentially murdered her best friend. This time, she was the survivor of a vicious attack, the survivor of an atrocious, despicable killer, the survivor of the schoolboy who had charmed her and befriended her after he had kidnapped and murdered her own best friend.

Her YouTube channel was taking some hits, too. Thankfully, most of the comments that were coming through now were positive. People were praising her for being a hero, congratulating her on surviving her encounter, sending their well-wishes and telling her how glad they were that she had survived. The videos with Jackson were now filled with comments similar to the things Matt had said—that the way he talked up killers as if they were brilliant was a tell-tale sign, and why had nobody suspected him before? *It's obvious, duh!*

Hindsight was twenty-twenty.

There were comments on her videos that actually related to their content now. Her views were going up and up by the day, and when she checked her subscriber count out of curiosity, she was floored to discover that she had jumped from barely six hundred subscribers to almost ninety thousand.

And that number was climbing every day. She'd been shaking when she pointed it out to Matt.

Matt

> That's what happens when you go viral. Your story is being shared all over the place, Audi. It's on Reddit; other YouTubers are talking about it. The story's spreading. That number is going to skyrocket even from here. People all over the world are hearing about this case.

It was nice being able to talk to Matt again. Although they had now met in person and exchanged phone numbers, their communication mostly remained through Messenger. There was something calming about that. It was a piece of her old life that had always been a comfort to her, messaging Matt all afternoon and into the evenings, and she was glad to have it back. And at an all-new level, too. She had always thought her relationship with Matt was fairly strong despite the Internet separating them, but now that she was experiencing it after having met him in person after he had helped to literally save her life, she was beginning to realise just how wrong she'd been. It may have been strong before, but that was nothing compared to what it was now.

Going back to school had been hard. All eyes had been

on her once again, and this time, it was for a mix of different reasons. There were a lot of sympathetic looks for what she'd gone through—everybody had heard the story by then, and the shock they were all feeling was palpable in the hallways and classrooms wherever she went. There were, of course, a select few students who were certain beyond reason that Jackson was innocent, that Audrey had framed him for this entire mess and had either killed him and done away with his body or framed him so well that he'd had no choice but to flee in fear of his own life. Thankfully, those students were in the great minority, so Audrey didn't have to hear from them much.

Despite the number of people trying to speak with her, hear her story first-hand, and apologise for the things they had said previously, Audrey kept exclusively to her tight little group with Lenore, Roxanne, and occasionally Peter, who had asked his friends on the soccer team to keep an eye on Audrey whenever she was making her way through the school. She hadn't yet found the words to let him know how grateful she was for that.

The hardest part of her week had come when Penny and Danielle had sought her out.

She hadn't known what to expect when their faces had come around the corner and made a beeline for the little shaded area that she, Lenore, and Roxanne had claimed as their new hangout spot. Roxanne had spotted them first and had been on alert at once, causing Audrey and Lenore to follow her gaze to the incoming threat. Audrey had tensed, sure that Penny had come to tell her that she was one of those who still believed that Audrey was guilty, that she would never forgive her for ruining their lives, that it was all her fault that Jackie was gone, and Jackson was on the run and—

"I'm sorry," were the first words to come out of Penny's mouth.

Audrey's jaw dropped in both shock and disbelief. Lenore's eyes widened. Roxanne's expression had gone hard, her lips pursing. Penny hurried to go on before anybody could interrupt her.

"We both are," she insisted, gesturing to Danielle beside her. Danielle nodded profusely, her eyes brimming with tears. "You understand why we said all of the things that we did, right? Jackie was gone, and we were mourning. We'd just lost one of our best friends, and a lot of the evidence pointed to you being the culprit. You can't deny that, so we had to believe what the evidence was saying! And we were under so much stress from school and the police and the media that we just couldn't keep our thoughts straight and see the truth."

"And what's that?" Audrey asked, her mouth dry.

"That you were always innocent, of course," Danielle said, her lower lip quivering. "We always knew it deep down, but we had everything telling us that we were wrong, so I guess we got confused with everything. You get what we mean, right?"

Yes, she did. Audrey knew exactly what it was like to have the whole world telling you one thing and feeling like you *had* to believe it even though it was against everything that you believed yourself. Her thoughts went back to Matt. Matt, who had so graciously forgiven her for her stupidity. Matt, whom she would never doubt again.

"Yeah," she said at long last. "I get it."

"Oh, thank God," Penny said, a smile spreading across her face. "So you forgive us? We really want to put all of this behind us and try to get on with our lives. And you're going to keep talking about Jackie on your channel, right? We thought maybe we could help you with th—"

"No."

The two girls stared back at her in surprise. "*No?*"

"No," Audrey repeated. "I mean yes, I forgive you. And yes, I'm going to keep talking about Jackie on my channel. But no, things can't just go back to the way they used to be. Having all of this happen, getting some distance from you guys... it made me really take a good look at my life and at the people in it. I think it's funny that all of a sudden, you're interested in supporting my channel right when it's starting to gain popularity, and the media aren't covering Jackie's story as much, so you've got no way to get your faces out there. I think it's funny that you were so ready to throw me under the bus all of those times, like at the funeral, but now you want to 'put all of this behind us and try to get on with our lives'. Well, I have every intention of moving forward. But it won't be with either of you."

"But," Danielle gritted out, "you just said—"

"I said I forgive you. But I don't want to be friends with you anymore."

Lenore looked at her in mild surprise. Roxanne's expression was smug. "Tell 'em, girl!"

"You can't be serious!" Penny cried. She and Danielle both looked outraged. "We just *apologised* to you! You can't just abandon us like that!"

"Like what?" Roxanne asked. "You mean like you did to her? Like you would do again in a heartbeat the second she stopped being useful to you? Get over yourself, Penelope. Audrey isn't your ticket to stardom, and Jackie wasn't, either. The things you did just to get your face out there are disgusting, and I hope people realise that about you now that this case is all solved and over with. I can't believe these two were ever friends with you. Two-faced bitch."

Penny didn't stick around to hear any more of it, turning on her heels with one last rotten look at the three of them before she stormed back towards the main courtyard of the school. Danielle was quick to follow, throwing a rude gesture over her shoulder as she went.

Delilah had sought her out, too, giving her another long hug when they'd met in the hallway.

"I hope your channel finds a lot of success," she said to Audrey quietly. "Even if we're not friends anymore, I'll be watching."

Those words had hung heavily on Audrey's shoulders as she'd suffered through the remainder of the school day. She did her best to pay attention to her teachers in every lesson, but she constantly found her mind wandering. It was halfway through her final period when she finally gave up on trying to pay attention, pulled a page free from her notebook, and started to make her bullet-point notes.

She got to work as soon as she got home, finishing up her notes, clearing a space for filming, and setting up her camera as best as she could.

She turned on her laptop and navigated to her YouTube

channel, needing to take a few moments to think this through, to decide whether or not she truly wanted to do it. Her numbers were still growing, going absolutely wild after the last video that she had posted, so for the first time in a while, she navigated to that page and started scrolling through the comments.

She was pleased to see that this time around, those comments were mostly positive. There were, of course, still the odd negative ones, but not anywhere near as many as the last time. She was about to move away from the page when one comment in particular caught her eye, and she stopped to read it.

"You're doing some wonderful work here, Audrey," it said. *"I can't wait to see how many cases you help solve in the coming years. Keep up the great work. I'll always be watching. - Detective Robert Flanagan."*

Audrey smiled. *Keep up the great work.* Well, that was all the convincing that she needed. She had to do this.

She'd been debating filming this video for several days. Much like with the first videos about Jackie, it was something she knew she had to do. Back with those videos, Jackson had given her all the push that she needed. This time, she had Lenore, Roxanne, Peter, and Matt telling her that it was her choice and that they would stand with her no matter what.

She'd wanted to wait for her channel to get bigger—well, it was bigger now. And she wasn't likely to be seeing this kind of traffic again. Waiting any longer might turn out to be a hindrance more than a help at this point.

Jackson wanted her to tell his story? Well, he could suck

it. She had a more important video to record.

With that final thought, she hit record, sat down in front of her new camera, and began to tell her father's story.

Acknowledgements

Audrey might not be the best content creator out there (they all start somewhere, right?), but I want to give a shout out to some of the amazing YouTubers who inspired her and this story: Bella Fiori, Danielle Kirsty, Brooke Makenna, Eleanor Neale, and Kendall Rae. These ladies are all wonderful true crime content creators, covering an assortment of cases from all over the world, and I highly recommend giving them a watch or a listen. You're sure to find a vibe that suits you.

It was while binge watching Kendall Rae that I started getting the beginning ideas for this story, about an aspiring true crime video creator whose unsupportive best friend becomes the subject of her work. And thus, in the span of the thirty days of NaNoWriMo 2021, *In the Days Before* was born. And then reborn again and again as I agonised over it for another three years. I hope it paid off, and there aren't too many inaccuracies scattered throughout the pages! (I did my best, I promise!)

As with most writers, I struggled a lot through this process. Mostly with Imposter Syndrome, but also with burnout. Lucky for me, my friends are a lot better than

Audrey's, and there was always someone there to hold me up and give me a push when I needed it.

SO THANK YOU TO...

My IRL bestie, Chanttel—for never failing to make my laugh when the first question is always, "What's your current body count?" My online bestie, Alex—for putting up with all my "will Americans understand this?" questions and never asking for context. My work bestie, Olivia—for being the best beta-reader a girl could ask for, and not being afraid to tell me when things are getting too Wattpaddy. My writing bestie, Nicole—for endlessly inspiring me, even when I can never comprehend how you write. so. fast.

Thanks Mum, for not constantly asking what I'm working on, because I'd rather write it than talk about it. Here's another one for the shelf. Thanks Nana, for swearing up and down that you loved the last one. Those words gave me the final push to finish this one.

Thank you to the co-workers that cheered me on, even if you're not a reader. Sometimes a cheerleader is exactly what's needed!

Thank you to Immy Grace, who edited this manuscript so quickly and so beautifully, even when I kept insisting you could take as long as you needed. Working with you was such a treat, and I hope we get to work together again in future!

Thank you to Kim at *The Author Buddy* for an amazing cover! I highly recommend *The Author Buddy* to anyone looking for cover artists, beta-readers, or author services.

They really are a wonderful addition to your publishing arsenal!

Thank you to Elle and Silver Shell Publishing, for continuing to let me be a part of the wonderful team. Setting out as an indie author can be as intimidating as hell, so it's always good to know someone has your back!

Big thanks to the members of the *Rebel Elite Book Club* and the *Pretty in Punk Book Club* on Wattpad, all of whom helped smooth out and shape this story with helpful comments and feedback. Also thank you to the readers who provided feedback and cheering on after this story was shortlisted for the Watty Awards in 2023!

And thank YOU for taking a chance on a little indie and her first attempt at a young adult crime novel. Here's to hoping you'll be back for the next one, and here's to hoping they only get better from here!

About the Author

Renée Shantel started writing at the age of eleven, for no better reason than she was tired of waiting for *Harry Potter and the Order of the Phoenix* to be released. She has entertained dreams of being published ever since. She has taken several short courses in creative writing, book editing and publishing.

When not writing (or thinking about writing), she can be found shooting analogue photography, casually learning to play the violin, or smothering her cats with love.

SILVER SHELL PUBLISHING

Stay tuned for more from
Silver Shell Publishing
in 2025

www.ingramcontent.com/pod-product-compliance
Lightning Source LLC
Chambersburg PA
CBHW020241010826
48973CB00006B/1604